THE
*J*OURNEY
PRIZE ANTHOLOGY

Winners of the $10,000 Journey Prize

1989
Holley Rubinsky (of Toronto, Ont. and Kaslo, B.C.)
for "Rapid Transits"

1990
Cynthia Flood (of Vancouver, B.C.)
for "My Father Took a Cake to France"

1991
Yann Martel (of Montreal, Que.)
for "The Facts Behind the Helsinki Roccamatios"

The Best Short Fiction from Canada's Literary Journals

THE
Journey
PRIZE ANTHOLOGY

M&S

Canadian Cataloguing in Publication Data

Main entry under title:

The Journey prize anthology: the best short fiction from Canada's literary journals

ISBN 0-7710-4433-X

1. Short stories, Canadian (English).*
2. Canadian fiction (English) – 20th century.*

PS8329.J68 1992   C813'.0108054   C92-094350-0
PR9197.32.J68 1992

Typesetting by M&S
Printed and bound in Canada on acid-free paper

"Bella's Story" © Diane Juttner Perreault; "The Bottom of the Glass" © David Bergen; "By the Big River" © Judith Cowan; "How Beautiful Upon the Mountains" © Steven Heighton; "A Man Away from Home Has No Neighbours" © Steven Heighton; "No Miracles Sweet Jesus" © Maria A. Billion; "No Rosa, No District Six" © Rozena Maart; "Rainy Day" © Guy Malet de Carteret; "Silence" © Carmelita McGrath; "A Theory of Discontinuous Existence" © Michael Mirolla; "Traplines" © Eden Robinson; "Travelling" © L. Rex Kay

McClelland & Stewart Inc.
The Canadian Publishers
481 University Avenue
Toronto, Ontario
M5G 2E9

Dear Reader:

The $10,000 Journey Prize, awarded annually to an individual writer of distinction in the early stages of his or her career, is made possible by James A. Michener's generous donation of his Canadian royalty earnings from his novel *Journey*, published by McClelland & Stewart Inc. in 1988.

The annual publication of the popular *Journey Prize Anthology*, now in its fourth year, is a statement of McClelland & Stewart's own commitment to supporting new and developing writers and the literary journals that first publish them.

The anthology comprises a selection from submissions made by literary journals across Canada (this year we received seventy-seven). These submissions were read, without benefit of author or journal name, by an editorial board, joined by the acclaimed novelist and short story writer Sandra Birdsell.

The authors whose pieces have been selected for the anthology are contenders for James A. Michener's $10,000 Journey Prize, which this year will be announced and awarded in October, as part of the International Festival of Authors at Harbourfront in Toronto. At that time, McClelland & Stewart will make its own award of $2,000 to the journal that has submitted the winning entry.

I am pleased that this venture has received the enthusiastic support of writers, literary journal editors, and the public, who join Mr. Michener and me in celebrating the emergence of new voices in Canadian fiction.

Sincerely,

Avie Bennett
Chairman and President

Contents

THE
JOURNEY
PRIZE ANTHOLOGY

JUDITH COWAN

By the Big River

Mme Chartier sat smoking in the hard sunlight of late February, looking out through her broad windows at the St. Lawrence River. The river seemed to be smoking too. The cold had not broken but the ship channel was kept open by the ice-breakers and the water steamed into the frigid air. It was probably thirty below out there. Beyond the pressure-tumbled mountains of ice which were half the river, she could just see a dark line of water, flat and dense, carrying its load of broken floes. She watched it as she watched everything now, from a centre of stillness in the midst of a destroyed and disordered world, from the fragile home-free of her seventy years and her four children (of whom one was dead) and of her widowhood. Her electric baseboard heaters, never off these days, clunked at her, drying out the air and cracking the sounding board of her piano. She stretched her fingers and looked at them, the stiffening of the enlarged joints, and at her diamond ring.

Her husband had died the summer before, at the end of a long hot night had simply gone into the spare room at the back of the house and lain down and died on the couch there. They had both known that his heart was bad, but had he known, had he ever guessed how frightened she was of waking up beside a dead man? Was that why he had gone and died in the spare room? She lit another cigarette. She was alone. And her heart was fine and she was only seventy and her own mother, well over ninety, was still very much alive. But Louis Chartier, her only lover and her husband of more than forty years, had been dead for six months now, gone, it seemed to her, before she had ever had a chance to talk to him. Had she even known him? Could one really know a man? Somehow there had never been time.

She tucked her feet up under her and scanned the river. The big ships went by in the channel all winter now, and the first captain into the port of Montréal, the winner of the gold-headed cane, always arrived on or around the first of January. No longer an event, really. Their backwash heaved more blocks of ice onto her breakwater and she read their names and countries of origin through Louis's binoculars.

Waiting for the telephone to ring, she picked up the binoculars and examined an ice fisherman who was climbing out through the blocks. She could see only his back, his heavy jacket and big boots, a wisp of his breath blown back over bent shoulders. An element of life in a lifeless landscape. In spite of the cold, he was a sign of spring. The tommycod were coming upstream into all the little rivers to spawn, although there had been fewer in recent years and there was always a lot of mercury in them. She wondered why he would bother, the ice here was so thick and the fish not really edible, if he ate them he would poison himself. But that was his business. Life went on, fish spawned in polluted water, people found the time to reproduce themselves before they died, the eternal processes continued even if there was no real communication among them, even if a man could live for forty years with a woman without ever opening his mind to her and then go and die in a corner. She dragged on her cigarette and thought of making herself a drink. She needed it while she waited for the telephone to ring.

It hadn't been her idea to live out here, twenty miles from town and five miles from the village. That had been Louis's idea, when they were first married. After that he had rarely been home though, and it was she who had spent her life here. And now she was committed to this place because her children had grown up here and her granddaughters expected to come here in the summers. How could she live in an apartment in town? What would they do there? But it wasn't getting any easier. With Louis dead, she had had to learn to drive all over again, angrily because she remained convinced that it was not her job. And then winter had come and the roads were sheer ice and at the best of times the car was too big for her. She couldn't see out of it properly even before the windows started to ice up. It was his car. And so she had parked it until spring and lived by telephone.

And as it turned out, it didn't matter how far out of town she was, the telephone would still have been her only link, because the call she was waiting for would be from Nicosia. This had been going on since long before Louis's death. Carole, her eldest daughter, was in Beirut, had married a Lebanese doctor when they were both just out of the Université de Montréal and had gone there with him. Now he was dead and Beirut was in flames. Mme Chartier had spent this morning, as she had so many others since the war began, trying to get through to Lebanon, and all of the afternoon waiting for an operator to call her back. There was nothing else she could do.

She and Carole had been widowed within months of each other and now, through the bombs and the rockets, Carole was going to have to try and get herself and her two daughters out of the country and back to Québec, back to her mother and her grandmother and her sister. But it was almost impossible. She had hung on there too long, in love with a man who had risked everything to stay in his own country. When he was killed she had found that her Canadian passport had expired. By that time, the Canadian embassy in Beirut was closed and she was supposed to send her old passport to Damascus to be renewed. Damascus. Madame clenched her cigarette. Did the bureaucrats not understand the terrible danger of that? Her hand trembled as she stared out at the ice. Damascus was in Syria and the Syrians were the enemy and the border was closed.

There was so little she could do for them, she who would have done anything. Her daughter and the little girls were going to have to get out without papers, run the gauntlet of the bombs and take the boat to Cyprus, but when to risk it was still a question. Would things get worse or would they get better? There was so much death, so much death everywhere. Mme Chartier had spent days and weeks on the telephone, to External Affairs, to newspapers both French and English, and to people in Beirut who might still have working telephones, yet she knew that she could make no difference. When she could get out of the house and find someone to drive her to the village, she went to the church and prayed.

She told herself that Carole and her daughters would

survive if only because they were women. For some reason it was always the men who died, no matter what the danger was, and it was the women who were left to carry on. She herself was a habitual survivor. Alone in her lonely house, she felt at times a comfortable fatalism. She was old, and, faced with a prowler or a burglar, certainly she was helpless. But so what, she said to anyone who would listen, I've lived my life. Let him kill me. What difference does it make? Like smoking, it no longer mattered. A friend had told her she was *un oiseau de malheur*, a harbinger of disaster and a witness to the calamities of others, a reporter who always lived to tell the tale, and it did seem to be true. She lived in this little house, buried in snow or cut off by high water for half the year, reading, smoking, seeing the world on television, watching international shipping going past in the river, isolated but never more than a few steps from her lifeline, the telephone, and always with a tale to tell. Although she saw few people face to face, she talked and talked. She lived at the centre of a web of contacts, giving and receiving information, passing on the latest bad news in a voice roughened by cigarettes and by familiar expectation of the worst. Was this the simple cumulative effect of living long? Surely gruesome events surrounded anyone who lived long enough. Neighbours died in car accidents, close friends died of cancer, other people's children committed suicide, her own son had died of leukemia years before.

But this war had touched her more recently. Her Lebanese son-in-law had been blown up in his car on his way to the bank. A doctor and not even on a mission of mercy, she thought. Just another man gone, leaving a family of three females to regroup without him. Well, they would, she thought. They always did. If only Carole could get them out of there and come home. If only Mme Chartier could have her daughter and her granddaughter safe, she would not grieve for lost men who could never be brought back, she would accept the reality of being a family of women only. Madame had not prayed for the impossible, but she had prayed to hold what she had, she had prayed for a phone call from Nicosia.

"*Que veux-tu…?*" she had said to someone or other on the telephone, "*d'une façon ou d'une autre, les hommes ne sont pas faits pour durer…*"

A man was not a creature made to last. A woman could try to get a response out of one of them but it was hardly worth it because he'd be gone before she had the time. On the other hand her ancient mother, still lucid and demanding, was a constant telephone presence, complaining day after day about conditions in her extremely luxurious seniors' apartment hotel in Montréal. Mme Chartier frowned through her smoke, contemplating the unknown man who was still out there on the ice, probably not catching anything. If he came to the house, she thought, she would give him hot coffee, but she knew he wouldn't come. She calculated that he must be at about the same distance from the shore as the stretch of water where her Lebanese son-in-law had water-skied a few summers before. How things change, she thought, how little we understand. They could have left Lebanon long ago, or they could never have decided to live there, he could still be alive.

While her immortal mother lived on, buying dresses and kid gloves, having hips and corneas replaced, going to the hairdresser and the dentist. Madame snorted. If only she could live in that palatial place herself, she thought, instead of in this shack by the river. In fact her mother, some years ago at eighty-nine, safely installed in what had seemed an acceptable nursing home, had high-handedly called a taxi and moved out because she found the cuisine uncivilized. She had refused to eat dinner at 5 o'clock, and she had refused to get up in the morning. That was not her custom, she said. And accordingly she had chosen a marble-floored *hôtel-de-ville* with gilded elevators and a limousine service and all the medical personnel disguised as servants, so that she could have dinner at 8:00, and brandy afterwards, and then a few hours of television or bridge, and the following morning sleep in. Born into the *haute bourgeoisie* of the last century, she expected all that. She was a lady, and moreover she had learned her expectations at a time when a lady did not concern herself about paying. Unfortunately she had outlived two husbands, neither of whom had left her provided for. Thus it was her daughter, an old lady herself, who had to pay the bills.

And when Mme Chartier tried to tell her the news from Beirut it seemed to make little impression on her. The great-grandmother, now so old that all the beautiful bones of her youth were showing again, was past caring about anything but her own comfort. So Mme Chartier was trapped between generations. When she went to see her mother, the staff in the hotel assumed that she herself was a resident. No such luck, she rasped, I'll die out in the snow one winter, or be washed away in the spring flooding, and no one will notice for a week.

The afternoon was beginning to lower when the telephone finally did ring and she fell upon it with her heart pounding. She stood holding the receiver, hearing connections going through, staring out at the river as if she could see Beirut and Cyprus, the ship, the bombs. But she saw only the man on the ice, still sitting there in the cold. Why didn't he go home? Some woman would be waiting for him. Then the telephone line seemed to open.

"*Oui, allô…?*" she said.

But there was nothing. More clicking. Then for a moment an operator's voice.

"Carole?"

And the line went dead. She stood holding the phone, gripping it, trying to squeeze something out of it. When it remained silent she put it back down and took the bottle of Scotch from the mantle. She went to the kitchen for ice. This had happened before. Eventually one of them would get through.

She sat down by the window again with her drink. This was the hardest season, the very dragged-out end of winter, when everyone was tired of snow and ice and of everything else because they had been deprived of sunlight for too long. People caught colds, then the flu, and coughed for weeks. Quarrels were worse at this time of year and despair was deeper. The really ill and the fragile elderly gave up hope of ever seeing another summer and died. The beginning of the suicide season, she thought, as if life were not hard enough to hang onto anyway.

The sun was dipping to the horizon and, as the temperature fell, the ice-fog over the river thickened. The ice fisherman seemed to have gone home but then she saw him farther off, lit up through the haze by the long cold lateral rays of the February sun. She thought again about how crazy it was to live alone out here. She might well be murdered. Why wasn't she afraid? She reached for Louis's binoculars. The man wasn't coming her way, he was climbing out through the broken ice towards the channel. At that moment the telephone rang and she dropped her cigarette as she leaped to seize it. She heard the line opening like a series of echoing doors.

"Maman?" said Carole.

In the rush of relief at hearing her daughter's voice, and

trying at the same time to pick up the dropped cigarette, she lost sight of the man out on the ice. But she had to look somewhere. Where was he? Downstream she saw him again. He had reached the edge of the ice and now he simply stepped into the dark, fuming waters of the ship channel. Then he was gone.

DIANE JUTTNER PERREAULT

Bella's Story

Rene comes down the street wearing green shorts and a light cap to shade his eyes from the sun. He is nocturnal and he roams the high walled space between fences, usually in shadow, an alley man and also a thief. He waits for Bella. He stands at the bus stop, ill at ease or simply ill, waiting, huddled against the wind, his twig legs too thin and twisted to support the weight of his responsibilities. He will use a cane before long, though he is young, maybe forty. Death sings in his ear and his life is frail and full of silences.

In summer, he sits in Bella's weed garden shelling peas for supper, or painting bits of junkyard furniture. They have a garage sale every other weekend. They sell trinkets: painted egg cartons, tin cans, and old cups; but really they merchandise stolen bicycles, radar detectors, and car radios, anything he can find. Rene drinks beer under the apple tree and plays with Susie, the love child. She is only three, and she likes to play butterflies. She flaps her arms like wings and twirls off the back steps. He catches her in midair and swings her round and round. Rene didn't need another child. He had trouble enough feeding Jean and Bella. But Bella wanted a girl. She wanted to buy dresses and braid baby-fine hair.

Bella has a weed garden three feet high and a picnic table in the shade, with a fresh cloth and flowers. She pays attention to detail. She has to or they would all starve. From May to September, she prunes and plants and rearranges things. She wears a straw hat and squats on the back step drinking coffee. Sometimes she goes into the garden to pick refugee strawberries for lunch. The soil is full of maggots, but the strawberries are sweet and full of flowers.

Since early spring, Rene and Bella have been outside, digging out dead grass, turning soil, crossing paths, and avoiding speech. Bella swallows his words bitterly and spits them back at him in the full sunshine of the neighbourhood.

"I will not sell wheels," she says. "The bicycles are stolen. I didn't know that, Rene."

"Where the hell do you think I got them, sister?" He stops, wipes his forehead with dirty hands, then stabs his fork into the mud. "Bitch," he mutters and goes into the house.

Many years of black eyes have taught her things, especially the value of silence. She watches him go but says nothing. Her eyes have sunk deep inside to a place where he can't get at them. Once, when he went to hit her, she ducked and he put his fist through the French doors in the living room. It served him right. She is not afraid. She says this over and over as she mops up broken glass and blood. Sometimes, the neighbours phone the police and when they arrive, she says they must be mistaken. Perhaps they have the wrong house.

They fight over trivial things: a late supper, a missed bus, a new pair of shoes.

"I need shoes for work," she says.

"We need to eat," he says.

"Damn it, Rene. I'm on my feet all night. I can't wear these. I'm worn out."

"So quit."

"God, you're mean," she says and turns away.

Bella works the evening shift at a Salisbury House, frying hash browns and burgers. It doesn't pay much but it helps. At least she gets her meal there, and sometimes stale buns to take home. And tips. She stashes the money in a jar and hides it behind the fridge. It's safe there.

Rene hasn't had a real job in seven years. He's worked a few months here and there: TV repairs, encyclopedia sales, even carpet cleaning. But nothing's come of it. He still dreams of going back on the road. Bella dreams of a day at the beach, hunting seashells with Susie, and lying in the sun with nothing to do.

In the autumn, Rene goes deer hunting with his brother. He doesn't like his brother and he'd rather not go, but he can't refuse. They need the meat for the freezer. As the two of them drive up the B-grade highway into the Manitoba brush, he is sullen, slouched down into his seat and thinking. He dreams of his former life: the endless flat of the Trans-Canada, the cheap hotels, the quick burgers, and even the miniature moccasins he used to bring back for Jean.

When he returns, they celebrate. They carry a picnic down to the old basilica and sit in the courtyard among the ruins eating roast duck and potatoes. Bella bakes bread and apples for the occasion. They eat outside one last time because after this the days are short and the wind is cold, snow comes and they put plastic over the windows to keep away the draughts.

But this is a time of celebration. They pass around the choke-cherry wine and lean against the cool stone walls and the stories come out like stars.

Rene tells the stories. "Things were really good back then," he says. He rolls up his shirt-sleeves and pours himself a drink. His arms are bony and it seems that his hands are too large. Susie crawls into his lap and he strokes her hair because Bella isn't available. She's busy packing up the picnic and scrubbing a stain out of her skirt. Duck grease from Susie's fingers. He pours a drink for Bella and watches Jean. "You want one too?" he asks.

"I guess," he says. Jean slumps against the wall, a little way off. He is absorbed by the grit under his nails. He pretends to be bored, but he isn't. He's seventeen.

Rene pours the wine, and begins again. "When I had the business, we had everything. Didn't we Bella? You name it: TV sets, radios, even a new stereo. I was the first one to get air conditioning in the car. See, I lived in my car back then, Jean. Had a trunk full all the time. Carload Bouchard they used to call me. I'd sell anything. Always hustling. Always trying to make a buck. And it worked too. People liked me. I wasn't pushy, but I had a feel for it. You got a feel after awhile. A taste. And the miles spinning by. It was like flying. Man, I was flying." Rene stops, and spreads his arms wide to take in the whole ruined courtyard. As if he owns it.

"And all the time I'm calculating all that money in my head. Just driving. God. Don't get me wrong, son. You've gotta be tough. Wasn't easy to work on commission. You see, people trust you. You've gotta be honest. But you've gotta hustle. It's all a balancing act."

Rene balances the glass on his knee, and waves for Bella to

come closer to him. Jean lights a cigarette. Through the smoke rings he watches Rene. He can almost love his father now. He can almost forget the beatings, the names he's called Bella: slut, whore, bitch, the way he steals cigarettes and won't admit it. Bella comes and sits down. Rene puts an arm around her, and Jean winces. At seventeen, he vacillates between love and hate. He pulls his black hair into a ponytail and kicks at a stone. He remembers the cool dives into northern lakes and his father's green eyes, which weren't as hard as stones then. He decides to stay for the stories. He has heard them so often that he knows they are true. He will defend them endlessly because he doesn't want to lose the memory of lakes, and fish, and his father's eyes.

"Tell us about the moose, Dad."

"Which one? Oh, the one I nearly hit. Yeah. That was nearly game over. The snow came early that year. End of September, we had sleet. Anyway, that was October and the roads were slippery as a skating rink. I was trying to make Thunder Bay that night. And here I am running out of gas. But I can't stop. No place to pull over, driving blind and already twenty cars in the ditch. I counted them to keep my mind off the gas situation. See I couldn't just stop. Some guy might plough into the back of me. I sure as hell didn't need whiplash. So, everybody's driving blind, white-knuckle country, and then up comes this bloody moose. I damn near hit the thing. Rolled the car and nearly broke my neck." Rene's hand goes up to his neck automatically. He rubs the spot and rolls his head, remembering another trip.

"Some guy picked me up and we spent the night in a ma-and-pa motel," he says. He squeezes Bella's breast and grins. "You know. The one with Zelda's buns. God, I was starving by then. But it worked out all right. Made a lot of money on that trip. Man, you were spoiled rotten, Jean. I always brought back presents. We could hardly walk for the toys all over the place. Bella used to complain about it. Eh, Bella?"

She nods. But she is far away. She is watching fireflies moving through the navy-blue night. The fireflies are all dead now, but she sees their orange streaks moving in the air, like illuminated frost, the illuminations of memory and pain. He will get to it, she thinks. When he is drunk enough, he will get to it. He will tell the long story. Jean will listen and Susie will sleep and the stars will fade.

That must've been the spring trip. He'd postponed it for her. Sales were bleak and he didn't want to spend the money travelling. The drought was terrible all across the Prairies. All that winter, the fields were bare of snow and the topsoil piled up in the ditches. He said sometimes you'd see patches of ice. Huge stretches of it. And you'd get a twinge of hope. And then when you got closer, you'd see it was only salt. They were losing money. And he was driving all the time, skipping meals, just to save a bit on hotel bills. He slept in the back of the car some nights, though he never said. But she knew it from the condition of his clothes.

"I'd been on the road three weeks," Rene says. "I was damn sick of those flea-bitten small towns. God, I wanted some city. I was heading home, and this man comes on the radio and says we're heading into a dust storm. He says to stay off the highways and keep the windows shut. I paid no attention of course. After three lousy weeks, it feels like forever and I just wanted to put my feet up on the sofa, have a beer, see Bella."

He squeezes her breast again, and pours another drink for

himself. Jean gets up, takes some wine out of the picnic basket, and drinks straight from the bottle. He has no use for glasses. It seems stupid, this ritual pouring of wine. What does he think he is? A bloody priest? He's a drunk. Rene frowns and Jean sits down, but only because Bella looks worried.

Rene continues. "That was some storm," he says. "The sky was yellow. Like it's made out of clay. I drove six hours. In the clear patches I could see little tornadoes rising up out of the fields. Like evil spirits. It was hard to breathe. I pulled over to a Shell station to get gas and clean the windows. I started feeling kinda sick. Guess I was about four hours into it. Was near the border. Yorkton maybe. I hung on till I got to Brandon and then I was sick at the side of the road. Sick as a dog."

Rene stops, lights a cigarette, and flicks the match onto the ground. The official story claims it was food poisoning. But Bella knows. She found the mickey of rye in the car that night, in the trunk under a blanket.

What if he hadn't been drunk? What then? The story rotates in her head, over and over with all sorts of endings. Like a dull headache. He murdered a girl that night. She went and saw her once, lying comatose, suspended between two worlds. And what she remembers is not human really. What she remembers is the mess of wires, and the little green lights which traced the movements of her heart.

"Jesus. I should've checked into a hotel. But what would Bella think? Two hours from home and I check into a hotel. Come on. So I drove. Damn. I put the radio way up loud and I ate sunflower seeds to keep from falling asleep. I needed a coffee. Funny thing is, I got to just outside Winnipeg. I mean, I was almost walking up to the front door. Then I saw the lights of her car coming at me. I guess I must've been over the line.

I don't know really. All I remember was lying on the gravel, looking up at the stars, and rubbing my neck. It hurt like hell. All I got was a bit of whiplash and a few cracked ribs. Jesus. That poor girl." Rene gets up and walks to the corner of the courtyard. He looks out over the dark church cemetery and says nothing. Bella listens to the silence and to the wind in the branches, and the rumble of distant traffic.

"It ruined me," he says. "They sued me for five hundred grand. I lost the car. Lost my licence. I didn't have enough insurance. No Autopac then to cover your ass. Shit. It all comes down to money in the end. You were so damn skinny, Jean. And hungry all the time. And damn it all, you wanted a bike for your birthday, Jesus, you wanted that bike."

It's late. Violence weaves in and out of his voice now. Jean is tired. He doesn't want to hear it anymore, but Rene makes him sit and listen. "I'm going to teach you something Jean," he says. "I'm going to take you hunting. We'll go next year. Just the two of us. That'll be something, eh?"

Rene hasn't been hunting on his own in years. He's got guns, but they aren't strictly his. He is only storing them for Bella's mother, Angela. When Bella's father died, Angela was so lost. She didn't know what to do with his guns, so Rene took them. He put them in the garage and told her not to worry. They've had the guns for so long now that Angela's probably forgotten them.

Bella hasn't though. After the accident, Rene told her that if she ever left him, he'd go and blow his brains out. She believes it too. She has seen the look in his eyes. She hears the tormented dreams as she lies beside him in bed. She puts ointment on the bruises at the base of his spine. She massages the shoulder blades which rise like sharp rocks from his back. She worries when he's like this, drinking too much. He gets moody. She wants him to get off this track. Put the bottle away and come home to bed.

It is late autumn. Most of the elms are yellow, or have already lost their leaves. The leaves rush down the lane, and it sounds like children, running or calling. Bella is getting ready for work. The window is open and a cool breeze floats into the bedroom. She is uneasy. Jean is outside, smashing a basketball against the garage. His T-shirt is full of holes. And black. Is that a marijuana cigarette he smokes? She wants to know. And will he come home tonight? Where does he go? Bella never asks Rene where he goes. She wouldn't dare. "Sister," he'd say, "I don't have to punch a clock around here."

Rene is out there too. He grabs the ball away from Jean and throws it. It hits Jean in the stomach. Rene goes over and punches him and the boy's cigarette slides down onto the sidewalk. Rene crushes it with the heel of his boot.

"You fuckhead," says Jean, and he turns toward the house. On his way, he spits, and grabs a beer from the picnic table. He goes to open it with his teeth, but Rene grabs him and knocks the beer onto the ground. Then he slugs him in the stomach.

Bella watches from behind the window. She is mute, but she feels the kick in the pit of her stomach. She goes on with her makeup. She needs to cover the shadows under her eyes. She wants to hide the lines which have crept in around her mouth. Mostly, she wants to hide. But she can't. She's late with her routines. Susie whines at the door. And still, she stands and watches. Jean is doing the slugging now. She'll be late. It's his turn. Rene has a bloody mouth. Bella goes to the bathroom, and when she comes back, Jean has vanished.

She gives Susie a quick hug and hurries out the front door,

so as not to see Rene lying on the grass in the yard. So as not to have seen anything. She runs to the bus stop, but misses the connection and is late for work. She has missed too many connections and the night is tedious, the café empty.

Rene is asleep when she gets home. Bella can hear him moaning as soon as she opens the back door. She goes in, closes the blinds, gathers up newspapers, and turns off the lights. She prefers darkness, prefers not to see the purple bruises which have already blossomed on his face and arms. She takes off her clothes and throws them on a chair. Then she sits down and rubs her feet. Gently, she rubs the damp, sweat-cramped toes which curl and callus against each other. She wonders if Rene will ever have a real job. She worries about Jean. She splashes cold water on her face and slips into bed beside him, on the broken side. She always sleeps on the broken side so that she will roll toward him in her sleep. He doesn't want the broken side. He is afraid he will crush her, though she doubts he weighs as much as she does.

He smells of whisky and onions. He's ordered a pizza. Must've taken the money from Jean, she thinks. There's nothing left in groceries. She won't say anything now. She is desperate for sleep. And if he touches her, if he wants her, she will cry. She will hide the tears in her pillow, so as not to show him. She wants only to curl away from him and sink into the night. When they make love, he is so thin, so small and bony, that she feels like she is molesting a child.

Sometimes Bella sleeps on the sofa. Sometimes they make love still. It all depends. Rene is moody. She skirts their room cautiously, checking for light spills, soiled clothes, indications. She does the laundry at night when he is out, when she doesn't want to lie down alone listening to the dry rustle of his absence. She hangs out clothes by moonlight. The white

T-shirts float down the line like ghosts of the family. In winter they will freeze stiff on the line and her fingers will be stiff and white too.

He sits in their bedroom now, drinking whisky and watching TV. He flicks from channel to channel, switching programs every few minutes: a glance, a snicker, a hand-rolled cigarette. He's rereading pocketbooks which lie in piles on the floor by his bed: spy stories, crime fiction, the history of World War II. They have the well-worn look of obsession. He knows all the plots. He marks passages and makes notes in the margins. His lamp is on all night.

"What're we going to do, Bella?" he asks. Jean has been missing for three weeks and Rene is desperate.

He hovers like a dark circle of guilt around her. She isn't sure what he's after. Is it forgiveness or revenge?

"You still love me, Bella?"

Bella shifts position, looks down at her feet, at his, at the stains on the floor and the small curve of light coming in through the window. Rene's feet are small and graceful. In the moonlight, they look almost like porcelain. He stands beside her chair and stares at the open oven. He watches the red coil of heat as if it were a fireplace. Bella pulls up a chair for him, then rests her feet on the oven door. In spite of the heat, she is shivering. Night after night, she puts extra blankets on the bed, but it does no good. She can't stop shivering.

"You still love me?" She tries to consider. How to answer? Little clips of conversation circle about in her head. Finally, he stands up and shouts. "Jesus Christ! Will you say something?" He throws a glass against the wall and glares at her. "Where is Jean?" he asks, but she doesn't answer.

Rene goes to the window and opens the curtains. He stands

there a long time, until the first light of day leaks into the room. His shirt is undone. Bella counts his ribs, tracing the scars which form a network of faint lines across his chest. She remembers the wetness of his skin. She remembers his hands tingling with desire, and the exact curve of his neck. His neck is tense now and full of hate, and she is afraid.

"Where is Jean? He's phoned, hasn't he, Bella?"

"No," she lies.

"You're lying, Bella. I want him home. I said I'd take him hunting. Where is he, Bella?" Rene sits down at the table and waits.

"Let's have breakfast," she says.

Rene begins to page through the paper. Bella puts bread in the toaster, and pulls out the butter and jam. She glances at him from time to time. His face is so white, she thinks. Like a mask. And the skin is pulled too tight around his eyes. His head seems too large for his neck, like a child. He is strange. And yet, she is sorry. She knows that underneath that flimsy shirt, he is all bones and red sores. He gets them from lying on the bed, from the buttons on the mattress.

"When did he phone?" he asks.

"Last week," she says. She butters the toast, puts sugar in his coffee, and takes it to him. "He wants to get his stuff."

"What stuff?"

"I don't know. Change of clothes, maybe. I haven't gone through his room."

"He phoned you. How many times?"

"Two or three. For heaven's sake, Rene. He's seventeen. Let him go."

"He's not going anywhere. He's not taking anything out of this house."

"Okay. I just said …"

"Shut up. He's not going. Christ!"

Rene goes out and slams the door. Bella sits down and pages through the paper. Her hand shakes a little as she picks up a pencil and begins to circle things. She is going through the want ads. She will find a good place for Jean to live.

Susie comes into the kitchen. "Morning, honey," says Bella. She opens her arms and the little girl runs up and jumps into her lap. She squeezes her and, for a moment, Bella is giddy. She wants to giggle. But then Susie squirms off her lap and reaches over for the cold toast on the table.

Perhaps Jean will phone again. Perhaps he shouldn't come back at all. Rene is so explosive lately. But Jean will say, "Don't worry. I can handle it, Mom." He is starting to talk to her the way Rene does. And she's caught between the two of them. Bella circles addresses for Jean, suites to let. She should run like hell. Get a room for herself too. But she could never leave him. Even as she thinks it, she knows it is only a fantasy. How could she ever leave him? He is like a shadow, a cloud, a comfort. It isn't fear. It's something else that keeps her here. She isn't sure what, though.

One week later, Jean comes home. He seems different. She hears him bragging on the phone. How he beat up his old man again. She slaps his face, but it has no effect. He stays out all night. He has dropped out. She tells him to clean up his language, clean up his room, get home for supper on time. But he doesn't hear. And Rene plays little mind games with him. "Go to your room," he says. "Sit in the closet. Have a cigarette on me. Drink my beer. Drink more. Drink till you're sick. Get bloody sick. You can't do it, can you?" And Jean falls for it. Jean is so abrasive. Like he's made of spikes. She never knows where to sit down.

It is November now. Rene is out in the yard one last time, pulling up plants and throwing them into the trash can. Now and then he leans against the fence, lights a cigarette, and tosses the match into the sandbox. Susie sits in the sand, digging holes with her yellow shovel and singing. Jean is out there too. In the lull between words, Rene goes on digging, turning over the soil for next year. Suddenly, he spins around and says, "I could cut your fucking tongue out and you wouldn't tell me, would you?" He slugs Jean with his shovel, throws it down, and turns toward the house.

Jean screams, "You bloody maniac. You're crazy, man." He stabs his shovel into the mud and stands perfectly still. "All right. I'm sorry," he mutters.

Bella runs out, grabs Susie, and runs back to the house. "For heaven's sake, Jean," she says. "Get in the house." But he doesn't hear her. He is watching Rene.

Bella watches them both from the kitchen window. She wants to scream too, but she clamps down and shuts up. She grinds her teeth and begins to peel potatoes for supper. Her mother is coming for supper and for once, there will not be a scene. Bella stuffs the turkey and hands a bit of bread to Susie without taking her eyes off the yard. She goes on chopping, peeling, cutting, and watching. But eventually, she throws the knife into the sink and runs outside.

Jean is bleeding. His head is cut from the temple to the ear and he's lying on the grass. Bella stands still and tries to grasp what is going on. The yard spins round and round. Her hands smell of raw turkey and dust, the dead leaf dust of November. She helps Jean to his feet, and Rene orders her back into the house. He goes into the garage and closes the door.

Susie whimpers at the back door, her round face scared and

streaked with tears. Bella goes in and picks her up. "Shh," she says. "Mommy'll give you a doughnut." Bella's hands shake as she unwraps the cellophane, but she tries to smile. "It'll be all right," she says, though she isn't sure. Things are coming unravelled.

"Come on, Susie." Bella's voice is strident. "We are going to Auntie Francie's house."

"Where Auntie Francie?"

"You know, sweetie. The lady down the street.... Nice lady."

"Don't wanna go, Mum."

"Please Susie. Listen to me." But Susie digs her fingers into Bella's thigh and shakes her head. Finally Bella picks her up and runs down the street with Susie's sticky fingers clinging to her hair. She puts her down on the neighbour's doorstep and rings the bell. Why don't they come? Eventually, the door opens a little.

"Jean is hurt," she says. She's an expert at half-truths. She refuses the coffee and runs back down the steps, abandoning Susie at the door. She is shaking badly now. Susie wails and the woman takes her inside. Bella stops. She measures her breaths and counts slowly. She counts the trees, one, two, three. She will walk slowly, slowly home. She will be calm.

She is halfway down the street when she hears a shot. And then the calm resumes, the boys across the street go on with their game. The wind is cool. Perhaps she should have put a jacket over Susie's dress. Perhaps she shouldn't have done this. She is just being hysterical, overtired. She is trying to work out what she will say, how she will confront him.

There is another shot. And then two more. Bella stops. Suddenly, she sees Jean. He runs out of the house. He is limping. He tries to run to a tree for shelter. He shouts, "Oh no. Oh no.

Oh no. Don't shoot!" And then, Rene comes out and shoots him in the back. Rene is as white as bleached bone. And calm. He turns and goes into the house. He closes all the blinds and locks the door.

She gasps. Maybe he will live? Her son lies on the sidewalk a few houses away. He bleeds. He will get cold, she thinks. She should bundle him in blankets. He is so cold. He is all blood-ied, like a newborn, like when he was born. But he is not cry-ing. It is curiously silent on the street.

An ambulance pulls up, but no one gets out. Everything moves in slow motion around her. Why don't they get out. Why don't they let go of her arms. She will get him. "Let go!" she screams, but they don't let go.

The police block off the street with cruiser cars. They evac-uate houses, scoop children off the sidewalk, and still, her boy lies there bleeding on the pavement. One thousand armed men in the city of Winnipeg and all they can do is wait.

Jean dies from loss of blood. She goes to the hospital and identifies the body. It isn't real. It's like a video without sound, freeze frame: Jean curled up in a puddle of blood on the pave-ment. Rewind. She can't rewind the movie or go forward.

It rains. All through the night, the police stand outside, watching the house, waiting. And the next night too. He keeps the police at bay. For once he is winning. He is high. He is tired. He says he will come out. He says he will shoot everyone in sight. He talks on the phone. He wants to talk to Bella.

"Are you tired?" she asks.

"Yes, I'm quite tired."

"You've been up forty-eight hours now," she says quietly.

"Yes," he says.

"Are you coming out of the house?"

"Yes," he says. "I want to write you a letter."

"Rene ..." Bella twists the telephone cord and looks around the room. "Rene, Jean is dead."

"You're lying," he says and hangs up.

Bella is sitting in a house halfway down the street. There is a police radio on the table and a little wooden rooster perched on a shelf over the sink. She studies the rooster: red and black with flowers painted on it. It looks Mexican. Like the things her mother used to buy on a holiday. "Jean is dead," she murmurs. And then she watches the clock.

For three days, it rains, a steady pouring of cloud, and the wind is cold. Spectators come to see the house. The street is a stream of umbrellas, windbreakers; a street in motion. And what do they expect to see? An open door, a few jackets hung in a hall closet, a lawn of shattered glass. Bella sits in another house with the blinds down. She sits in the sorrow of starless nights where no sleep is possible.

What do they want? she wonders. Those people who stand there pressed up against police lines? A yellow ribbon circles the street. It is like a fair. And they bring beer and baby strollers and stand there in the rain, watching. Waiting for him to come out. Do they think he will walk out, head down, meek, like a dog? They don't know him. She knows. Rene is dead.

She knew it when he pulled the phone out of the wall. She knew what he did, too. He went up into the attic and shot himself in the head. Like he said he would. So why did they throw in the grenades? Why did they shatter her house? Where will she ever live now? There are worse things than death, she thinks.

Later, she will walk down the street. She will walk down all the streets which curve and wind their way down to the river.

She will stop at the ruins of the burnt-down basilica, go into the courtyard, and sit there. Up above, the sky will pass through the perfect circle in the old stone wall. There will be a crispness to the clouds and the sky will be deep blue. She will sit until she's numb. Mute as marble. And the Virgin Mary will stand there in the cemetery, with benevolent arms outstretched, forgiving all abuses of doubt and snow and irreligious leaves which crust around her feet.

STEVEN HEIGHTON

A Man Away From Home Has No Neighbours

I.

AMANOGAWA AMERICAN ENGLISH SCHOOL, ŌSAKA, AUGUST 1987. The day's last lesson was over. Hashimoto and I drank tea at a small table beside the school's main window, which looked out over broken ranks of factories and warehouses, Love Hotels, tramlines, baseball diamonds, and tenements. In the late afternoon light Ōsaka was dusty and dry and flattened, like a neighbourhood after an air-raid.

"You are a carnivore, yes?" Hashimoto-San eyed me through the steam rising from his tea cup. He was my best student by far, and a kind of friend, so I'd asked him to stay and help clarify something that had come up in the lesson.

"Actually I don't eat meat," I told him. But I wasn't being completely honest – I did eat a little now and then, on special occasions, or when it was offered by a host or visiting neighbour.

"Yes, of course," he said, "but I mean 'you' in the general, collective sense. Most Westerners are meat-eaters, is that not so?"

I hesitated. Clearly Hashimoto-San was about to advance

one of those sweeping racial theories so popular here. Months before, after a few whiskys, he'd asked if my penis really was as big as a bottle of Johnny Walker and if Western women were all nymphomaniacs. No, I'd assured him on both counts, and he'd seemed both disappointed and relieved. Now, quite certain I was making a serious tactical blunder, I admitted that this time he was right: most of us *were* meat-eaters.

He blinked triumphantly. "We Japanese are not," he said. "*We are grain-eaters.*"

I raised my tea cup to my mouth to conceal a frown. "In that case what about the meat you had with your noodles a few hours ago?" I looked for support to Principal Kobayashi, who had eaten with us earlier at the Café Pittsburgh and now sat at her desk grading papers. But she was engrossed in her work and did not look up.

Hashimoto-San dismissed my objection with a gentle lifting of the hand. "An anomaly. A temporal exception. I am speaking in broadly historical terms. A thousand years ago your ancestors were roasting whole oxen over bonfires, while mine nibbled on cooked seeds, mushrooms, and mountain tubers."

Mystified, I replenished Hashimoto's cup.

"Now, *Sensei*," he continued, "surely you do not deny that slaughtering and consuming live creatures is a more violent activity than the gathering of seaweed, pulses, and fungi?"

"I suppose that depends on whether you're an animal or a fungus."

Hashimoto-San furrowed his brows and then said, "You are being facetious. My point is that on a visceral, intrinsic level Europeans have been habituated to violence and so we must expect them to be more aggressive than their Oriental counterparts."

"You're a talented linguist, Hashimoto-San, but I'm afraid your biology leaves something to be desired."

"The opinion is not mine alone, Steven-*Sensei*. It is widespread in Japan, and few scholars dispute it. And with all due respect, *Sensei,* your knowledge of science may be inferior to theirs."

On the table by my fist a puddle of spilled tea quivered with green flecks, like a pool of primordial soup.

"So," I said, "this is what Mr. Takaoka was talking about in the last lesson?"

"He did not mean to offend you. He did not mean necessarily that you are violent."

"I realize he wasn't saying that. It's just that … well, I'm not sure how to put this.…" I paused, then decided to press on, instead of skirting the issue in the discreet style I was now accustomed to. "*All* human beings are violent," I said, "or at least they learn to be." And I shot a glance at Principal Kobayashi to make sure she wasn't listening; her English was mediocre but I knew her family had suffered during the war and I didn't want her to hear what I had to say. "The problem with your theory is this: while my meat-eating forefathers were busy butchering each other with spears and daggers, your rice-eating ancestors were doing just the same thing – riding around the countryside with their pretty flags, carving up the peasants, assassinating rival lords.…"

"Certainly, they were, but when the Samurai killed it was always in the line of duty, always out of a sense of *giri,* of obedience to a higher power. I was talking about violence as a natural inclination.…"

"That's an interesting distinction. I'm afraid it might be lost on the victims."

"Nevertheless it exists."

I picked up my empty cup and put it down again more loudly than I'd meant. To my friend this gesture would probably seem a declaration of war.

"Look, Hashimoto-San, if you force me to do it I can cite all sorts of atrocities committed by both sides in World War II and you won't be able to explain them away as handily as you just did the Samurai." The volume of my own voice startled me; I tried to calm down. Hashimoto examined his cup, no doubt seeing my outburst as conclusive proof of the very theory I was attacking. But what a theory! After all, hadn't Hitler been a vegetarian? Hess? The Khmer Rouge? What would my prize-student have to say about the grain-eating pacifists who bombed Pearl Harbor? Had they started their day with a nice big steak, or did somebody lace their breakfast tea with animal proteins?

But I couldn't say these things to a man who'd been a small child at the time of the war, nor could I mention the death marches and the torture of Allied prisoners and the sacking of Nanking where one hundred thousand women were raped in the space of a few hours after the city fell. No, it would be unfair to cite these things, whatever my reason.

Hashimoto was watching me. He'd pointed out before that like most Westerners my thoughts were transparent, like a child's, and now he said, as if reading from a teleprompter lodged in my forehead, "You are thinking of Pearl Harbor. And perhaps of other things as well."

I was not surprised that he'd managed to intercept my train of thought, but I hadn't expected him to say anything outright. Like most embarrassments, national or personal, Pearl Harbor was not to be mentioned in sober conversation. I thought I might as well go on.

"The rape of Nanking," I said. "I was thinking of that too. I guess I don't have to remind you what happened. There've been similar cases in the West and it'll happen again, probably, there or here or someplace else because nothing ever seems to change and people behave the same way no matter where they live or how they dress or what kind of food they eat. *One hundred thousand unarmed women.* How do you square them with your stupid theory?"

Hashimoto glanced over my shoulder at Kobayashi, as I wanted to do but could not. Like me, he would be anxious about the effect our words were having. I felt a stab of remorse. The ultimate savagery, I reflected, was the dropping of not one but two atomic bombs on Japanese civilians – and though she'd never said it outright, Koyabashi had managed to imply that her parents had been killed at Hiroshima.

"Yes, well, about the rape of Nanking, as you call it, the cruelty is obvious and undeniable. But not impossible to explain."

"Explain it," I told him, leaning across the table. I could hear Koyabashi rising from her desk and pacing towards the back of the school.

"A man away from home has no neighbours," Hashimoto said, squinting as he looked out over the enormous city. The sun was going down. "A Japanese proverb, Steven-*Sensei*. I know you take an interest in our sayings, but this is one with which you may not be familiar. In fact I can see by your expression that you have never heard it."

"Never," I said softly. My remorse and my surprise at his change of tone had disarmed me altogether.

"Even peaceful, unaggressive men will commit atrocities when they are far away from home and the eyes of their neighbours...." Hashimoto explained the proverb with pedagogical care, perhaps feeling that since it was Japanese I would not be able to interpret it myself. But maybe he was right to do it? At first I saw his little gloss as needless and patronizing but that night as I rode the subway home to Nagai, as the car rattled rhythmically and station lights pulsing through the window alternated with the dark in that way so conducive to meditation and dream, it occurred to me that he may have wanted to specify a particular meaning because the proverb contained more than one. As my mind drifted over the past hours and over the last century – most of which I knew only at second- or third-hand – I began to see that the proverb was explosive, that if you held or touched or turned it in a certain way it would burst open and scatter meaning in all directions, like the white-hot particles of a new galaxy. Like a universe or a grain of sand – a fistful of desert sand turned to glass – it contained all the past, the present, and maybe the future too.

A man away from home has no neighbours.

Hashimoto-San turned from the school window and almost looked me in the eyes.

"Much, I think, can be explained by this."

II.

A WARTIME ROMANCE. Matsuo Koyabashi joined the Imperial Japanese Army in the winter of 1931 and was shipped with his regiment to Manchuria in late spring. He was twenty-three years old. His duty was to help defend a Japanese-controlled railway from the Chinese interference his officers referred to as "imminent." Matsuo was proud of his uniform and his rifle and of being stationed so close to Mukden, where his father had fought bravely twenty-six years earlier in the

Russo-Japanese War. To his parents, who had a tiny farm on the outskirts of Hiroshima, he sent monthly a portion of his negligible pay cheque, along with blurred photographs of himself and his comrades posed stiffly in front of steam locomotives or in the barracks yard or on dry hillsides behind the fort. He did not tell them anything about Yang, the Chinese farm girl who sometimes brought eggs to the fort and whom Matsuo had fallen in love with soon after his arrival, because the Chinese were the enemy and fraternization of any kind was strictly forbidden.

Whenever Yang came to the fort it was Matsuo's job to meet her and collect the fresh eggs, and their exchanged glances soon became shared words. Before long he contrived to meet her in private. He could hardly contain his excitement but he forced himself to say nothing even when his comrades teased him or made indelicate remarks about "the pretty farm girl," because he was quite sure they would not approve of his tightening involvement, and he was afraid they would report him.

He was deeply embarrassed and shamed by his actions. He had always been an obedient son. But after several weeks of torment (during which *seppuku* loomed as the only dignified solution to his troubles) he resigned himself to the situation, and admitted he was not ready to end his life.

(He vowed that if he was discovered he would admit his guilt at once and offer to kill himself, because his actions had brought shame on the regiment and set a poor example for the men.)

The continual chatterings of his conscience created such tension in Matsuo that sometimes, after making love with Yang in the dry hay-strewn ditch behind her village, he was possessed by a blind rage and imagined strangling her then and there and freeing himself of his lust and shame. But glancing down into her lambent eyes, half-open in the moonlight, trusting, he was overcome by tender feelings and then a deeper shame that such ideas could occur to him. She knew some Japanese and he a few words of her dialect and between them they managed to make themselves understood. In her stilted but strangely lyrical way she told him her heart glowed like the full moon when he was present, but that watching him creep home over the furrows and then awaiting his return her heart waned to a sliver.

Because Japanese characters are borrowed from the Chinese and he thought she might understand him, he decided to write short poems for her on army stationery; when he handed them to her she pretended to read and then praised and thanked him and pulled him close. Actually she could not read at all, but she understood his gesture, because the folk traditions of her region were full of lovers who came from far away and courted village maidens with their poetry.

By late summer Matsuo was obsessed with Yang. At first it had been enough to trade looks and endearments twice a week when she appeared at the gate with her eggs and to meet on certain nights in the fields behind her village, but now he crept from the barracks as often as three times a week in order to see her. Though the other men were always dead with fatigue and slept soundly, his manoeuvres involved considerable risk, for as he stole through the barracks yard toward the rear fence he had to dodge a sentry and a spotlight from the guard-tower. But he could not stop himself. He was often sluggish on parade and more and more he incurred the censure of his drill-sergeant when he reacted slowly or clumsily to commands. Yet as night approached he felt an inexplicable energy returning to his limbs, a feverish tingling in his lower belly, an electric numbness in the hands and scalp that seemed to presage the sweet, freezing blast of oblivion that swept through him when he made love to Yang. His cries, her cries – they were getting harder to muffle as their love and their knowledge of each other's bodies increased....

By now it had become customary in the barracks for the men to compare dreams on waking. They had only a few minutes to prepare themselves for parade, but most of them stubbornly observed this ritual. As they shook and stretched themselves awake, washed, straightened their bunks and dressed, they would holler out coarse commentary on sexual dreams, trying to outdo each other with graphic details or boasting about the traits of dream-partners. Gentler domestic fantasies in which a mother or father appeared were also common. Some of the men admitted, with uneasy fascination, to violent reveries where they bayonetted real Chinese instead of the stuffed dummies in the barracks yard. Matsuo said nothing. The sexual bravado that seemed so accessible to other men had always been foreign to his nature, and now he had finer reasons to absent himself from his comrades' exchange: the coarseness of their banter jarred him since he had experienced real earthly love, and besides, it seemed he no longer had dreams to talk about anyway.

He thought probably he'd stopped dreaming because of his fatigue and the tension, anger, and foreboding that more and more oppressed him. Probably, he reasoned, his body saw sleep as its only chance to escape ... but one morning he did remember a dream, and it was horrible. He had been yelling as he raced through Yang's village, swinging his rifle like a primitive club, cracking the skulls of the faceless civilians who had rushed from their huts to see what was happening....

"Koyabashi," a half-dressed soldier leered, "how come you never let us in on your dreams? Sounds like you had a good one last night – I heard you squealing like a sow. Dreaming of that pretty whore who brings the eggs?"

"I don't dream," Matsuo spat out, lowering his face to the basin and brutally rinsing with icy water.

"Not the way we do, anyway," said another soldier, the one whose bunk was closest to the door.

The first soldier cocked an eyebrow. "What do you mean by that? You mean he doesn't dream of women?"

"Don't think he needs to," the second one said. "You don't have to sneak from the barracks in the middle of the night just for…."

The man snapped to attention and bowed as the stocky drill-sergeant, who had entered the barracks as he spoke, paused in front of him and glared up at his face. Very softly he asked whom the man was referring to; who had been leaving the barracks in the middle of the night?

Scratching the dry scalp under his thinning hair, Colonel Morita inspected the handsome boy standing at attention by his desk. Several times in his career he'd had to deal with this kind of problem. He'd hit upon several disciplinary expedients and now as he watched the boy he turned them over in his mind, as a distracted hand will spin a cup of tea to see how the leaves settle.

His alternatives:

1. Punish the girl so terribly that no Chinese woman will ever dream of tempting Japanese soldiers again. Have the boy go to meet her in the usual place but escorted surreptitiously by his whole platoon. After the boy has had her, let the other men emerge from hiding and have her too, one after another.

Have the boy observe everything. After that he will beg to be allowed *seppuku*.

2. Destroy the girl's village so that she will be held responsible and punished by her own neighbours, who at the same time will learn at first hand about the fury of Japanese reprisals.

3. Have the boy sent home in disgrace.

4. Have the boy executed before the whole regiment.

5. Have the boy beaten, absolved, and then shipped to another sector of the Manchurian line. After all, what recruit hadn't dreamed of doing as this one had done? Despite himself the Colonel couldn't help admiring the boy's courage, resourcefulness, and tenacity. No, he could never again trust his obedience, but his bravery was beyond doubt and in coming weeks it could prove useful.

On the other hand....

Colonel Morita sleeked back his thin hair and examined the boy's smooth, impassive face. From far off the faint cry of a troop-train, arriving.

It had been almost two weeks since he had come but he saw at once that she was waiting for him in the usual spot. She was curled up in the ditch, wrapped in a wool cloak, the skin of her closed eyelids vivid in the full moon's light. She must be very tired for she did not wake at his approach as she always had before. Perhaps she had given up hope, or no longer desired him....

But here she was. He knelt beside her and watched the delicate rippling motions of her eyelids, which showed she was dreaming. He kissed the closed eyes and they opened as he pulled away. They did not look startled or afraid but wakeful with recognition, and love, and the certainty that he would return.

As he studied her features his heart began to race and stammer. He found it hard to swallow. She wrapped her arms round his neck to draw him down and then held him with such strength that for a moment he felt like a bound prisoner, or like the stuffed bayonet-drill dummies lashed to their posts in the barracks yard. He kissed her repeatedly, his eyes tightly closed. He had come here determined to obey his orders but now his body was betraying him for he felt no sexual stirrings, only fear and remorse and bitter self-hatred. She wanted him, he could feel the insistence of her desire, and it terrified him and made him want to run from her, or with her, quickly, to escape this sordid ambush and free himself of dishonour. The Colonel had warned him that should he betray his orders both absolution and *seppuku* would be out of the question and he would be executed publicly, shamefully, before the whole regiment. "My heart is full," she was saying in her strange Japanese, "I love you – " and he was afraid his platoon, concealed a stone's throw away, could hear every word. Now they would have even more reason to taunt and bait him, though in their hearts they must be envious, and angry too – in fact he was sure he sensed their anger, a chafing, rank miasma like poison gas, rising from the ditch where his comrades lay.

But he could not do it. It was impossible. And he saw now that they would not be able to do it either: they felt nothing for her, to them she was nothing, no one, not even a dream-partner, and surely desire cannot be made to follow orders. There was no danger here. Disarmed by their own bodies they would disobey, and they would face the consequences together.

"I love you," he said in plain Japanese, loudly, so she would never forget the words and his comrades would hear them in their hiding place and they would carry in the crisp autumn air across the fields to the village and back towards the railroad and the fort. He stood up so he was clearly visible to his platoon. He drew Yang to her feet and tried to explain what was happening. She looked confused. Run, he said, and he pushed her away towards the village. She came back and he pushed her away again and this time she seemed to understand, she started to run and she glanced back at him as she went, once – twice – and the moonlight flashed off her smooth forehead.

The men of his platoon had begun to yell. Matsuo turned to confront them. Like shock-troops rising from a trench they burst from the ground with terrifying resolve. Two of them began to scramble after Yang. As Matsuo turned away and urged her to hurry, the platoon sergeant pulled out his revolver, as he had been ordered to do should complications arise, and fired three rounds.

Matsuo crumpled into the bottom of the ditch where the straw was still warm and held the imprint of Yang's body. He did not move again, and he never learned that Yang managed to reach the village, where the soldiers were forbidden to follow, or that he was wrong about the well-trained members of his platoon, most of whom could have fulfilled their orders if they'd gotten the chance. He did not know that within two days ago his regiment would blow up a stretch of track an hour north of the village, blame it on the Chinese (and claim Matsuo as a casualty) and on this pretext invade and overrun all Manchuria within a few months. He didn't know, as we do, that the surviving members of his platoon, along with several hundred thousand other trained men including his brother

Haruo, would prove years later at the fall of Nanking where thousands of women were raped that *a man away from home has no neighbours* – that a man without neighbours is no longer a man but a menacing bundle of explosive fibres, fugitive customs, homeless and camouflaged desires. These are the things that were not known, or could still be denied, just sixty years ago.

To a man with a hammer, the Chinese say, *everything looks like a nail.*

Better that Matsuo never had to learn it.

They buried him in the ditch.

III.

TACTICAL MANOEUVRES: A TRUE STORY. Anyone who knows will tell you this is the biggest, finest Love Hotel in Ōsaka. The quantity and diversity of our rooms are quite unmatched, the video selection is encyclopedic, the staff skilful, courteous, and discreet, the location convenient but not conspicuous. If your reasons for using our facilities are the usual – overcrowded apartment blocks, nosy neighbours, live-in relations, rice-paper-thin walls – you'll find plenty of plain, serviceable rooms available at decent hourly rates. And if you're interested in something a touch more exotic – well, anyone who knows will tell you this is the finest place in the city. There's simply no question: it's only when you're away from home and neighbours that you can truly relax.

Shall we take a look around?

Some people, of course, see Love Hotels as an unfortunate

necessity, a symptom of the crowding and domestic incon-venience of modern Japan, but in fact the idea comes from the West, where recent statistics show that a skyrocketing propor-tion of all sexual acts occur in rented rooms rather than at home. The inference we are forced to draw from this figure is plain enough, is it not? Clearly the appetites of today's sexual consumer are dampened by the routines of home and com-munity and aroused by things anonymous, generic, and ex-pensive. Our studies actually show customer satisfaction ris-ing in direct proportion to the cost of the room! So that our new prices symbiotically benefit both client and proprietor.

Summer Moon? Yes, that's the name. We chose it to remind potential clients that we're more than just a business. Like any good Love Hotel we provide our guests with amenities as per-sonal and indispensable as the moon is to a lover on a summer evening: consider the romantic atmosphere, the privacy, the freedom from pressures, the quiet, the space to dream. And there's no denying that our Theme Rooms can spice up any marriage or affair gone stale, as they inevitably do....

Take this room, for example: our "Cadillac Ranch." These days it's a big hit with the university crowd. The walls, as you see, are decorated with glossy black-and-white posters depict-ing various vintage models from the heyday of American auto-manufacturing, while the big "drive-in" style video at the back of the room features a staggering assortment of vehicular entertainment including highlights of last year's Indy 500, exciting footage of road tests, medleys of the best car ads from the last decade, and endless repeats of *The Love Bug*. And there in the centre of the showroom, if you will, the pol-ished gleaming pink chassis of a vintage Cadillac Eldorado. Were I to retract the convertible hood you would find instead of seats a plushly-appointed queen-sized bed. The mahogany dashboard rising above the pillows behind the mattress has various switches and gauges which control the room's temperature and lighting (including a set of high-beams which shine from the cciling and illumine the bed at opportune moments) and the soundtrack, which includes hundreds of the best-known automotive hits of the past decades. A "speedometer" allows the couple to assess their performance in terms of pace and frequency and to compare themselves with previous visitors. There is even a species of vibrator built into the bed which, when activated, simulates aurally and sensually the smooth, soporific progress of a Cadillac Eldorado over an American superexpressway. All this for only 10,000 *yen* per hour.

There are other Theme Rooms, of course. I might mention for example the "American Dream," a bedroom designed to resemble the inside of a multinational bank. The king-sized bed is nestled inside a mock-steel vault behind the teller's cages at the back of the room and the toilet paper is attractively stamped with the currencies of the world's leading industrial powers. The video features various recent Hollywood films which we find we can choose almost at random. Needless to say (laughs) no security guards are present.

"Grand Central Station," just up this hall here, is another popular one: with its high, echoing ceilings and piped music and travel announcements it could be anything from a rail terminus to the departures level of an international airport. The twin berths are in a sealed compartment as luxurious, we believe, as anything on the Orient Express or the Tokyo-Ōsaka bullet train. We consider the room's appeal to lie in its promise of escape, of distance from the domestic and familiar.

But in the last few years it's this next room here, that has generated the most interest in clients both foreign and local. We call it "Tactical Manoeuvres." As you can see, the walls are sheathed over with guerilla netting and painted entirely in camouflage; those hanging vines are artificial, but I think you'll agree they look genuine enough. One of the room's soundtracks offers the martial anthems of every nation in the civilized world while others feature impressively authentic sound-effects including gunfire, battle-cries, the rumble of approaching tanks, the roar of jet-fighters, and all manner of explosion. What – you don't believe this room is popular? Well, I can't honestly say I see the appeal myself, but believe me "Tactical Manoeuvres" is doing very well for us, and we're not about to meddle with our bottom line.

Some people, I suppose, just come for the videos. Naturally we've got *Rambo. Rambō* is everywhere, though, isn't it? (Laughs) [*Rambō* happens to mean "violence" in Japanese. The proprietor is making a joke.]

We have all the Rambo clone films, too. And we have some local efforts – historical numbers like *Ran* and *Nihyaku-san-kochi* – though these days, oddly, our Japanese clients don't seem too interested in the country's past. Still, there's lots of other material to choose from – we have ten channels that play non-stop twenty-four hours a day! But the most striking attraction of the room, as you can see, is this beautiful reduced-scale replica of a Tiger battle-tank constructed of sturdy, life-like plastic and acrylic and authentically decorated. I can tell you're impressed. Please, go ahead and touch it. Now if you were to climb this ladder and lower your-self into the tank you'd find a comfortable twin bed and above it where the gunner's sights would normally be a video screen. There's a sort of dashboard too with the same kind of controls as in our "Cadillac Ranch." It's expensive, but you'd be surprised at the number of U.S. Navy officers and men who come up on leave from Kōbe to try it, and then all those Japanese recruits from the bases up north – they could spend a week's pay on a few hours in "Tactical Manoeuvres" (not to mention the cost of the girl, if she's hired) and most of them are delighted to get the chance. But mainly we deal with tourists and businessmen.

And look – here's the latest. We're importing them from the States as a novelty: *Camo-Condoms*. That's right, the rubber is actually embellished with a military-camouflage motif, but the really clever thing about them is the slogan here on the wrapper: DON'T LET HER SEE YOU COMING. As you must know, here in Japan we say "going" in reference to the sexual climax, so the joke is lost even on Japanese who have a little English, but North American clients never fail to make appreciative remarks upon checking out. One imagines a muscular camouflaged guerilla with a knife between his teeth creeping up on an enemy's woman in the jungle – like Rambo, I suppose? Yes, I think that must be part of the item's allure: here is a condom that Rambo would use....

So you are interested in "Tactical Manoeuvres?" Fine, that's fine, I thought perhaps you might be. Yes, we do require a deposit, and we need you to sign the register. But where is your wife?

You have checked into "Tactical Manoeuvres" alone. Once the proprietor realizes you intend to do this, he asks no further questions. He has seen everything, everything – and no doubt seeking to spare you embarrassment, he confides that in recent months quite a few people have done the same thing.

You climb down into the belly of the tank and make

yourself as comfortable as you can. You try to imagine couples making love in this claustrophobic mock-steel womb, but it isn't possible to imagine. Or perhaps for you it is possible – how can I say?

On one channel you find a movie that looks a little different from the other fare. It is a Japanese film, *Nihyaku-san-kochi*. Numbed, you stare at the screen while wave after wave of soldiers in pillbox-caps and white spats swarm up a hill into gunfire under the murderous moonlight....

IV.

NIHYAKU-SAN-KOCHI: THE FILM. So Shoji Kobayashi and Hideyuki Murata will be in the second wave for the first night-assault on 203 Metre Hill. This is something of an honour, though both of them had hoped their company would be placed in the front line; their commanding officer has advised them, however, that in his opinion even under cover of darkness the terrible new guns will demolish the first wave, so for all intents and purposes their attack will amount to the same thing.

A young boy scurries up the trench-line with an ornamental decanter, half-filling the men's mugs with hot *sake*. "Three minutes," he whispers to Shoji, and the decanter, painted with scenes of Samurai at rest under blossoming plum trees, quivers in his tiny hands.

The camera pans away from the crowded trench and focuses on the battlefield: Nihyaku-san-kochi, or 203 Metre Hill, looms above the darkness, its barren flank coldly metallic in the full moon's light. It is a chilly night in late autumn soon after the turn of the century. The summit of the steep hill bristles with Russian trenches in which riflemen and machine-gunners (most of them in their late teens) and their terrible weapons (some of them newly invented) await the Japanese assault, which they will be expecting after the long barrage that has just lifted.

Shoji gulps his *sake* in one draught and instantly it goes to work on the twisted, griping pain in his lower gut. Unconsciously he presses up against Hideyuki. Through the thick, itching wool of their uniforms he feels the heat of his friend's arm. Hideyuki has finished his own *sake* and now rests his forehead on the sharp lip of the mug, his downcast eyes a few inches from the earth. He is weeping, or trying not to weep. So as not to shame him Shoji looks away and concentrates on the moon and tries to compose a haiku, as he knows great warriors are meant to do before battle, or after. He can think only of Bashō's famous lines:

> Ah, summer grasses –
> All that remains
> Of the warriors' dreams.

The order to fix bayonets is coming up the line in furtive murmurs, man to man, and Shoji thinks of the children's game where a secret phrase is passed round a circle by the whispering players and then repeated at the end, by which time it has changed into something quite different, something absurd, garbled, comical, or monstrous. But he knows that when the lethal gossip reaches them and his friend turns and gives him the order it will be the same one he is expecting, and he will obey.

Fix bayonets –

CUT to behind the lines where Count Kiten Morosuke Nogi, the Japanese commander, is composing his own haiku as he waits with his officers and scans 203 Metre Hill. It is the key to Port Arthur and for several days he has been struggling to take it. So far he has lost 10,000 men, and last night Hashimoto, one of his officers, pardoned himself but insisted on observing that the Count was, perhaps, being rather more stubborn and wasteful of his men's lives than was quite necessary, for now. Nogi dismissed the objection and reminded the Colonel of their duty to the Emperor.

"*In this world,*" Colonel Hashimoto said, quoting the present Emperor's dead father, "*all men are brothers. Why then this constant war?*"

"A moving sentiment, no doubt," said General Nogi, "but a rhetorical question all the same. You are a good man, Colonel, but a dreamer."

An explosion on the far hillside lit up Nogi's face. He said, "If men were capable of grasping the full horror of war, every one of them would go mad. But they would not stop fighting."

Hashimoto was nonplussed by the General's remarks. He wondered if the man's personal losses were unhinging him.

"And the Emperor, General? Is the Emperor a dreamer?"

Nogi thought for a moment, then said, "The Emperor is a dream – an invention. And, like all monarchs, a dreamer. Kings do not decide the course of history. It is always the soldiers who do that."

"You mean the generals," Hashimoto said. "The soldiers decide nothing."

"They decide with their lives. They're an extension of us, of me. Like sons...."

Embarrassed, Hashimoto looked down at the muddy boots

he had not removed in three days. "Then please, General, call off this foolish attack. Or you are killing us both, son by son."

Nogi turned away from Hashimoto and the smouldering hillside.

"I have my orders, Colonel, and officially they come from the Emperor. Good night."

Hashimoto paced off to the edge of a knoll and stood watching the barrage, like festival *hanabi* – fire flowers – in early spring: sprays of poppy and indigo, Japanese lanterns, molten chrysanthemums bursting out of the dark slopes. *Mottainai,* he mumbled. *It is a waste. Away from his home a man has no neighbours to watch over him and keep him from harm. There is no one to plead his case, none to object to the wastefulness of his death....*

CUT to the front lines where an officer leaps from the advance trench a stone's throw from Shoji and Hideyuki and rears his samurai sword in the moonlight. It flashes like a line of grinning teeth. Yelling *Banzai, Banzai,* or *A Thousand Years for the Emperor,* the first wave of men surges up and hurtles away into the shadows. Then suddenly the whole hillside is flooded with light: two brilliant silver eyes, far bigger than the full moon and brighter than a thousand suns, burst open, wide awake, on the summit above them. The confused officer pauses, spotlit, his upraised weapon slowly falling as he tries to make sense of things. There is a clatter of machine-gun fire. The brilliant eyes move, like human eyes, or the watchful brotherly eyes of Buddha, and long tapering paths of light begin to sweep over the hill. The first wave of men is silhouetted like a row of leaf shadows on an autumn sidewalk and now as the machine gunners pick out their targets the leaves begin to fall. *A Thousand Years,* a second officer cries, his useless blade gleaming in the harsh new light as the second wave rises from its ditch and advances at double-time up the steepening slope, Shoji and Hideyuki unconsciously leaning together, shoulder to shoulder, not realizing that now they offer an easier target. Their eyes are virtually closed against the glare of the television lights. *A Thousand Years for the Emperor,* they gasp as they stagger over fallen comrades. Then all of a sudden CUT.

Sorry, I can't go on with this. Can we see what's on the other channel? Or better yet, let's just turn off the whole fucking machine. But you want to know what happens, right? I sure do. So how about this? Hideyuki was wounded, but he survived. Shoji survived – and so did the whole platoon. They all survived! The whole army went on, miraculous, immune to the blinding light and the whistling bullets and the rocket's red glare, and the Russians disarmed and met them halfway and everyone embraced and sat down for a picnic on the hillside and drank each other's health with *sake* and plum wine and vodka and exchanged whatever gifts they could dig up: green tea and microchips from the Japanese, rye bread, eggs, and back-issues of *Pravda* from the Soviets, and the officers fumed behind the lines and drew up new orders that no one would obey, and they gave themselves Purple Hearts, promotions and raises, and they mentioned themselves in dispatches and they snapped their flint knives over their knees when nobody applauded. No one got hurt at all.

(Much of this actually happened the day before, when a two-day truce was called to clear away the dead.)

Three Moons, Shoji whispers to himself, spotlit in the field alone, Hideyuki wounded behind him, *Three moons above the barren hill: the body is a falling blossom.*

V.

BETTER HOMES AND GARDENS. A few years after the end
of the Russo-Japanese War, Shoji Kobayashi's cousins, the
Takaokas, took leave of him at Kōbe. They were bound for
America, where other relatives had already gone, and though
they had urged Shoji to come and bring his new wife and baby
son Haruo, he would agree only to accompany them as far as
the port. In fact, he was already planning a move to Hiroshima
and the farm of another cousin.

Mr. and Mrs. Takaoka and their newborn twins, Shoji and
Masanori, set sail on a beautiful midsummer day and docked
in San Francisco three weeks later, then sought and found an
apartment in the Oriental quarter of the city. After working
together in a canning factory for two years, while their elderly
Japanese neighbours minded the boys, the Takaokas saved up
enough money to buy land in a small valley near Rio Vista,
where they intended to farm. The Takaokas had farmed all
their lives, and the new land was fertile, but at first they experienced problems because the soil and climate of the valley were
so different from Japan's. But after a few years, with the help of
their neighbours (who were mainly white), they managed to
make a go of it.

Their life in the twenties was pleasant and successful in a
modest way, and before the Oriental Exclusion Act was passed
in 1924 they managed to convince several Japanese relations to
immigrate to America. The Act itself was something of an
insult, but it did not affect them directly, and like many com-
fortably assimilating migrants they preferred to ignore the
whims of their adopted land instead of making trouble. For
though at first they had found the open, empty spaces of the

valley draining and inhospitable, the idea of a return to the finite rice fields and jammed living arrangements of their old Kyōto home no longer seemed attractive. Shoji and Masanori were growing quickly on the plentiful food and now towered above their parents; once in a while there were troubles with the local children but for the most part their neighbours seemed tolerant and neutrally helpful, if not exactly welcoming.

Things changed, of course, in the thirties. The valley was not so badly affected as other agricultural regions of the continent, but the climate was no longer benign and dependable and some of the Takaokas' crops began to fail. Faced with debts and failures of their own, the attitudes of their neighbours seemed to change. Some of them made it clear that the Takaoka twins were no longer welcome in their homes and when incidents at the high school between the two boys and certain white students became common, Shoji and Masanori, who had always been rather placid, were usually blamed for the trouble.

A man away from home, Mr. Takaoka concluded one evening over whisky, has no real neighbours.

To make ends meet, Mr. Takaoka was forced to take a night job at a local factory while continuing to work in the fields with his wife during the day. After a year of this taxing regimen he became ill. In June 1937, a month before the Japanese Army crossed the Marco Polo Bridge en route to Nanking, he died of pneumonia. His sons cremated him and buried his ashes under a small tombstone at the edge of the fields.

The harvests were much better in 1939 and ' 40, and the mood of many of her neighbours changed, but Mrs. Takaoka grew increasingly anxious about political developments in

Asia. Still, she was pleased that her sons had graduated from high school and that they worked now with such diligence on the farm and in the factory – though when Shoji met a Mexican girl there whom he wanted to marry, Mrs. Takaoka felt she had to object. After a brief but heated argument the boy gave in.

In '41 the harvest was the best ever, but all that autumn Mrs. Takaoka was oppressed by a sense of foreboding: it seemed increasingly clear to her that Japan and the United States would soon be at war. She mentioned her feelings to the two boys but they paid no attention – they were busy with the farm and with work at the factory, saving money for their futures, talking of marriage and of trips to San Francisco to find wives. For their sake, she told herself, she would make a point of visiting the neighbours more often with her gifts of tomatoes, beans, green tea, and Japanese pickles.

Soon after the attack on Pearl Harbor the Takaokas' lives changed dramatically. Because of the valley's nearness to the coast and their presumed sympathy for the Emperor's cause, they were removed from their farm, first to a racetrack where they were billeted in horse stalls, and then, after a twelve-hour journey in cattle cars, to a concentration camp in Utah. They took only the most basic possessions.

The camp was called Topaz, but the suggestive elegance of its name was belied by its harsh, scarified environs. Dust-devils hissed in the barbed wire of the perimeter like wind through thistles, and beyond the guard-towers a salt plain stretched away for hours, ending on one side with the skyline and on the other at a distant range of mountains. At the time, Mrs. Takaoka could find nothing to compare it to because she had never seen a landscape like it, but years later she would be startled by a jab of recognition when she first saw photos of Hiroshima's flattened remains.

It was now early spring and Mrs. Takaoka set to work preparing a small garden. To coax life from the dense, resistant soil she composted whatever scraps she was able to obtain from the kitchen, collected manure from the chicken pens, and scrounged constantly for extra water. She had brought seeds with her, and now she planted onions, tomatoes, beans, cabbages, sunflowers, a little corn.

Her sons, formerly so helpful, had become idle and withdrawn and showed little interest in the garden. They loitered each day on the stoop of their lodging and walked the camp's perimeter at dusk, rolling cigarettes as a sun red as the Japanese ensign sank behind the far peaks.

In early summer a group of U.S. Army recruiting personnel arrived in the camp and asked for volunteers to fight the Germans. Shoji and Masanori were quick to offer themselves. After passing a brief quiz and pledging their loyalty to the flag they were accepted. Again Shoji and his mother found themselves at odds, but this time the boy refused to acquiesce, and Masanori insisted on accompanying his brother.

Dressed now in the uniform of the recruit, they resembled grown men.

A few weeks later Mrs. Takaoka escorted her embarrassed sons and a score of other boys to the camp gate and wished them farewell. She allowed her presence to speak for itself and did not shame them further by begging them to be careful. Standing by the barbed wire she watched dust rise in a thickening cloud from the wheels of the truck taking them to the train, and she did not turn back to her garden till after the dust had settled.

That first autumn Mrs. Takaoka's harvest was negligible, but over the next three years she found ways of improving her yield. Her compost heap was now considerable and she encouraged newly arrived internees to use the rich, flowering humus to grow produce of their own. The fresh fruit and vegetables from these "victory gardens" were a welcome supplement to the camp's meagre, monotonous fare.

Periodically she received letters and photographs from her sons, who were now stationed in England. They told her they were not being treated too badly, though for a while their lieutenant had refused to believe they were twins because, he said, all Japanese look alike, and they must be playing a joke on him. On leave their movements were restricted, but they managed to see a bit of England; her favourite picture, which she framed and hung above the stove, showed the two of them looking festive and rakish, with cigarettes drooping from their grins, arms linked as they stood on the platform of a train under a hanging sign that read GATWICK. But they were some distance off and the photograph was overexposed; she had to admit she couldn't tell them apart.

The winter of '44 was a bitter one. Icy winds, like the ones from Siberia that blew south over the Sea of Japan each December, rushed unimpeded across the salt-flats and drifted dunes of fine snow against the barbed wire, the camp gate, the pylons of the guard-towers. Several of the old people died in February, including a fisherman from the coast whose last words were *umi ga natsukashii* – I miss the ocean.

Spring came late that year but Mrs. Takaoka's garden was already thriving when news came of the Normandy landings. Soon after that, a letter arrived from Shoji assuring her that both he and Masanori were unhurt, and telling her with a disappointment she could not share that their regiment had been consigned to the second wave. This, she reasoned, was a promising precedent, a good omen.

The summer was long and hot and Mrs. Takaoka's garden flourished prodigiously. The gentle, apologetic white woman who taught the camp's school-aged children often stopped by to ask for gardening advice or to share a pot of tea. She never failed to ask about Shoji and Masanori. Mrs. Takaoka liked the woman, and sometimes forced her to accept an apronful of cherry tomatoes, peas, or long beans.

Near Christmas, long after the camp's humble harvest was in and the victory gardens were fertilized with a dusting of snow, news came of another battle in France. Hitler, it seemed, had gathered his legions for a last great offensive against the Allies, and the American troops were bearing the brunt of it. Hourly the radio carried cautiously phrased reports on the U.S. Army's "tactical retreat" through the Ardennes and the "stiff resistance" of encircled troops at a place called Bastogne. Mrs. Takaoka listened carefully to these reports, though the nuances of euphemism, which she sensed but could not always interpret, made it difficult for her to gauge the situation's gravity.

The day after American New Year, a tall slim man in an officer's coat appeared on the edge of the compound. Mrs. Takaoka watched him through her half-frosted window as he marched across the grounds and stopped some playing children, then a hunchbacked old man, to ask some kind of question. He was looking for someone, that much she could tell, and slowly it dawned on her whom it must be that he'd come for, and why. He seemed to look up and peer toward her lodging, then at the window with her face behind it, but she could

not be sure where he was looking because of the frost and the
weakened condition of her eyes. He was approaching now but
his features were still unclear. She turned from the window
and went to the stove to prepare tea.

That spring a delegation of smartly uniformed officers
arrived in Topaz to bestow posthumous awards on the mothers of two boys killed in the Battle of the Bulge. Mrs. Takaoka
was one of the mothers. As he presented the small, burnished
Legion of Merit the presiding officer assured her that Shoji
had died bravely in the service of his country. He regretted
that Mrs. Takaoka could not leave Topaz to receive the medal
in more appropriate surroundings, but trusted she understood such things were temporarily impossible.

Mrs. Takaoka bowed to the man and turned away, clutching
the medallion to her breast.

That evening was clear and mild, but instead of working in
her garden as she liked to do when the days were growing
longer, Mrs. Takaoka took a walk to the camp perimeter and
stared west toward the mountains. Despite the warmth, her
joints ached, and she had to wrack her memory for several
seconds to recall her age. She opened her hand to look at her
son's decoration: it was luminous and star-shaped, like a gem
or a talisman, and its keen tips had cut a pentagon of lesions
into her palm. The bright scarlet ribbon that hung from it
twitched in the breeze. She wished she could place it over the
modest stone they'd set above her husband's ashes but the
farm was days from here by train and lately she'd begun to
wonder if it would still be hers when the war ended....

The sunset was no more vivid than usual. The Legion of
Merit gleamed like a coin in the ruddy light. For a moment she
pulled back her arm in a clumsy wind-up as if to fling the

medal over the barbed wire and into the desert, then clenched her fist more tightly around it and hugged it to her chest.

Masanori was still alive, she told herself. She repeated the words several times under her breath, dropping the medal into her apron like an amulet and turning back to her garden.

VI.

... AND IN EVERY ANSWERING MACHINE A ZEN KOAN. A Japanese businessman shook me awake as I reached my station. He said he watched me get off at Nagai every night and didn't want to see me carried to the end of the line the way a drunk or exhausted commuter would be. I thanked him, stumbled off the train, and made my way to the exit.

It was late, and a slim, metallic moon was balanced over the city. As I walked home past the darkened banks, the *pachinko* joints, the Love Hotels and bars and office buildings and into the vacant sidestreets of my neighbourhood, I thought about the apartment I'd left early that morning, how alien and unsettled it always seemed because I spent so little time there. Suddenly I wished I had someone – anyone – beside me. Except for Hashimoto and the principal I had few friends here, yet I wondered if someone might have called while I was out and left a message on my new machine; I thought of voices, a touch hesitant, shy and distorted, their timid invitations wasted on the empty bedroom; I pictured sound-waves stirring a few grains of dust on the *tatami* floor. My Japanese neighbours were as busy as I was and I hardly ever saw them – and what is a neighbour anyway if you're never home? Someone away from home has no neighbours because people are neighbours only when you're there. Like the tree tumbling in the forest, like the sound of one hand clapping; when I reached the alley that leads to my apartment I turned back towards the lit-up sidestreets and bars around the station.

VII.

THE SUN FLAG. *A man away from home,* General Nogi muttered to himself, *has no neighbours; and away from his neighbours he has no home. Strangers must bury him, and he will sleep in ground his family can never visit....*

It was dawn. With hands linked behind his back the General paced slowly over the smoking battlefield. His officers followed at a tactful distance, but he was aware of their gaze. Stepping with careful respect over the corpses of his men he looked up and felt a stirring of pride at the sight of his ensign rippling in the winds above the hill. A pale moon surprised him in the morning sky, and he began to weep.

"A dream in the mind of a dragonfly," he quoted under his breath, searching for the right words. But they would not come. From somewhere far off there was a wail of a train arriving or departing and he thought of his two sons, one of whom had died earlier in the year in the opening assault on Port Arthur, and the other three days in the first daylight attack on the hill. In both cases he had given the orders.

He turned on his officers. They were waiting for him to recite the poem a victorious Samurai is obliged to compose after battle. He raised a hand, as if for silence, and spoke.

L. REX KAY

Travelling

Four days after his twenty-seventh birthday my brother took an overdose of his antidepressant medication and died. Our family physician, Dr. Powell, had been prescribing the pills for three months, the second time David had been treated for depression. The bottle we found at his bedside had been filled a week earlier and held a month's worth of medication. They assume my brother swallowed sixty tablets.

My father's brother had flown in from Vancouver. He offered to help with the funeral arrangements but I had done everything by the time he arrived. The big question was what to tell my grandmother. She was seventy-nine years old and living in a nursing home. She had a failing heart and Dr. Powell didn't think she'd last another year. He didn't think we should tell her about David. He thought we should tell her that David had gone travelling again. My uncle agreed. Tracy, David's girlfriend, agreed. My girlfriend, Brenda, didn't agree. She said lies like that have a way of backfiring. Personally, I was undecided. I didn't want to lie to my grandmother but I could appreciate Dr. Powell's point.

Two days after the funeral I drove my uncle to the airport. He told me what a waste it all was and that I should call if I need anything. He said he'd always been there for us kids and would still be there for me.

In the end I lied to my grandmother. I thought it would be easier on her. Nobody visited except Dr. Powell and me, so I didn't think it would be all that hard to preserve the fiction. I told her that he'd quit his job and gone travelling on the spur of the moment. She was upset that David had left without telling her but he'd done that before. She told me not to worry, that he'd always been more affected by my parents' deaths than I had, and that this was his way of trying to deal with it. She also told me that she was looking forward to his letters.

David always wrote such fine letters, she said.

Brenda said she'd told me so. I called Dr. Powell who told me to read her some of David's old letters. He said she'd never recognize them. I said she would. He told me to make some up. She couldn't see, her memory wasn't that good anymore, and she'd be dead in a few months. She'd worked so hard, raising David and me, it wasn't fair to tell her that David had killed himself. She'd suffered enough for one lifetime, Dr. Powell said.

I talked to Tracy. Tracy and I had found the body together. She'd called me up on the Tuesday following my brother's party to tell me that David hadn't answered his phone the previous night and hadn't shown up for work that morning. My brother had managed an upscale café since returning from his last trip overseas.

"Oh, hell," I'd said. "He's taken off, again. I'll meet you at the apartment in an hour."

My brother had gone travelling without warning before. Usually, it was for a few weeks, once it was for a year. He'd also go travelling with plans. I'd recently calculated that he'd spent more than half of the last decade on the road.

But this time, of course, he hadn't gone anywhere. Nowhere tangible, at any rate. He was curled up in bed, looking pretty peaceful, and his skin was quite cold. His limbs were immobile, so I guessed he'd been dead for a while. I called an ambulance but told them not to hurry. Tracy went a little hysterical but pulled herself together, sitting on the couch while I did a few things, taking the pill bottle and note and turning off the stereo. He'd been listening to a tape of The Beatles when he went to sleep. The note said that he didn't blame anybody, that he loved Gram and me and was coming to love Tracy, and that he hoped we'd forgive him. When I went back into the living room Tracy was watering the plants. I showed her the note.

"Stupid, isn't it?" she asked. "Watering the plants in a dead man's apartment."

She turned to another plant but put the water down and began crying again. I held her until the ambulance attendants arrived. It bothered me that Tracy seemed more affected than I was; my brother was dead, my closest living relative. I figured I would have a delayed reaction.

When I told Tracy about the letters she began to laugh. It sounded hollow. "I didn't expect that," she said. "What are you going to do?"

"Well," I began, "I've got a bunch of the old letters together."

"I can give you a few of mine. If you want."

"I was sort of hoping you'd write them, Trace."

"Me?"

"Well, yeah. You're better with words than I am, and it would make it easier for me to read them to Gram, if I didn't write them. More natural."

"He's your brother, Andy," she said.

I didn't want to have to say what I said next. "I didn't really know him that well, Tracy. I mean, we grew up together, but I never knew him very well. I think you knew him better. I don't think I could write a letter like he would, even with the old ones."

Tracy wouldn't write the letters. She said if she knew him that well, why was he only "coming to love" her after two years? Why did he commit suicide when she thought he was finally settling down? If she knew him that well, why couldn't she make him happy?

I spent Sunday night at Brenda's. I lay in bed and told her that I didn't think I could write the letters. I was angry that I had to. I asked Brenda to write them for me.

She twisted onto her side and propped her head up on her hand. Her breasts fell together. She pushed her dark hair back and looked at me. She didn't say anything.

Monday night, at work, I began the first letter.

I'm the night manager of a small downtown hotel. I do the books, throw out the drunks, and supervise a staff of two. Dianne handles the desk and Neil the rooms. The work is generally quiet and easy and the food and beverage manager is retiring in two years. Dianne, Neil, and I work well together, shooting the shit and playing computer games. Right now we're in the middle of a computer Risk phase, trying to take over the world after the books are done. Neil's a bit flaky, he's a nineteen-year-old guy who takes some philosophy courses at the U during the evenings. Dianne says he's probably a genius. Dianne's a single mother in her early forties. She's a little heavy, has short, blonde hair and wears garish green eye-shadow. Neil says it's the sort of colour that when other women see it at a cosmetics counter they think, "Who on earth buys this stuff?", but on Dianne it looks okay.

"Yo, Andy," Neil said when I showed up at work.

"'Yo," I said. "Yo, Di."

"Yo. How are you doing?"

I told them about the letters.

"Man," said Neil. "This is clearly a problem."

"Thanks," I said. "That helps."

That night after I finished the books I closed my office door and spent several hours rereading my brother's letters. Gram was right – he did write good letters. I hadn't really noticed at the time, but his letters were funny and evocative. There was something of a pattern, for which I was grateful. He always began by describing where he was as he wrote. "As I write this I'm sitting in my favourite café in Paris, looking at Notre Dame Cathedral when I'm not busy looking at Parisienne women," one began. Or this, from his first trip to Asia: "The noise of Bangkok is so oppressive I had to splurge for an expensive, indoor restaurant to write this or you wouldn't be able to hear the words." Or, "At this moment I am sitting on my balcony in Kalkan, Turkey, watching the Mediterranean do nothing, doing nothing myself."

After the setting he told us about the people he was travelling with. "I'm with quite a cosmopolitan group these days: John is a doctor from New Zealand, Fred is a photographer from London, Sarah and Elspeth are teachers from Vancouver, and Rudi is a typesetter from Munich." Frequently, he placed his companions in the current setting: "Also on the roof are Peter, a chef from New York, and Asa, the Scandinavian girl he's travelling with, plus Soncalm (sp?), whose family owns a hotel in Thailand, and Jennifer, whom you heard all about last letter. Peter and Asa are hanging laundry (not mine, unfortunately), Soncalm is writing a letter, and Jennifer is reading a guide book, trying to decide where we'll go if we ever leave this place."

Generally, David would then tell us about what had happened since his last letter, telling a funny story or describing some of the people he'd met or places he'd been in detail. He'd end with his future plans, reminding us of the next post office we could write him care of. Then he'd send us his love and sign his name.

My first problem was where he'd gone this time. It had to be somewhere he'd been, of course, but that still left Asia, South America, the South Pacific, and all of Europe. I decided to start him off in London, since there were a number of letters from there and it seemed easier.

"Dianne," I called, "what's the goddamned temperature in London, please?"

"How the hell should I know?"

"Could you check the paper for me, please?"

"Overcast with a high of fifteen celsius," she said a minute later.

"I wish it'd rain on him," I said.

"Dear Gram and Andy," I typed. "Here I am in a restaurant in London, looking at the overcast skies, though it is mild. 15 or 16 celsius, I'd say."

I reread what I'd written and deleted everything after "Dear Gram and Andy." After three more attempts I lifted the opening paragraph out of a 1981 letter, changing the weather and the names of the people he had met. Then I decided I wanted him alone, so I deleted the others. Then I made it rain, after all.

"I'm sorry I ran out on you guys like that," I typed, "but I turned 27 and suddenly felt like I had to move on. It's good to be travelling again. Don't miss me too much. I've asked Tracy to sublet my place and put my stuff in storage. Andy – you can have my CDs, and anything else you want. Except the leather jacket, at least until you lose some weight." I thought that all sounded pretty authentic.

I worked on the letter off and on during the week. Friday night I wrote it out longhand on airmail paper and stuffed it into an old envelope. Monday afternoon I went to the senior citizens' home to visit Gram.

"Letter from Dave," I told her.

"Well, it's about time. Read it to me."

I read the letter while Gram closed her eyes and listened. When I was finished she was silent for a long moment and I began prickling with sweat. I was certain she recognized the forgery. My heart began pounding and I tried to think of how I'd explain it to her, whether to admit that he was dead or just to say I was afraid she'd be upset because he hadn't written yet. Maybe I could just deny it, smile indulgently at her senility, but that scared me even more. At last she opened her eyes and I saw tears in them.

" 'With all of my heart, David,' " she quoted. "He always ends them that way. He's such a loving boy. He's such a treasure."

I should have been pleased but felt instead a rise of anger. He's such a treasure. So loving. I visit you two, three times a week. I call every day, I don't leave you for more than two weeks for my entire life, and he's the goddamned treasure. If he's such a loving boy why can't he stay here with you, why couldn't he visit you more than twice a month even when he is in town? What the hell does that make me? I'm not the fucking one in fucking London! I stopped myself, and went still. The inner voice continued, much softer now. I'm not the one who's dead, it said. The one you'll never see again. I'm just the younger brother, the dull one, but very nice, actually. The one who's here for you. Who's always been here for you. Evidently things like that don't count for a whole lot in this world.

I felt ashamed, not only because David was dead. David was not to be criticized. He was, somehow, beyond it. He always had been. David was to be appreciated, respected, thanked for being himself in your presence. He was the bearer of life and adventure, of wisdom and beauty. He brought stories and photographs, true, but long before that he brought poetry and novels, music and promise. He soothed deep hurts by his existence. He was beyond criticism: it was a quibble.

"Before my parents died, when I was about five years old," I told Brenda that night in bed before going to work, "I remember once crying to my mother about something David had done to me. I can't remember what it was. He was always getting me to play with him and then, I guess, getting bored and sending me away. I'd go to my mother for comfort. It's my strongest memory of her. When I was five she held me that time and told me not to be mad at David because she and Dad wouldn't be around forever and then David would be the one to take care of me. Three years later they died. She was right, but … Jesus Christ …"

I'd been looking up at the ceiling but now I turned to look at Brenda. Our faces were inches apart on the pillow. Her eyes were still. "What were you going to say?" she asked.

"Nothing. Just that … that was an awful thing to say to a kid."

Brenda nodded. I saw in her eyes that she understood but I could take no solace. I'd committed an act of betrayal.

Things stayed pretty bad for David after that. The weather

continued to be cool and wet, and he caught an awful cold. He decided to go to Paris but that didn't help. He had to spend all day inside his cheap hotel rom, and the heat was broken. I felt a little guilty, making him stay indoors in his favourite city, but I was enjoying myself.

"Poor David," Gram said after a Monday letter.

"I know. It's awful," I answered.

He went to the riviera and got over his cold but got dumped by a Swedish girl named Inga.

"Oh, how sad," said Gram.

Six weeks into his trip somebody stole his wallet and there was a subtle but clear reference to a shot of penicillin.

"This is getting sick," said Brenda.

'I know," I said. "I know I'm taking out years of anger. But there are worse ways to do it. At least I'm not hurting anyone."

"You're hurting me. It hurts me to see you acting this way. And you're worrying your grandmother."

"Oh, Brenda. Lighten up."

Two months after his death my brother played a tennis match against the son of an Italian clothing designer. The challenge was issued when it became apparent that David, despite his clothing and rather inept Italian, was charming the heir's girlfriend at a café. David was never a good athlete but tennis made sense to him. He out-thought more skilled opponents and frustrated them with an array of piddly drop shots and lobs with eyes. He showed up at the club in a tennis outfit designed by a rival clothing designer and brought a thermos of coffee with him onto the court. He lost the first set 6-1. This Italian was good. But David was accustomed to losing first sets: it took him a while to figure out his opponent's weaknesses. In the case of the son of the Italian clothing designer David could find no weakness in any strokes, but was able to exploit his temperament. He settled into a pattern of deep lobs, towards the baseline, but shallow enough to tempt his rival into trying overhead slams more frequently than he should have. The Italian began thudding balls into the lower third of the net and sending others bouncing off of the far court fences. The assembled friends began hooting and David sensed support from some of them. He won the set 6-4. The girlfriend cheered.

He began the third set in the same way, but then judged his opponent sufficiently unnerved to merit a switch in game plan. He began to play an aggressive, attacking game, hitting the ball right at the Italian. He wanted to win in style. He wanted to pound the ball down his throat. He did play with style, and bravely, but lost 7-5 nonetheless. His opponent was not magnanimous in victory: David went back to his *pensione* alone, regretting the money he'd spent on clothing he didn't need and a quite useless coffee thermos.

"Wow," said Neil, when I read him the letter. "That was great! I was well and truly excited."

"I didn't think you could write like that," said Dianne.

"Neither did I," I said. "My heart was pounding. I'm exhausted. I didn't even know what was going to happen."

"But he lost," said Brenda, when I told her that. "He's lost and he's still alone."

"Stop accusing me, Brenda. Do you think I like doing this? I'm writing these letters for my grandmother's sake. I'm doing it for her. Okay?"

Brenda was leaning back against the window ledge, her hands gripping the sill. Her voice was soft, as it was when she was most intense. "Sure," she said. "And you're not getting anything out of it yourself."

I rarely lost my temper but, when I did, it almost always

involved David, one way or another. I stared at Brenda and felt myself growing dizzy with rage. "Okay," I said, my voice loud and beyond control. "So I'm having a little fun. What's it matter to you? What the hell do you want from me? Do you want him to marry the girl and bring her home to meet the family? Good thinking, Brenda. Fuck you. I think you care more about my fucking dead brother than you do about me!" I stormed out of her apartment, slamming the door on the way.

That November my brother went to Crete and my grandmother went into hospital. Till then my subterfuge had given my life a comforting rhythm. I thought about and researched the letters through the week, then holed myself up in my office Friday night and wrote. Over the weekend I'd transcribe the letter into longhand and read it to my grandmother sometime early in the week. But in the first week of November she went into heart failure and required an admission. It had happened several times before, the laboured breathing, the clouded mind, the blue and cold lips. Entreaties to let her die. Then the intravenous medication followed by a sudden then a gradual improvement. The rounds of bloodwork that left her thin arms stained with ink-blue bruises. Changes in medication I couldn't understand, though I tried. And each time, her eyes re-set further back in her skull. Looking into them I wondered how many rounds she had left.

"Read me the letter, again," she asked.

The last letter, written during my grandmother's first week in hospital, was a sad one, full of a new kind of loneliness David had never written of before. It was a tired voice, and reflective. For the first time in any letter, he mentioned my parents, wondering what they would think of the reconstructed ruins of Knossos. My father had had several books of archaeology in his library; David thought he would have found the site overdone. David had never been to Crete. I was now working on fresh research, information culled from guide books and encyclopedias.

David was living on the south coast of the island, in a town whose prehistoric caves had been inhabited, off and on, for millennia, most recently in the sixties and seventies by hippies on the lam. Currently the town was full of travellers suffering from what he called "Sixties Envy," trying to recreate a period they had romanticized out of all proportion, trying to escape into the past. He wondered if he had ever looked like them; if he did now. He wondered what they were all afraid of.

"He's beginning to grow up," my grandmother said. "I think he's beginning to forgive himself."

"Forgive himself for what?" I asked her.

"For hating your parents."

"Hating them? Why, because they died?"

"Of course," said my grandmother.

"It wasn't their fault. They were hit by a truck."

My grandmother looked at me from her hospital bed. "You were always so different from him," she said. "More logical. Maybe he's learning now."

My parents were killed in the late winter, when I was eight and David was thirteen. They had gone away for the weekend, driving to visit friends across the border in the States. My grandmother was staying with us. Sunday night, when my parents were due back, David decided to surprise them and shave. He had a noticeable peach-fuzz moustache, but had never shaved it off. That night we went up to my father's bathroom and I watched as he wet his upper lip, applied shaving cream, and dragged a razor through the foam. He rinsed his face and looked first to the mirror, then at me. It was a shock – I hadn't realized how prominent the moustache had been. While I looked at him a small orb of blood began to form on his lip. I giggled and pointed it out to him. He dabbed at it with a Kleenex. "Nicked myself shaving," he said in a deep voice, and we both laughed. A moment later the police rang our doorbell.

My grandmother had a healthy December. David stayed in Crete, because the south coast of Crete is the warmest part of Europe in the winter, but moved on to another village. In the middle of the month Brenda and I broke up. It was a quiet thing, with no intense anger or remorse. I guess it had been coming for a while. She told me she thought it was best for both of us and I didn't disagree. At a quarter to eleven I left her apartment. It was too cold to walk so I took a cab to work.

I didn't talk about it for a week but then I told Dianne. I talked for a few minutes, not really sure of what to say.

"I'm sorry," Dianne said when I'd finished. "She seemed like a nice girl, that time she picked you up here."

"Yeah, well. She was. It's not that big a thing.'

"How long had you been going out?"

"Almost two years."

"And it's not that big a thing?"

"I guess it should be. I'll tell you what I do miss. Having someone to phone every day. Every morning, I'd get home from here, shower and call her at work. Just to tell her about my night. I don't even know what there was to tell. What the hell ever happens here?"

"Loneliness is a terrible thing," Dianne said.

"It must be tough for you, sometimes," I said.

"Tell me about it," she said.

"It's funny," I said. "I'm not really sure that I've ever been lonely. Not even now. I'm not sure I can be lonely."

"You're one of the lucky ones," she said.

In late January David went to Egypt. I spent a lot of hours in the library, researching the inland route he'd be taking down to Kenya. His Egypt letters were filled with the details of the crowds and pollution of Cairo and the wonders of the ancient ruins. I stared in awe at pictures of the pyramids and the temples of Luxor and Karnac, pictures I'd seen before but that now possessed a sense of immediacy. I tried to see them through David's eyes and felt this urge to communicate my impressions, which spilled into the letters. And I realized that writing letters wasn't enough, that he would want to share this with other people. Suddenly I understood why his letters always began with descriptions of where he was followed by whom he was with. They complemented each other. Far from home, touching photographs from childhood, these travellers would need someone to share the experience with, to make it real. So David met up with an American couple and an English guy and they travelled Egypt together and he and the English guy, Nick, hitched the long road south through Sudan. The letters became irregular, none for a few weeks, then three together. He and Nick had spent the time slowly moving south, waiting two or three days for a lift, sitting on the side of the road drinking sterilized water and spending easy time, talking about their lives and swapping travel stories. Nick was from London. He was one of those solid, dependable guys with a lot more on the ball than you first think.

"This Nick sounds like a good person," my grandmother said after the third letter. "He reminds me of you." My spine shivered and I blushed for the first time, I think, ever. "Don't be embarrassed," she said. "I'm sure David misses you." Two letters later, in Kenya, Nick flew to Johannesburg to visit relatives.

David went on a photo safari in Kenya. I pored through books on African wildlife and described what he was seeing. For the first time I began daydreaming about travelling myself, but quickly pushed the idea away. But I now began to understand why my brother had travelled so much. He met an old man in Malindi who told him stories from before World War II, of the land and the animals before they were destroyed by greed. I stole most of the details but the actual words were mine and both Dianne and my grandmother cried when I read them the letter.

In the early spring David went to the Seychelles and fell in love. It was a sudden realization, that I was having more fun writing letters in which things went well for him. And that his happiness was mine to grant. He met her in a bar on the beach. He was sitting at a back table reading a book when she walked in wearing a Panama hat over her long, dark hair, a bikini top and a sarong, tied to reveal her tanned left leg as she moved. She ordered beer, in English, and sat down without glancing at him. David walked over and asked if he could join her.

"It's about time," she said. "That must be some book, David."

"What?" David asked. "Who?"

"I've been sitting around here for two afternoons waiting for you to notice me."

David laughed. "Why didn't you say something."

"What, and be forward? My mother would kill me."

"She's got something, that girl," my grandmother said at that point. "Where's she from?"

"Massachusetts. He's coming to that," I answered.

Katherine Rowe, from Newton, Massachusetts. She was twenty-six years old and taught modern dance in Boston. They fell madly in love.

"It's so strange," David wrote three letters later. "I'd been alone for so long. I'd actually convinced myself that I didn't need a woman to share my world with. And then this person walks into my life and it's as if the past months I'd been sleep-walking. The world has come alive, the feel of the breeze, the salt-smell of the ocean, the slow dance of sunset colours. I don't know how I lived without this for so long."

"What about Tracy?" my grandmother asked.

I was caught off guard. "She's got another boyfriend," I said softly. "Don't worry about her."

My grandmother nodded. "I'm still worried. It's too fast. He'll get hurt."

"They're in love," I answered. "Besides, nothing's going to go wrong."

And of course, nothing was. I was in a fabulous mood. It was spring, the snow was melting, David, Katherine, and I were all deliriously happy. I couldn't wait for Fridays, to prove that joy doesn't have to end.

"Yo, Neil," I said, bopping into work one night.

"Yo. Holy Stars! Your head, man! You're in definite danger of denting the ceiling. Check this: new program. We're about to land on Normandy."

"Lemme at those Jerries. Actually, let me do the books and make sure the lovebirds have another perfect week in paradise, and then lemme at those Jerries."

It was a wonderful spring. Dianne, Neil, and I outfoxed the Germans, my grandmother was healthy and David and

Katherine made plans to finally leave the islands, to return to Kenya and book a flight to India. David described Katherine in terms he had never used before. He said that she made him feel totally accepted and loved. That she believed in him so intensely that he was coming to believe in himself.

I read that letter to Dianne and Neil. "I used to believe in my ex that way," Dianne said. "It was misplaced."

"Why doesn't some woman like that find me?" Neil asked.

Ten months after he left for London, ten months after his suicide, and one week before he and Katherine were to leave for India, my brother's travels came to an abrupt halt. My grandmother, three weeks before her eightieth birthday, succumbed to her third heart attack. They rushed her to the hospital in pain, but by the time she arrived she had no spontaneous heartbeat. I was there in twenty minutes, just after Dr. Powell. The emergency team laboured to restore her heartbeat, giving her drugs and electric shocks. I saw her briefly, lying naked on a stretcher, surrounded by efficient young people in white. Dr. Powell spoke to me, then to the doctors. Five minutes later they stopped trying to revive her. They covered her up and allowed me in. It seemed like she had been dead a long time.

It was a small funeral, even smaller than my brother's had been. Again, my father's brother flew in. He asked me to move out to Vancouver. He had a chain of one hour photo labs and he wanted me to manage one of them. He said that family should stick together. I realized that he was now the only blood relative I had any contact with. I told him I would think about his offer.

The funeral was on Monday. The following night, because it was easier than not, I returned to work. The week went by with a surface of normality, except for a visit to my grand-mother's lawyer. She didn't have a large estate, but I inherited a modest sum of money. Enough to travel on for a long time, I thought, then stopped myself. I wasn't ready for where such thoughts led.

Friday was difficult. I should have expected it, but this was the first Friday in ten months I wasn't writing a letter. I did the books then printed out copies of all the letters I'd written during my brother's travels. I sat in my office reading them, thinking about David and thinking about my grandmother. And my parents. After a time I felt the need to escape my own memory.

"I'm leaving early," I said to Dianne. "Will you make my excuses?"

"Of course," she said.

It was a little before 7:00 and the air was still cool, but the feel of the sun on my skin predicted a warm day. I began walking in the general direction of home but didn't want to get there. As I approached the bridge leading from downtown I loosened my tie and slipped off my windbreaker. I was walking quickly and my calves began to ache as I moved uphill but I found it difficult to slow down and stopped trying. There was a pressure inside. Things I was trying too hard not to think about. I turned off at the foot of the bridge and soon found myself in a residential district of old, restored homes and towering oak trees. I became aware of the houses, stirring with early Saturday activity: a young man, not much older than me, edging his sidewalk; a middle-aged couple drinking coffee on a screened veranda. I felt an emotion rise in my chest I could not identify as simple grief. I turned the corner onto Brenda's street.

MICHAEL MIROLLA

A Theory of Discontinuous Existence

I.

When Giulio awoke, he found he no longer had an appendix. At the time, the humour of the situation escaped him. It was only years later, as a freshman in college, that he'd come up with what he thought was an appropriate pun for the occasion: Why did the textbook leave you hanging? Because they'd taken out its appendix! While lying ever so still on the hospital bed, he felt each day the stitches that prevented the rest of his insides from spilling out. He wanted desperately to scratch that spot, to satisfy the itch that tormented him the moment he thought of it – an unholy combination of pain and desire. But he had been warned the stitches might come undone – with a subsequent outpouring of guts – and so all he could do was lie on his back wondering if some other organ – taking pity on the missing appendix – might not slide over to fill the cavity.

The hospital seemed full of kind, smiling people, willing to go out of their way to keep him happy and make him feel at home. But it was the nurse who sponge-cleaned him daily that made him realize, at last, the emptiness, the inadequacy, the

78

serendipitous nature of his nine-year-old existence. He fell in love with her hands, those cool, long, thin fingers that pampered and delighted him, those glossy red nails that made his hair stand on end as they stroked his skin ever so gently, leaving only the slightest of traces. Years later, when searching through his dreams for surrogate lovers to fill his bleak bedroom (straw-hatted wife labouring mightily in the garden), he had but to shut his eyes and there she was, starch-sparkling white, entering the room with a cheerful "Good morning" to break the fall of dust-laden sunlight, and then vanishing again with only the scent of lilac left to linger over the rest of the suddenly miserable afternoons.

And, except for that first, brisk "Good morning," she seldom spoke, seldom engaged him in conversation, preferring to hum softly to herself as she changed the sheets and pulled back the blinds. So it came as something of a shock when, the morning before he was scheduled to leave and while spongebathing him, she asked right out of the blue: "Do you believe in God, our Almighty Father, Creator of heaven and earth?"

After a moment of face-scrunching, Giulio nodded, hoping to make her so happy that perhaps she'd never go away, never stop squeezing that sponge.

"You shouldn't," she said ever so quietly, before walking out of his life forever.

It was as if a blurred image had, for a moment at least, been pulled into razor-sharp focus, the clearest focus imaginable. And then it was gone again — as if it weren't meant for him after all. For, when everything else had been removed from that frame, what was left in the crystal-clear emptiness was simply his own confusion, one that would hover over him, on and off, for the rest of his life.

And that confusion, Giulio remembered, was definitely still

there during a first-year introductory course in philosophy, his choice for the mandatory arts subject science students were obliged to take.

"Ugh! Philosophy," Giulio would admit one day, long into a future that at the time seemed so preternatural. "Whatever was I thinking? I must have been crazy." He giggled. "Sorry, I didn't mean that." The person sitting across from him in the dark didn't react. "Anyway, I thought maybe it might be a break from my heavy science load. Besides, I'd heard good things about philosophy, that it had answers to the important questions. I don't know who was responsible for that crock? You?" Giulio reached over and patted the person's leg – then quickly pulled his hand back before it too vanished in the dark. "Where was I? Oh yeah. This professor wanted to get to know us better, so he held the class at the local university tavern. Well, there we were, this bunch of bright-eyed and bushy-tailed freshmen, waiting for the professor to let us in on some of the secrets of the universe. You know: God, existence, and free will or reasonable facsimiles thereof. Imagine our surprise when this creep brushes these aside like so many annoying flies and launches into a discussion of logic. And it didn't get any better. Next, he was saying that truth had nothing to do with morality, that it was only verification brought to its logical – there was that word again – conclusion. That's when I said to myself: He must be joking. Later, he's going to tell his colleagues how he suckered those freshmen yokels into believing that the mysteries of the universe were nothing but expressions of logic. And I looked around, searching for a way to prove him wrong. All I saw was a drunk slumped over a pool of beer, a veteran of the place, gurgling happily to no one in particular. I found myself thinking: Has he too misplaced his appendix? I guess I lost track of what the prof was saying because suddenly he was into billy goats. Something about billy goats and Socrates. From then on, I avoided philosophy like the plague. But I've told you this story before, haven't I? That same night, in fact. It was you I called, wasn't it?"

Yes, it had been though Giulio by then was too drunk to be coherent. He had told his friend – the one now sitting so motionlessly in the dark before him, a friend he'd known since first grade – to meet him in front of the tavern. And, as dusk fell, the two of them had wandered about the campus, holding each other up and shouting at the statues that had been donated through the years by well-to-do alumni with visions of immortality. It had given Giulio a rare sense of belonging but in no way cleared up his confusion.

"Do you know," Giulio's friend had said, plopping himself down on the damp grass, "that statues are dangerous?"

"No kidding!" Giulio had replied, gulping down the last of the beer smuggled out of the tavern. "I didn't know that. Should I have known that? I should, shouldn't I?"

"Yes, yes, yes! And do you know why?"

"No, I don't know that either – but you're going to tell me, right?"

"Ah, Giulio, ignorance is bliss, studied ignorance even more so. The truth is that statues move when we're not looking, that's why."

"A fifth column, as it were? Gothic or Baroque?"

"You may joke but I think they should all be blown up. The only good statue is a headless statue. That way, although they might still be able to move around, they certainly couldn't do very much damage, now could they?" He had stood up and raised his fist. "Yeah, that's it. Off with their heads!"

At this point, Giulio had to restrain his friend from attacking the statue of the Three Bares, a campus landmark.

"Hey, you can't do that," he had said, steering his friend away from the statue. "If you take off its head, it won't be able to see itself jerk off. That would be too cruel."

"Okay then," his friend had said. "So let me kick the bastard in the balls. Huh? Let me do that, at least. If he doubles up – even ever so slowly, then we'll know, won't we? Come on. What's hurting one statue compared to saving mankind? Come on. We've got all night. We can wait it out."

"Oh yeah?" Giulio had said. "What if he's like that uncle of mine? You can kick him in the balls all you want. It won't hurt him in the least."

"Why, does he sing in the choir?"

"No, no. He just sucks them right in. Right into himself. Like a big slurp – and they're gone."

"Sure, I know all about that. In fact, I can do that with my brain. Every day from 7:00 to 3:30. Slurp – and it's gone."

Later, a great deal later, Giulio's grade-school friend was committed by his own family. And not for wanting to blow up statues but for actually believing he himself had turned into one. He would stand in one spot for days on end, moving only imperceptibly, face covered with chalk to make it look like alabaster, eyes fixed forward or forced back into his skull, as if in a desperate attempt to see inside himself.

Giulio heard about him then for the first time in years. The phone rang in the middle of the night, like an exclamation point. Giulio sat up with a jerk, not knowing for a moment that the person beside him in his brand-new bed was his brand-new wife. The phone rang again. It was his mother. She was crying and asking him if he could go over to his friend's house. Something awful had happened. The two hadn't seen each other since that night under the statues but apparently, before his friend sank into what would turn out to be a lifelong stupor, he left a scrap of toilet paper with nothing on it but Giulio's name.

"But Mom, what can I do about it?" Giulio protested. "It's not like we're still friends or anything. I hardly know the guy anymore."

"Who is it?" his wife was asking, still half-asleep, a pool of heat beside him.

"It's nothing. Nothing, really. Go back to sleep. Yes, Mother. All right, Mother. If you want me to. But he probably won't even recognize me."

Giulio kissed his wife, still giving off her unnatural heat. Then he dressed and went out into the breathtaking winter night. A thin layer of snow squeaked underfoot as he walked to his car, smug in its affluent, tree-lined driveway. He tugged at his ears to keep them from freezing, clapped his hands together before reaching for the door handle. Overhead, he could hear the sound of the street lights as they sparked. The stars themselves looked ready to crack. Even though the car had been plugged in, the engine whined and moaned before finally turning over. I feel exactly the same way, Giulio said to himself.

He sat in front of his friend's house for several minutes, getting up the courage to knock on the door. This was the first time in years he had set foot in the area where he had spent most of his youth. On the surface, little had changed – the same tired-looking, lower middle-class duplexes; the same ice-encrusted puddles reflecting oily light; the same crippled neon signs buzzing like angry bees in store windows. Even the same corner cinema – only now displaying another alphabet over the same B-grade horror movies. But the sameness wasn't enough to make him feel at home. In fact, he had the impression of being unwanted, as if he'd suddenly become a foreign object this body's immune system felt obliged to reject out of hand.

His friend's parents, expecting perhaps a flash, a miracle cure, at first greeted him like a long-lost saviour, forcing coffee, grappa, anything they could find, down his throat. But they soon began to look at him askance when they realized he could do nothing for their son. They pleaded for help, for God's help, for his help. He was an educated man; he knew medicines; he had contacts who knew medicines; he knew government officials who knew short-cuts to health and long life. They pleaded half in Italian, half in broken English. His friend's mother sat crying at the kitchen table, her hair dishevelled and soaked with tears. Giulio tried to get through to his friend for more than an hour – to no avail. He talked to him, shouted at him, jabbed and pushed him. Then, he stood up and walked back and forth in a daze, as if running on automatic. Finally, when no one was looking, he slipped out of the house, not even daring to say goodbye. Afterward, thinking back, he would remember only the sickly yellow glow from the kitchen lights, the mother's frantic tears, and his friend's look of piercing non-recognition, a stare that could freeze the world itself.

"What the fuck could I do?" Giulio later would ask no one in particular when he was drunk and capable of bringing the subject up. "What exorcism did they want me to perform? 'Rise, my son. Push back the stone and follow me.' He was beyond help, beyond grief, beyond hope. Any fool could see that. I no longer knew him. Who, in fact, did? Was he the same

guy I had played pick-up football with as a child? Had got
pissed with as a teenager? Was he the same guy who pulled me
out of an empty swimming pool one night after we'd raided
the houses of our more affluent neighbours across the tracks?
Had showed me the escape hatch in the bushes as the police
cars trained their lights on us? Or was he someone else,
mutated and psychically disfigured? Fragmented beyond recognition? Or maybe he was no one else by that time, a vanishing trick that had left the rest of the world believing he was still
there? You tell me. I've gone to university, landed a good position, started a family – ready at thirty to move up the career
ladder if one is to be cynical. He was never any good at school,
took it as a long-winded joke, once beat up on a teacher who
insulted his typing technique, quit the moment he was
allowed to, could imagine nothing better than a job in the
shipping department of a food plant, and lost all his friends.
While the rest of us were busy forging lives for ourselves, he
stood still. Let's put it this way: I might have known him once
before he became a statue, but that was it. The best thing you
can do now is kick him in the balls."

II.

His appendix gone forever and not yet even the hint of a joke
to replace it, Giulio left the hospital on an immaculate June
day, ready to face a summer of slow convalescence. He
remembered squinting into the late-morning sun and then
looking back from his wheelchair at the mirrored windows of
the hospital, hoping to see a pale white hand wave or a curtain
rustle, even if only slightly, to let him know he'd be missed.
And he didn't care if it were purely by accident – someone's
dying breath, for example. That would have been enough for

him. But the reflected light was too blinding, the signals too overpowering and impossible to read. Was it a message or a plea for help? One more tear in the fabric or the start of a healing pattern?

His mother and father smiled at him as they lowered him gently into the back seat of a relative's borrowed car. His father had come straight from work – the graveyard shift in a brewery. He had the glazed look of a man who doesn't get enough sleep. Or was it something that went beyond sleep? Giulio never did understand his father, just as he would never understand the vast majority of what went on around him. The things Giulio did understand – the workings of atoms and molecules, their combinations and decimations – were things his parents didn't even believe existed, like trips to the moon and the probing of our subconscious. And, as Giulio grew older, what he had in common with his parents grew less and less, shrinking till, at the end, all that was left was the bond of birth. Giulio often described it in one of the few ways he could – mathematically: "We're two intersecting sets that were once practically identical, practically overlapping, but are now slowly drifting apart. What we've been left with, the only connection we have, lies within that ever-diminishing intersection. As for the rest...."

But for that summer at least Giulio still had everything in common with them, including dependence. Because he couldn't run around – or even go for a walk the first few weeks – he found it best to stay indoors. That way he wouldn't see his friends playing and get jealous. He lay on the sofa and watched movies all day long – June Allyson, Errol Flynn, Cary Grant, *The Scarlet Pimpernel, Robin Hood*. And when he grew tired of watching movies, he read.

His mother made him feel comfortable, propped a pillow beneath his feet, ushered his closest friends in and out, brought him the hot soup she had just finished meticulously making, opened windows and curtains to let the sun in, and generally flitted about him like a guardian angel. He felt warm and secure, a warmth and security he would never feel again.

During his reading, he discovered Tom Swift, Jr., son of a science fiction mastermind scientist detective who chewed up alternative universes and intergalactic criminals like ordinary mortals chewed gum. This, in turn, awoke in Giulio an interest in science. At the time, it was science only of a childish sort – the science of flying on fantastic ships to the outer star systems, of destroying vicious monsters in time warps. But it soon became more bookish in manner, more circumscribed, more ordered until Giulio found himself registered in an Honours Chemistry program at the local university. And that set his course in life, excluding a few dead-ends such as the introductory philosophy which he quickly dropped in favour of Introductory Italian for Beginners.

His father slept in the morning and worked in the garden in the afternoon. Sometimes Giulio would sit in the backyard and watch him turning over the sod. He worked skilfully, wasting little of his energy on showy display. And he enjoyed what he did – whether crushing clods of earth between his fingers or spraying pesticide on his grapevine. Giulio saw only a hunched-over man, a little grey about the temples, stern in his demeanour, often impatient with his family and always in a hurry, always engaged and moving like someone who feared the stillness. In no way, with no amount of imaginative straining, could Giulio identify this man with the much younger one standing next to a brown motorcycle, army cap tipped jauntily back, and looking like the very incarnation of Rudolf Valentino. Giulio realized later that was the photographic style in those days and couldn't be helped.

As he healed through the long summer days, Giulio spent more and more of his time out of doors. His favourite pastime was wandering through the huge field behind his house with a glass jar in his hand. In it, he caught whatever he came across, but mostly the bumblebees attracted to the rich array of flowers. The first was the easiest. After that, the art consisted of being able to snare other bees without allowing those already trapped to escape. Giulio provided the bees with clover and punched holes into the metal lid of the jar so they wouldn't die from asphyxiation. But in the long run it didn't help. If the bees were kept in the jar for long periods of time, the survivors were left invalids, unable to fly when released. Instead, they crawled along the cement lip of the patio, swatted left and right by the family cat. Occasionally, their last act before dying was a vicious sting that would send the cat howling and jumping down the garden path. On his death bed, that would be one of the scenes that flashed before Giulio's eyes – the bees buzzing frantically, circling in one spot, stingers sliding spasmodically in and out, the cat hurtling through the air, and the heavy, overpowering smell of pollen in his nostrils.

It was the same odour left imprinted on his brain the following summer when, playing cowboys and Indians, he had to watch helplessly as his brother slipped from a branch he was climbing and was left hanging in the fork of the tree, his neck mercifully snapped so that he suffered only for a moment. And, when Giulio bought his own first home twenty years later, he cut down every tree on the property, refusing to listen to any argument to the contrary, refusing even to discuss the matter.

While it was his mother who seemed to collapse under the weight of his brother's death, the long-lasting effects were actually felt by his father. When it was reported to him, he merely shrugged and descended into the basement, there to be lost amid the casks of wine and the onions braided for the winter. He became suddenly a meek, yielding man, ready to acquiesce to whatever came his way. Often, in the years that followed, Giulio waited for him to show flashes of his old anger, the fire that made him blaze in argument, that surmounted an education that had never gone beyond the second grade and that forced others to bend to his will. He waited in vain. Giulio himself became more and more belligerent in the face of this calmness, this self-atrophy. He took to answering rudely or saying something cruel about his parents' lack of education. And then, good Catholic boy that he was, he would immediately regret the words. But, through rudeness, cruelty, insults, and guilt, his father sat there drinking his wine in silence, a docile, smiling man – a Zen monk perhaps, focused on an object no one else sees, the only object of importance in the entire universe.

It wasn't long before he, too, succumbed to "that weight that pushes down on all of us, that pull of indecent gravity from which no laughter can deliver us. No bursting supernova can have as much effect as one death, a great philosopher should have said. That's what it should be about. Not billy goats that look like Socrates."

"Ah, you're so full of shit," his friend was saying as he leaned against the statue of a nude, inspecting it closely in the dark. "What do you expect – that we should all stand on this planet shoulder to shoulder forever? And when we become too many for that, what then? Gymnastics, human pyramids, standing, eating, sleeping, dreaming, fucking, kissing, moaning, crying, laughing, pissing, defecating on top of one another? Ah, you fool. I understand perfectly."

"What! What do you understand? Sweet fuck all, I bet. You telling me that death is acceptable to you? That you see nothing wrong with it?"

"Giulio," his friend said, tumbling drunkenly to the ground once again. "That's why I love you so much."

He stopped and turned away. Giulio found himself getting more and more angry – as he usually did when he'd had too much to drink and no longer felt in control.

"Well, for Christ's sake. I'm waiting. Why do you love me? Why is death acceptable to you? Why do you make statements like that and then stop? Who do you think you are? Prick! You remind me of my father after Johnny's death. Like some stupid cat that's swallowed a canary."

"I have a theory," his friend said, standing up and walking away. "I've thought about it long and hard while moving pallets of strawberry jam and plastic cup cakes. I call it the Theory of Discontinuous Existence – in capital letters. Like your capital 'T' Truth."

"Discontinuous Existence, eh? That's brilliant. Does it have anything to do with your theory of statues?"

"It might. It just might. I haven't thought it through that far yet."

"So tell me. When you do think it through, are you gonna present it for your doctoral thesis or are you saving it for some post-doc work?"

"A low blow, Giulio. A crushing blow. For that, I'm not going to tell you."

"Oh, come on. Don't be childish. I admit it was a low blow, but you had it coming after all that theory bullshit. Okay, okay, I apologize. There, are you satisfied?"

"Too late," his friend said, stopping under the lights at the university gates. "Someday, somewhere, you might be fortunate enough to find out what the Theory of Discontinuous Existence is all about, but not from me. Never from me. In fact, this is the last time you'll hear me mention it."

And that was the truth. There were times when Giulio actually believed he had discovered on his own what his friend had meant. But he couldn't be sure. And the moment he felt sure, the seed of doubt was planted. It was as if someone else had the key to Giulio's self-knowledge.

One day, not long after his friend had been admitted to the hospital where he would spend the rest of his life, Giulio got a brilliant idea. He would kill two birds with one stone.

"Why don't you leave him alone?" his wife insisted. "First, you don't talk to the guy for years on end and now you think you can save him."

"I happen to believe it's a good idea. Besides, it can't do him any harm, can it?"

"Are you serious? You're fooling around with someone's head, emotions, his insides – and you say it can't do any harm."

His wife, a clinical psychologist who often dealt with people whose emotions were in shambles, should know. But Giulio was not to be deterred. That same night he sat in the hospital visitors' room with his friend. He looks like a piece of play dough, Giulio thought. Like Gumby – was that his name? He stays in whatever position they place him and when he moves, it's as if it happens in another dimension, one where a moment represented hours of our time.

"Listen," Giulio began, not looking at his friend, but at a large plate-glass window instead, through which he could see the lush grounds surrounding the hospital and a waterfront jogging path. "Remember that time you told me about your theory, that time under the statues? Yeah, a long time ago, I know. Now, what did you call it? It seems to have slipped my mind."

He finally looked at his friend's face. There was absolutely no response. Of course not. Even if one came, it would be hours or days later. Or in that other dimension. And who then would recognize it as a response to that particular question?

"Oh yeah," Giulio said, placing a hand on his friend's lap. "The Theory of Uncontinuous Being, wasn't it? No. Discontinuous Existence, not Uncontinuous Being. That's right! How could I forget! So stupid of me, isn't it? You have a real *stupido* for a friend."

Not a flicker. Not the least stirring. Either he was in complete control of his body or had lost all control. He sat there like stone, like the great Buddha, like a tremendous weight that held things down, kept them from floating off into space. Giulio stayed with him a few minutes longer, admiring the view, then got up to leave. As he was walking out of the visitors' room, a haggard-looking male nurse intercepted him.

"Excuse me. Are you his friend? I mean, do you know him?" he asked, hands stuffed in his pockets.

"I used to be his friend, yes. And I guess I knew him once, a long time ago."

"So you must know he writes, then?"

"He what? Writes? Is this some sort of joke? How can he write when he doesn't even move?"

The nurse pulled out a wad of paper from his pocket – a thick wad of crumpled up blue toilet paper – and handed it to Giulio.

"He writes at night when no one's around. I guess he steals

the crayons when he has therapy sessions in the autistic kids' ward. We've tried to catch him in the act but so far we haven't succeeded."

Giulio sat in his car trying to read the childish scrawl on the toilet paper. It brought back memories of a crystal-clear winter night and the cracking of stars. After the third one, he realized they weren't separate writings but an attempt to get one coherent sentence, one orderly thought, out of what must have been some horrible, dreaded fog. The first note had a huge "You" scribbled across it. It was followed by "You must not." The third reverted to "You," then "You can't." Giulio had had enough. He wouldn't put it past his friend to play games with him. He searched through the rest, looking for one that, if it didn't make sense, at least made a complete sentence. He found it near the bottom: "You can't outrun the cheese-slicing machine – not even on your best day." And then wished he hadn't found it. For his own confusion was absolute now. He returned shamefaced to his wife who was working in the garden. She didn't say a word, didn't even lift her head but simply continued snipping the roses.

He walked by her as quickly as possible, slipped into the house and headed straight for the washroom where he relieved himself and then flushed the toilet. But not before he had tossed several scraps of paper into the swirling water. They didn't speak for the remainder of the day and it was past midnight as both lay in bed before Giulio had the courage to say something, the first thing that came to mind.

"I'm getting a promotion," he said, talking into the dark that was occasionally brightened by the wind rustling through the curtains.

"That's great."

She turned and brushed against him for a moment, then moved away again.

"Well, you certainly don't sound too enthusiastic about it. I thought you'd be happy."

"I am happy. I'm very happy for you. What will you be doing now?"

"They're putting me in charge of my own lab. That's quite a step forward. I'll be able to initiate projects and work on my own stuff."

"Your own lab? Wow, that's really great. Isn't it?"

The curtain rustled again. They didn't say anything else. After a few moments, Giulio reached over to place a hand on her breast, making it seem almost like an accident. He was attentive for the least sign of rejection, the least murmur of discontent. But she lay stock-still, neither yielding to his touch nor fighting it. Emboldened, he shifted his hand across her body, in a line down over her belly button, thinking: This is how the butchered animals are gutted, with a fine slit so as not to damage the insides. Still angry at her, he eased his fingers between her thighs, found the clitoris, and started to rub in a semi-circular direction. Within seconds, the lower half of her body began to arch and jerk: snake-like hisses escaped through her clenched teeth. Giulio pushed himself length-wise against her, slapped back and forth against her side. Her body now moved by itself, caught in a rhythm from which it could no longer escape. Only her head and feet still touched the bed as she made tiny doll-like noises and shuddered to orgasm. Giulio lay back then on his side of the bed, feeling the perspiration cooling beneath him. Still in silence, she reached for him and pulled him on top of her. His penis twanged like a tuning fork as he used it to ease her legs apart. She touched the hollow at the base of his back. All his anger dissipated then and the first waves of sperm began their long, one-way swim.

Giulio never discussed his friend with her again. He was the secret they kept between them, the wish that prevented total commitment. Of course, she knew when Giulio had gone to see him. He would return sullen, itching for a fight. And they would avoid each other for the rest of the day. As the years passed, Giulio visited his friend more and more. Toward the end he was seeing him once a week – always in the visitors' room, always the one-sided conversation. And always Giulio came back with a note, some scribbling or other, which he read and then destroyed.

He eventually left the university lab and started a company of his own, becoming a successful manufacturer of plastic molds. He took up photography and spent countless hours in the basement darkroom. His wife died of cancer, an awful, horrible death where they removed one at a time her left breast, then her right, and last of all her stomach. She, too, handed him a note before she died, not on toilet paper but from her deluxe, perfumed writing pad, the one she used to make appointments for her patients. His son, after two years spent cruising the South Seas as a crewman on a twenty-metre sailboat, returned home, stayed at the house for a while, and then entered a seminary.

Giulio hadn't lost any of his limbs to disease. His back was straight and his mind sharp. His life was an ever-rising arc with no gaps.

"Healthy as an ox. Full of vim and vigour."

These were the words his father used to describe both him and his brother. The funeral mass for his brother took place in the same church where, years later, Giulio would wed. Back home after the ceremony, the immediate family sat mourning in the kitchen. Although it was midday and the sun was shining brightly, the house lights had all been switched on. The kitchen table had been removed, revealing four discoloured marks in the linoleum; the chairs had been placed so they formed a circle, ringing the walls. A pot of water, spaghetti slowly melting in it, boiled on the stove. There was the familiar smell of meat bubbling in sauce. But it wasn't Giulio's mother who cooked or rushed about keeping everything in order. Someone else had supplanted her, a Cassandra-like head of the official mourners. The smaller children played sullenly in the backyard, sensing something, their natural good spirits subdued, throwing stones at the blackbirds that hovered overhead or settled on the telephone wires. Whenever a rock flew uncomfortably close, they all burst into the air and the sky was filled with black wings. Giulio leaned against the back door, midway between the kitchen and the backyard, as befitted his ten years.

A voice called him to come in and eat. A hand led him into the dining room. A chair was pulled beneath him. Later, much later, when the scene was recreated time and again for various family members, including his father and mother, he would realize the meaning of that meal – the wine and the laughter amid steaming plates of spaghetti. But not then. He sat quietly at the table, not eating or daring to look up, the anger swelling within him till he could stand it no more. He burst into tears and rushed upstairs to his room. No one tried to stop him but he could still hear the laughter even as he drifted off into a vast, dreamless sleep.

III.

There was no Christmas that year, no snowy angels hanging twisted from the tree, no manger with its oversized Christ child, no spindly, cotton-batting sheep with a tendency to fall on their sides at the least hint of wind. Giulio listened to the yuletide songs on the radio with a new bitterness, a crisp cynicism. Was there really a world outside the 4 o'clock darkness that descended daily on everything – leaving only the tiny oases of light amid phantasmagoric drifts of snow?

Of course there was. Why, wouldn't Giulio get married on precisely such a day, pulling his new bride through a howling storm, through a vacuum where only death seemed appropriate? The priest spoke to them – them alone in the hollow empty tintinnabular church – of man's future, of planning an ordered life, of computers that would guide their every step with benevolent concern, of appropriate social behaviour, of driving from one place to another using the least possible energy and a mapped-out strategy from which there could be no deviation. But they were happy nevertheless. Nevertheless....

They raced out from the church, giddy, hand in hand, the wind growling all around them. Who was with them that day, that dark permutation snickering when the snow whistled up the bride's dress? She was so young and fresh, her cheeks like ... like.... They ran together, hand in hand, stumbling, plowing through the drifts, toward the warmth, toward a glowing neon sign that read Hsin Nho Chinese Restaurant, barely visible in the white swirling godless mocking ferment outside. They ran thus from the blizzard into the blizzard. Into the ever-darkening afternoon. How beautiful and supple her breasts! How delightful to snuggle in, to lick, to suck! What thought then, what unthinkable vision of amputation, of mauling, of maceration and cutting away? Dear God, that he might have died in that operating room, anesthetized forever. And not come to this.

The first wail of Giulio's child.

"It was a roar in my ears, unacceptable," he said. "Death must be much easier to face."

But this was another time, long before he'd met his wife-to-be, longer still before that child shredded his way into the world.

"That was her dream come true," Giulio confided to his somnabulant friend as they sat facing each other. "And her recurring nightmare. Do you want to hear it?" Nothing. "Well, I'll tell you anyway. In her dream, she was a young woman in billowing white who stood at the top of a winding staircase, full of innocence. And she wanted nothing more than to slide down those stairs, to feel the hard smooth wood between her legs. Instead, halfway down, the banister became a gleaming razor, unutterably cold steel. Sometimes, its horn pointed at her, a unicorn waited at the bottom."

Giulio thought he saw his friend smiling but not at the right places. Never in the right places.

"Yes, I know, I know," he said, snapping pictures with his new camera so that he could have at least one image of his friend. "It's so Freudian you could cut it with a knife. So my wife happens to have Freudian dreams. Can I help that? It's the reason she went into psychology, don't you think?"

And all the winters melted together. There was the mother and child to be taken home from the hospital – the same hospital and another light dusting of snow creaking beneath his feet. Had he not caught a glimpse of his nurse, unaged, turning the corner? How ridiculous! Could there be anything more idiotic than this idea of suddenly closing twenty years, of compressing them together like plywood so that the first would eventually come within a hair of touching the twentieth? Still, it didn't prevent Giulio from excusing himself for a moment and following the nurse to see if it were really her exactly the way he remembered her, to feel once again the texture of her smooth hands, the palms coated in Vaseline, the gentle scratching of her ruby nails. She had vanished. Of course, she had vanished, stupid. She was never really there. He slipped into the men's room and stood before the urinal, flushed and straining, unable to urge out the least dribble from a suddenly swollen penis. He returned to find his wife hadn't even missed him, so occupied was she with the new child. But her smile was all radiance, the smile of her wedding day, the smile of.... Ah, of such things are past lives made. Or invented, he thought bitterly.

"You mean to tell me you're willing to make up a life for yourself just so you could have memories of it?"

It was a drunken, rhetorical question tossed out in the middle of a table full of beer. They – childhood friends and he – had met to celebrate a stag. The night, begun on familiar tavern ground, would soon move to a club where strange women swivelled their hips and stripped to nothing in a monotonous mimicry of human lust.

"There's no need for me to invent a life," Giulio yelled, slamming his fist on the table. "I have a life. A bit disjointed. Maybe not the best or most exciting life. But it's a life. Can any of you say the same?"

He stopped abruptly. The others at the table were looking at one another. Then, someone laughed. Attention turned once more to the woman on stage – and the python whose tongue darted out from between her legs. Giulio got so drunk that night they had to stop the car several times so he could throw up without spewing all over the back seat. It marked the end of those friendships.

"What the hell," he told his wife when she asked what had become of his last, remaining friends, "all they do is drink and tell stupid jokes anyway."

He sank deeper and deeper into his work, first at the university lab and then with his own firm. There was a great future in polymers, he was fond of saying at the cocktail parties he now went to, and trying to imagine what he would have done without chemistry was like walking around in an inexorably dark room knowing all the while there's an open trap door somewhere that led to an even darker, even more uncharted basement. He knew, he said, that if he walked around blindly he would sooner or later plunge into that basement, together with the potatoes and the onions.

Potatoes and onions? Now where had they come from? The damp smell after a storm when the sewers backed up and water surged through the drain pipes and out the overflow. He was there in that basement, a vague pain in his side, a faint urge to scratch. The porous walls were crawling with spiders and sow beetles and millipedes. He bent over his retorts, a Bunsen burner flaming and bubbling. A ghost stood beside him, its throat raw and bleeding. Wait a minute! He wasn't yet dead, that ghost. He still had one glorious summer to live – of baseball, of marbles, of cowboys and Indians. But aren't ghosts eternal? They were there in the beginning and will be there when it comes to an end. Not true! Giulio hunched slowly over, as if pretending to ignore it, and then swung viciously about, hurling a test tube against the whitewashed wall. The liquid, bright crimson, flowed gently to the floor, leaving an uneven blotch. The stain was still there when they sold the house after his father's death. Like a memory but not quite. Like a forgetting but not quite.

And maybe that had been a ghost, too, that night when he and his wife slept peacefully in their upstairs bedroom, the child in the crib beside them, still too young for his own room.

"Giulio," his wife hissed all of a sudden, nudging him out of deep sleep. "Giulio, I heard a noise downstairs."

"Huh? What! What is it?"

"Giulio!" She shook him. "Wake up! There's someone in the house. I'm sure of it."

Giulio threw off the covers and sat rigid on the side of the bed, listening. He shivered. It was cold in the room, the thermostat automatically lowered at night.

"Maybe it was just the wind," he whispered. "It's blowing pretty strong tonight."

"No, no. I heard footsteps. And something that sounded like a door. Giulio, I'm scared. Go see what it is."

"Okay, okay. Just take it easy."

The hardwood cracked under his bare feet. He slipped into a pair of shorts. If he had to confront someone or something in the night, he preferred not to be completely naked. He stopped at the top of the stairs, allowing his eyes to get used to the dark. This is it, he thought. I will walk to the bottom of the stairs to my fate. Arms open – or akimbo, I will be greeted by the flash of a gun, the sting of a bullet where my appendix should be. The perfect coward's death. Freedom at last.

"My wife heard a noise coming from downstairs," Giulio

explained later to the police. "She asked me to see what it was. Well, you know how it is. I told her she'd probably been dreaming – my wife's a great dreamer. But I decided to humour her. Otherwise, she'd never get back to sleep. So I went downstairs and that's when I heard something like the sound of glass being moved across a table. I went to turn on the light but, before I could, someone ran by me, right past me. I called out. I don't mind telling you I was scared shitless. But whatever it had been was gone."

But was it really gone? The opaqued window in his dark-room stood open, swinging in the harsh wind. Giulio reached up to shut it as snow swirled about the room. Ruined negatives and half-developed prints recoiled in their trays. He checked to see if there was anything missing. Nothing that he could spot. Although no footsteps coming or going were ever found, the house was never the same again. There were now dark, unfamiliar shadows everywhere. Or so it seemed to Giulio. He installed more lights, even a large security spotlight for the backyard, sensitive to the slightest motion. The shadows became sharper and more defined. But they never completely vanished, having returned, Giulio surmised, from his childhood, components of a magic trick that had been left unfinished, dangling in its own confusion.

"You must bring all the cheese slices back together," the note read. Each and every piece of toilet paper read.

After several years of silence, his friend, grey-haired now and with a new sparkle in his eyes, had written again.

"I think it's because we ran out of baby-blue toilet paper for a while and were using white instead," the same male nurse, now even more haggard-looking, told Giulio. "He only writes on baby-blue toilet paper, you know."

And that was the truth. The weeks that followed led to a plethora of notes. Every time Giulio went to visit his friend, he found notes waiting. They were everywhere – piled neatly on the chair where he'd sit, stuffed into the pockets of his friend's pyjamas, scattered about the floor of the room, even left in long trails from the bedroom to the toilet.

"You're making fun of me, you old scoundrel," Giulio said at last, squeezing his friend's knee. "Aren't you? I've known you for over fifty years and I still have trouble figuring out when you're kidding."

Giulio would tell his friend about problems at work, how his business was prospering at the same rate as his ulcer, how his son had sailed off into the sunset without even a how-do-you-do and then had reappeared out of nowhere.

"Sometimes I think you made the right decision, my friend. You just sit there like a bump on a log, watching, smiling, writing weird notes. The rest of us ... well, the rest of us ... we're just like electrons around a neutron-proton core. We spin and we spin and every once in a while we make a quantum leap. How? Who knows. To what? Ah, probably to another atom or maybe yoked to a demanding molecule. And then we spin around some more. Yet, do you know what the loneliest electron of all is? You guessed it – a free radical. That's what I call them, all those lonely electrons. All charged up with no place to go. Well, maybe tonight, for a change, we'll swim across an electrolytic solution. Why? Just to get to the other side! Oh, to be discharged, de-energized, defunct – "

Giulio stopped in mid-sentence. For the first time in as far back as he could recall, he found himself talking about something other than his immediate work – even if the language he had used was that of his familiar surroundings. He felt disconcerted and looked around to make sure he hadn't been overheard. The nurse was too far away to hear. Besides, he was totally engrossed in the latest Germaine Greer. And his friend grinned, his smile beatific and unknowing.

"Sometimes, I get confused and run off at the mouth," Giulio said. "You know how it is. Last night, I thought my wife was still alive. It was a wonderful moment. I lay in bed, a young man again, and we were on the verge of making love. She smelled of musk and was warm, oh so warm so very very warm … like standing before a huge fireplace, all crackling radiant heat. I wanted her so badly … I wanted her so very much that my own lust woke me up. That's what lust can do for you."

But it was a remembered lust only and Giulio was all alone in his home, reading a letter from his son. He sat at his desk in the upstairs study. A cork bulletin board was covered with photos he'd shot and developed himself. It was the developing that he'd always found the most fun. The chemicals naturally. There were pictures of his mother, one taken only a few days before she'd died; of his wife; and of his son. None of his friend, however. The photos he'd taken were all ruined that night the ghost ran through their house and Giulio never dared take any more.

Outside, in the backyard, a midget-sized apple tree hung frozen. A flock of wrens, puffed up against the wind, huddled together on its bare branches. After his wife's death, Giulio had relented a little. No longer did he rip up any sapling that dared spring from the earth. But he did prune carefully, making sure no branches formed dangerous v's. And now this well-kept apple tree waited patiently for the warmth, ready to bud, to bring forth its wedding-white blossoms, the juicy fruit that rejuvenated anyone who ate it. Or almost anyone.

Dear Pater:

Thank you for the money you sent. It was greatly appreciated by the diocese – and particularly by me. With your help, we were able to repair the church roof without borrowing more money.

How are you? Ulcer acting up again? You should retire now when you're still healthy enough to enjoy yourself. Take a trip. I highly recommend the South Seas. You'll really like it there and that's from someone who oughta know. But I happen to know you even better and taking a holiday would never cross your mind.

Anyway, my duties are keeping me very busy. There's the responsibility of the retreat coming up in the spring (if that ever comes!) and my parishioners are always doing something or other that requires my attention. I know this sounds trite, father, but I feel fulfilled. And happy. Hoping you are too,

Yours sincerely,

Your son

A sudden wind shook the wrens from the apple tree. Giulio, feeling incapable of answering his son's letter – several attempts had already been crumpled up and tossed on the floor – rose from the desk. In the middle of the afternoon, the sun was close to setting. A red glow spread across his yard, the glow of an alien sunset. What was once familiar had become for him life on another planet. In the bubbling ferment of chemical processes, Giulio thought he saw a progression of some kind, but it was a progression that had nothing to do with him, that was leaving him behind. He walked slowly toward his bedroom; walked slowly toward that other well-worn note he kept under his pillow, this one from his wife revealing a capricious infidelity of long ago; walked slowly toward the still centre of his life. I'm an old man, he said lugubriously. There's only one thing left – and that's to decide the time of my going away.

Everything became a miasma of colour, a plastic explosion of light. Could it be what …? No, no. Just the chemicals going haywire in his brain. Just the neurons frazzling at the edges, causing the reactions to be slowed down, causing the memories to pop up out of the solution like prismatic bubbles. He lay on the bed, creaking. But I am me, now. Now! I am not what I was yesterday or the day before or the day before that. There is no connection between Giulio today and Giulio yesterday, between Giulio-lying-on-the-bed-creaking and Giulio-leaning-under-the-statue-singing. You fool. There is a point in time when there is no point in time. He felt a pair of fists kneading in his stomach, fists needing his stomach. Oh no, those weren't fists and they didn't knead/need his stomach. Oh no. Those were the gentle caressing hands of his mother, the gentle caressing touch of his wife, the gentle caressing motions of his nurse. Say it! Now! Say it! Now!

"Oh father, dear father. Please forgive me. I have spent my life trying to say something to you. But I had to wait until you were dead, till the slow poison filtered through your brain and seized you in its grip. And I had to wait till I was nearly dead, till the neurochemicals were no longer firing properly. Please forgive me. I loved you always – even in my hate."

The fog searched about for him and then settled before his eyes. He could hear a voice droning, a voice as far-off as the stars, as near as his own mind. A warm wind from the South Seas blew open the curtains. There, in the daylight, it was suddenly summer, the morning after vacations started. The streets were full of children, shouting and raising the dust, Giulio's unmoving friend among them; full of the milkman making his rounds and proudly showing off his new van, the van that had replaced dapple-grey Boxer, now in chevaline heaven; full of the street cleaner, sending forth a gush of cold water and mud across the sidewalk. Out of nowhere, an ambulance careered into view. A small boy, all wrapped up in blankets, was hustled by stretcher down steep stairs. A distraught mother huddled beside him, tears streaming down her face as the entire street came to a halt. Statues one and all. Poor boy. The ambulance sped away before Giulio's incredulous eyes. Poor boy. What had he done to deserve such pain, to feel as if someone were stabbing him repeatedly from within, to see the faces of his friends flash by as if they – not he – were being carted off?

That boy had never been inside a hospital before and now he was being wheeled into the emergency operating room. Doctors and nurses bustled about him. They were scrubbing, holding their hands in the air, smiling worriedly, probing, peering down at him from great distances. Poor boy. Something resembling a cup was lowered slowly onto his face. He resisted at first, fought it off at first. But then the warmth settled in, the feeling of retreat, a gap in the universe like the first time, the time no one is supposed to remember. And he fell away, the vision of his friend an anomaly sitting there in that sun-speckled room, blowing his nose on blue toilet paper and holding a picture of himself in his hand. Now, where did he get that? But he fell away before the answer came to him. Perhaps never to awaken. Perhaps to dream forever. Perhaps to invent the rest of his life after all.

Poor boy.

CARMELITA MCGRATH

Silence

Here is a closed space, closet space. Hidden things, dust and cobwebs, hinted space full of rolled scarves and yellow forgotten underwear, always too good to wear. Another's house, another's room, another's place, trying to imagine a partner gone and would that be worse than this? Have to clean up, clean out, amongst the boxes, the curtained shelves like confessionals because no one else can stand to be here among her absence and all the things she hoarded. A ghost of dust clinging to the mirror's edge, soft like sponge, liable to float off, a hat hanging cock-eyed off the edge where the sponges of dust dip and float, dip and float. Novenas pasted on cards stuck in the mirror frame which should be filled with pictures of the grandchildren her own were too spiteful to give her. How did she pass those sponges of dust, she with her rag permanently attached to her hand – perhaps because they were on the mirror, and she never had the time to look at herself. Floating dust, up, downward – where are the drafts coming from with the house insulated so tight – the mirror corner, the hat of felt.

Felt. What is felt? What in her room, the soft hat or the

softer darkness, was felt. Did she rub the hat ever and think of wearing it? Like a caress on her head, a felt kiss. Her friend Marina told her that hats were the cure for depression. On the real dark days, she said, when you can't think what to do, buy a hat for yourself and wear it out to Bingo. Darkness covered her like a hat, covers her now.

Once. Then. I remember her wearing a hat, once. So long ago it might have been grey or brown, so time has melted the colours. I remember her lying there, the silence that had been the content of her days. I remember the budgie that never sang, only screeched, a poor asexual budgie without a mate although she was told it wasn't right. That was before the silence blossomed in her like a tumour, cast a net around her, became her halo, her aura, her amniotic sac, her oxygen tent, her penumbra. Protection.

Just as she had come, she was returning, as soft, as silent. In April, the cruellest month, the same time coming and going. She had not, she said once, even let out a cry when she was born; instead she had hung there suspended, quiet, while they rinsed away the vernix, and tapped her, then harder. Stillborn, so they thought. And tapped her harder still, and she wouldn't speak out, wouldn't protest; that first cry took her a long time. She might have been the baby who invented the slap she was so quiet.

Mary make me meek and mild. Take me as your little child. She used to almost sing her prayers, wanting to be forever humbler than the dust motes rising up from under the bed in the sun, the silent afternoons with the sea crying in the distance. She wanted to be as contained, as silent, as Sunday afternoons in the 1930s in her village in the time before saucy American soldiers and automobiles.

When she married *him,* she spoke with a firm voice for a

while. It was as if marriage freed her tongue. She said "I do," and affirmed something, and whatever it was, it gave her authority. In one afternoon, with the end of the war making everyone giddy, with a veil made from curtain lace, she became an adult. That day she looked her father in the eye for the first time. Gloves and flowers. Men in shiny-assed and ancient suits that nowhere shade between brown and black hung on her every word and wished her the best. She the bride, the once in a lifetime thing to be.

Authority on a summer day, a week before the Feast of the Assumption. Authority came with the man, her glove in the crook of his arm, and later in the four children who bawled from the day they were born and couldn't be shut up with a dumbtit. In those middle years, noise bloomed around her as she stood among the begonias; the yard was full of it, the house always sounded like footsteps. When she heard her own voice coming out of her, it was like the voice of someone else, her great-Aunt Sara she had admired, her Aunt Sylvia she couldn't stand.

Now which of them did she take after? Whose voice? Who's the boss around here? She learned to boss well, the man with the sun-browned neck, his uneducated hands, the children with their minds like little flints, and even the chickens and the sheep in the yard. Shoo, shoo.

Discovering her voice. Get in! Get along! Move! Quiet! You'd just better try! Not in my house. Not in my yard. Not in my time. Later, after television caught up with her, over my dead body.

That was all before the silence blossomed in her like a tumour, like a flower. Then when she spoke, her words left a residue, harsh and bitter like ashes, to fall on those around her.

She never swept up then, never swept anything away, although she moved the dust and the ashes from place to place, although always the broom sang swoosh swoosh over the endless field of beige linoleum, the kitchen, the dining room, from morning to evening and to morning again like a restless pendulum in the long sleepless nights, nothing ever really got accomplished.

Nothing then could ever be kept clean enough. In the world full of filth, in the grimy Vale of Tears. They got a new radio. The radio on, the radio took over for her, each song was about bitterness. And then the television, and from 1 o'clock until 5 o'clock, all the stories were about betrayal. She called them "my stories," although what the handsome young doctor in his white coat cheating on his languorous, blonde wife had to do with her was anyone's guess.

There were awful threats. Insomnia, silence, the blooms of tension among the geraniums, everyone else's fears. When she came to spend the long hours between the doctor's visits, I tried to get her to piece it all together, the words, her history, but she looked at me and in her grey eyes I saw how foolish I was, always looking for words to say it when there were none that mattered a damn.

"Who are you?" she asked me once, not remembering that I was the one who cried the loudest. She sat on the edge of the antique daybed and squinted out into the room, projecting into the middle distance what I had told her, trying to piece me together and probably coming up with great-Aunt Sara. Or Aunt Syl, for all I knew. What was I, in pieces, a puzzle, a book for fine-tuning the television translated from Japanese so that no one could pick head nor tail of it. How was it that I could drink tea, have crumbs on my mouth from the floppy jam-jams, all travelling so liquidly through the esophagus, through the endless complicated viaducts of the guts; how could I when I was in pieces? In order to help her, I'd have to be as round and hard as an apple. But I was too worn out from it all. I don't think she ever really recognized me again, me crumbling and falling apart on the chair.

Sometimes individual words fell out of her mouth and hung in the air; in bad need of a joke, I used to call them Random Islands. This was usually between meals; she needed her nutrition badly, and she took her food as if it were imperative that she not starve now. How many meals a day, nobody knows. In her silence she was remembering the Great Depression. No sugar – no butter – once near the end of the month – no flour even. Bugs in the old brown flour sent out by the government. Six cents a day. The cow drying up, like all the females, attrition in her dry tired body. Once, raisins. They had eaten duff with raisins for a week. Stuffed themselves. Once, pork. Crying over the slaughtered pig, eating it with their eyes red over the plates. No more where that came from. Everything final.

Then she would eat the endless slices of lemon cake and stare at the ceiling. The cow, finally driven mad from eating hallucinogenic grasses, had jumped over the cliff. Waves washed over its body, pickling it whole in the moonlight.

Between the doctor's visits. "My head is full of the queerest things – you wouldn't believe it. I can't say."

"I have to go to work now," I would say.

"Listen!"

What she wanted. An electric dryer. A trip, I don't know – somewhere. To leave once and come back and turn the key in the lock and go in and make the neighbours lust for her account of it. To pay off the stove bought on instalments. High leather boots that didn't pinch her calves. To hold her head high. A house with children in it to visit. No heartburn. A frost-free refrigerator.

When she mumbled, half asleep from medications, I used to ask, "What did you say?" and she'd give me a black look. But her words spread out as if melted, dripping around the sharp edges of things in the tidy house, so organized, the silence constructed so well with its mitred corners, its cabinets and drawers with their liner paper and balls of camphor.

The TB. She hadn't gotten it, but a big crowd did. Sometimes everyone around her was coughing. There wasn't a glass fit to drink from. The germs lived everywhere, in coat pockets and barn rafters and chimneys and tin dippers left by the sides of wells. In closets, in drawers, among your best blankets, blankets not needed anymore, blankets pulled over heads, faces, big ones, small ones. Too many gone, the house next door shut up, its trapped germs barred up to live forever. Don't go near it. Survivor's guilt, like memory, like a nightmare, could come back on you anytime.

Like a lot of women, she found that when she had something to say, someone always interrupted her. Snotty children, growing fat and lippy on education, feigning superiority that the parents themselves encouraged only to get slapped in the face with it. And the man of the house – *him* – sitting on a kitchen chair pulling his boots off and snipping off her long sentences with his cold eyes and his pocketknife, making a little whistle out of wood, whittling away as if he had all the time in the world. Or him sitting there barefoot waiting for her to pick up the cue that *he had no socks on and where were they?* She going on about pinch-pleated drapes and sickness and letters from her sister Paula who was married – away – to a stationary engineer, and who had everything.

He would suck in a long breath through a gap in his teeth and cut her off just like that. It's no wonder what she said sometimes sounded childish, monosyllabic, and full of bits and pieces.

She had a habit of saying, "What?" You could be in a parlour sitting down and talking among yourselves, and she'd walk in with the broom or the mop dangling from her hand as if it lived there, and she would lean on the door frame and say, "What?" And everything would go silent. You didn't know where to pick up, what to fill in, what she had already heard. There would be a quizzical look on her brow, and you wouldn't know how to respond. She wanted to be a part of all the conversations that happened around her, and she would walk away offended. Someone was always hurting her.

Him. He was the one, I suppose, who hurt her the most. He would go through the trouble of cutting her off, leaving her sentences hanging in midair, all to utter something short and crackly, like static, of his own. Like the battery going in the radio just as the announcer yelled, "He shoots, he…" There was always the unpleasantness of the unsaid thing, a frustration that something else should have occurred, some breakthrough or climax. Such impotence. In them both, their surroundings, the things they made with their hands, in the fruitless children travelling in endless circles around the globe fooling themselves that they were trying to do good, were looking for something better. Such stillness. Out of the rocky soil, the thin earth.

In the apartment. She couldn't adjust, the place so sterile even I could hardly negotiate it without feeling like an interloper. Not a cooking smell ghost to linger in the cupboard, nothing that needed to be thrown out. In that place, the shiny and unused kitchen of a single woman, middle-aged, who ate out all the time. Who never had need of an orange peel baking in the oven to mask the cabbage. No smells, no wonder she got lost on the second floor and stood all day in the window, facing the alley where nothing ever happened, unable, it seemed, to turn around. She tried to find her way, tried to put a mark on the place. Date squares, cut glass squares, jelly roll, lemon doughnuts, all melding in the pale grey carpet, hitherto untouched.

Her prayers. Spilling, like her head, over the end of the couch, the words dipping out into the night. Awake, asleep, you couldn't tell sometimes except for the dribbling words. The Magnificat. The Sorrowful Mysteries. One night, falling off the end of the Glory Be to the Father, "Take your hands off me!"

I brought tea, and drank it until my kidneys floated away and I was left lightheaded. "If I had my time back, I'd be like you, I wouldn't have no one," she said.

In this room now, the silence, the dust. I can hardly believe the sheer amount of it; what was she, a myth of a housekeeper? What irony: me rejecting everything and becoming more her than she was, me with the place where not a mote was left to write itself in the sunlit air when the window was open. Me developing an allergy to dust, finding it now hard to tidy up, suffering like a martyr, the unmarried daughter with her modern, idiosyncratic diseases left to shake out the old coats and pile the old shoes in musty boxes. Here, in the closet, dried flowers she must have thought would make a potpourri. Not quite dried, the dew too heavy and persistent, they are turning to violet mildew in my hand. Why even throw things out? No one will ever live here again.

I suppose in the end I should take it all to *him*. Him in the nursing home, floating in and out of the transient's world of an Alzheimer's sufferer, him jumping onto every boat of an idea that comes his way and jumping off again just as quickly. I could take down the boxes, now destined for the Salvation Army, and unfold her history piece by piece, the panorama of half a century stored in clothing and memorabilia, and tell him that she is gone. Does he know? Who is it that he cuts off now from their long reminiscences? He had, she said once, in the end found his own way of leaving her. I want to tell him now it's a game that two can play.

Yet all I feel is a queer, directionless sorrow, for her for him, for their mutual struggle, the legacy of hardness they gave me falling away, me spilling over the edges where it girded me like a belt, kept my figure and my mind intact, for all these years. Ripening in this room – me of all people – only it is too late to change a damn thing. I, too, am set in my ways, and the mirror, the one she never looked in, tells me this. My mouth, its straight line. My body, ramrod posture.

Sometimes, I look in the mirror in my bedroom now, looking for signs of age. I am an ageing orphan, or nearly. This is proof of age. Naked sometimes, I cup my breasts in my hands and feel that loss of elasticity. I turn and see on my thighs the finger indentations of time, the stuff euphemistically and disgustingly called "cottage cheese." And I have to turn my head in certain ways to the sun for the light to make it young again, brilliant, the same colour as hers. Becoming her, finally, the fate of the child who has just buried a parent and will soon, inevitably as November, bury another.

What to do with the little cards, her exercise books saved from childhood, the scapulars and magazines and the Royal Reader with her name written proudly inside the cover? Leave them here? For it strikes me that someday this will be my house, and I could leave everything the way it is, a document to the dying century and forgotten stories. And yet I will never live here, will never sleep in this long, narrow room with its dust-furred mirror, not lie here where she slept with him and then dreamed herself into oblivion alone.

It is simply too engulfed in her silence. Like the houses she told me about, the houses that were shut up after the TB carried away the children, this house will remain closed, its windows as dark and as unrevealing as shutters until the peonies on the curtains fade from the sun and the young children of the village will dare each other to go up and look in, scared and titillated that they might see the old woman's ghost sweeping or staring, looking out the window at them in silence, until the grass grows through the front steps and no one remembers who they were who lived here.

ROZENA MAART

No Rosa, No District Six

Mummy and mamma always say dat I make tings up and dat I have a lively e mag e nation and dat I'm like der people in der olden days dat jus used to tell stories about udder people before dem and dats why mummy and mamma orways tear my papers up and trow it away but tis not true I never make tings up I orways tell mamma what happened and mamma doan believe me and I tell mummy and mummy doan believe me too and den I write it on a paper or on der wall or behind Ospavat building or in der sand at der park and Mr Franks at school he don't believe me too cos he says dat I orways cause trouble wi der teachers and I talk too much and I jump too much and I laugh too much and I swear too much and I doan sit still too much and I orways have bubble gum and I orways have pieces of tings and papers and my hair orways comes loose and mamma toal Mr Franks dat I'm under der doctor and dat I get pills cos I'm hyper active like mamma say, "someone who is restless all der time" but Mr Franks doan believe dat I'm under der doctor cos I make too much movements and today Mr Henson ga me four cuts cos

he says dat I was dis o be dient and dat I cause trouble in der
class but tis not true cos you see last week we celebrated Van
Riebeeck's day on der sixt of April wit der flag and we sing "Uit
die blou van onse hemel" on der grass for der assembly and
four weeks ago Mr Henson teached us about Jan Van Riebeeck
and Mr Henson toal us dat Van Riebeeck made Cape Town
built a fort and erecticated a half way station for food and sup-
plies for der Dutch people and der European people so dat dey
could have a rest at der Cape after a long journey and den Mr
Henson also toal us dat Van Riebeeck's wife was Maria de la
Quelerie, dis is true I dirint make dis up like mummy and
mamma orways say I make tings up and den Mari der big girl
in my class, she has her periods oready she toal us she wondered where Maria de la Quelerie put her cotton clot wi blood
on it in der ship from Holland cos Mari's mummy toal her not
to tell her daddy her broder or her uncles about her periods
cos men mus never see or know dees tings and den we all
laughed cos Mari's very funny and today we had to give in our
assignments on Van Riebeeck and Mr Henson ga me four cuts
on my hand cos I drew a picture of Maria and not Jan and Mr
Henson say der assignment was about Van Riebeeck and not
Maria and I say is der same ting cos it was all part of der same
history lesson and Mr Henson screamed at me to shut up and
his veins was standing out and he say dat I was not paying
attention and dat he is going to write another letter to
mummy about my bee haviour and I ask Mr Henson if Van
Riebeeck and Maria had children and Mr Henson says dat I
want to play housey-housey all der time and not learn history
and I say dat if Maria was Jan's wife den dey must've had children and den Mr Henson took me down to der office to Mr
Franks cos Mr Franks is der principal and Mr Henson tell Mr

Franks I was causing trouble and Mr Franks believe him and tells me dat he know I should not have been at school in der first place and dat I've made trouble since Sub A cos when I was in Sub A Mr Franks found out dat I was 5 and not 6 and he sent me home and der next day mummy went to school and made a big performance and Mr Franks took me back cos mamma doan wanna look after me der whole day and cos I start to write when I was four and mamma say I make too much mess on der walls and on der tings and now der school doan want me back no more and Mr Franks say dat I mus bring mummy to school but I dirint do anything wrong all I wannit to know was if Maria and Jan had children dat's all.

r.   29 April, 1970

❑

A warm April afternoon greeted the child standing with both arms on her hips. Her sticky fingers cupped the flesh around her cheeks as she eagerly observed the friendly wall upon which her writing spoke her truths. Her eyes, notable for observing several activities at the same time, moved over the written area, sealing it with a narrowed look of approval while her mouth pouted in a somewhat revolutionary way. Rosa took the sides of her dress and tucked them into her panties. It bubbled like a fluffy pancake as the Cape Town afternoon wind encircled her body; her brown cinnamon legs sweetened its appearance whilst also holding her rebellious posture together. She giggled as she saw her reflection in the sun. Rosa lifted her schoolcase and threw it over the wall and pulled a face as it sounded like one of the rats she threw across the gravel park. The stones were filing her case smoother and her shoes now had to suffer the grinding the brick wall were to put them through. The crevices between the stone bricks of George Golding Primary School knew Rosa well. She climbed with no difficulty. Once at the top she leapt like a grasshopper and knelt on the ground for a while pretending to sort out pebbles. Rosa undid her buckled black shoes and knelt forward to pick the thorns off her socks, throwing them one at a time at the row of marching ants. She removed the pieces of her dress still caught between her bloomers. Her plaited hair, tentacled in spiderly fashion, lay scrunched up between her legs. Its web of discomfort awaited the mystery that only Rosa could decide. The black balls of her eyes surveyed the area and alerted her to her peers some yards away. It was nobody she knew and no one who would complain to Mamma Zila. Upon deciding whether to go home through Hanover Street or down Constitution, Rosa chose Hanover. Verbalizing her decision to herself, she exclaimed, "In Hanover Street there are lots of busy people and nobody watches your feet, only your face!"

❏

The shuffling of feet, the racing of pulses, the screams of little children being bathed by older sisters and brothers in the backyard, the green hose pipe curling itself up among the plants, the sound of several litres of urine being flushed down the toilet in the backyard, where its circular swashing motion competed with bundles of early morning hair awaiting its disposal, the sound of creaking floors as boys and men raised themselves from their place of sleep, the smell of fire as the stove brewed its first round of morning tea, the ravenous chirps of gulls circling the street for morning bread crumbs, the sound of peanut butter jars being emptied by eager hands clenching sharp knives, the smell of fresh tobacco as working women and men light their first weed, the aroma of freshly braised tumeric onions from homes already preparing the base for tonight's supper, the ripeness of tomatoes, onions, potatoes, Durban bananas, and Constantia grapes shining like jewels in Auntie Tiefa's cart, the disgruntled noises of dockyard men walking the charcoaled streets, their feet removing chips of wood and cigarette butts from the previous night's fire, their eyes looking ahead matching their place of work – the sea, with the sky above the heads – and spotless Table Mountain – grey with not a speckle of white on its top – these formed the backdrop of this early morning Black experience.

Rosa was searching for a place to hide until the streets were clear. She "morning Auntied" everyone in sight as women took their children across the street and set them on their way to school with older children from the neighbourhood and others carried their day's produce, bundled on their heads or packed in their carts for purchase, to Hanover Street. There was a regional meeting for teachers at George Golding Primary School and Mr. Henson, Rosa's class teacher, was not attending the meeting and would be supervising their class the whole day. Mr. Henson and Rosa had a history of conflict, where the former had asked for Rosa to be expelled from school. The female-child recollected her thoughts and smiled to herself, remembering how Mamma Zila, Rosa's maternal grandmother, had asked politely that Rosa be readmitted. Mr. Henson, being a rather stern man who, on many occasions, demanded far too much respect than Mamma Zila thought he deserved, asked that Mamma Zila sign a written document for Rosa's conditional reacceptance and, in addition, state that Rosa was to behave and do as she was told. Resenting his authoritarian tone, Mamma Zila held Mr. Henson at the collar, lifted him out of his shoes, and insisted that Rosa be readmitted without conditions, mentioned a few of her relatives' names – suggesting a larger, family gang fight – and upon stating these, Rosa was reaccepted. Mr. Franks, the principal, warned that if Rosa was found doing anything unlawful, like writing on walls, engraving graffiti on the wooden desks, influencing other female-children, or throwing stones, she would be expelled permanently.

Deciding where to run and hide was not very difficult at 7:30 in the morning. The men from Ospavat factory were all outside waiting for the two sirens before the start of their working day, the wooden chips on their overalls still visible from the previous day's work. The women one usually saw at 7:45 rushed towards the red-faced Mr. Stowe waving their sandwiches to their white doorman and supervisor. For many of the men, it was their first opportunity to look between their prepared sandwiches and bargain with Auntie Tiefa for some tomatoes or maybe some homemade mango pickle. "Don't kick the bloody tins. You two boys better start walking before I come down with my stick. I mean right now you two devils." Motchie Tiema shouted at Wasfi and Ludwi to go to school. "Morning Motchie, the children being troublesome again," three men shouted. "Ai tog, you know when these boys start to grow hair on their balls." The men all laughed, shaking their heads in agreement and for fear of not wanting to disagree with Motchie Tiema. "See you men later, the beds are waiting for me." "Salaam Motchie," Auntie Tiefa greeted. "A leikom

Salaam Tiefa. I'll give in my order on Thursday, the usual you
know. Send Krislaam to Galiema from the Seven Steps."
"Okay Motchie," replied Auntie Tiefa. The two women waved
goodbye. Auntie Tiefa loaded the cart for the day's sales of
fruit and veg. A few men gathered round to buy some fruit
before Auntie Tiefa took off to Hanover Street. She hit their
hands away and made sure nobody was helping her load or
themselves with fruit. "No focking hand-outs for anyborry. I
dirint ask you to help, okay." Some of the men grumbled a bit
and reluctantly they moved away. "Are you talking to me or
chewing a brick Boetajie? Your father went with my father to
the war, so don't try your kak here," Auntie Tiefa reprimanded
the man. "No, no, no, Auntie T, it's time to leave now and the
siren is going off any minute and I jus wannit to save you der
trouble." "Gmmm! Okay take der tomato and skoot!" And so
they did. The men were pleased when the first siren rang and
they could move towards the big white building. Children
walking past the factory automatically kept their ears closed;
others yawned the full duration of the siren – some exercising
their jaws; others competing with the loud factory sound.

Rosa, hiding in the lane, pretending to fasten the buckle on
her shoe, saw the opportunity to run. The Free Dispensary
van came to collect Uncle Tuckie. Mrs. Hood and Auntie
Flowers were standing at the door waiting for the driver to
come to a halt and open the van. Both the women lifted Uncle
Tuckie into the van, dragging his lame legs one at a time. Rosa
noticed that the two women were dressed like they were going
visiting or shopping. Mrs. Hood was not wearing her apron
and Auntie Flowers wore her stockings. The elastic garters
were visible to Rosa as she watched Auntie Flowers bend to lift
Uncle Tuckie's legs. Hiding inside their house would be a

wonderful idea, she thought. She could always leave and since nobody locked their doors anyway, it would be as easy as chewing bubble gum. Rosa removed her shoes, held them in one hand, and entered the home of Mrs. Hood without the two women noticing. The second siren rang at 7:45 a.m. Now everybody would be inside attending to household chores. Auntie Raya was late, so was Mrs. Benjamin. Both women were shouting at Mr. Stowe to wait for them. "Meneer, we're coming now-now … meneer." Mr. Stowe smirked in his usual arrogant manner. Auntie Raya folded her apron and tucked it up under her armpit, nodding thankfully to Mr. Stowe for waiting on them. "Ai, Tuckie was really a handful dis morning, der man jus doan stop talking about der war." Mrs. Hood stooped to pick up Uncle Tuckie's plastic gun and shook her head, still communicating to Auntie Flowers.

Rosa heard the two women coming into the house. She was at a loss for where to run to now. She ran into Mrs. Hood's bedroom. Both women were approaching the kitchen, or maybe the bedroom. This she was not sure of as both rooms were close to one another. Rosa slipped under the bed. Ai no! Mrs. Hood dirint take the pee-pot out yet, Rosa sighed, and cursed the sight of the urine-filled pot sitting boldly beside her. The female-child fitted her shoes like gloves into her hands and placed them, rubber facing downwards, onto the floor. She soon realized that she would be needing both hands for protection. She wriggled them out slowly and stuffed the shoes in her unbuttoned bosom, placed both both hands over her mouth like a mask, and stared at the two pints of urine in the cast iron pot. She lay virtually immobile. When she lifted her head the diamond pattern wire from the bed caught her hair. When she tried to wiggle to each of her sides, the shoes, boxes, and other stacked away household goods prevented her from moving in the limited space. Auntie Flowers always dragged her feet and when Rosa could not hear them any longer she knew Auntie Flowers was standing still. Auntie Flowers placed herself on the unmade bed, right in the middle of it. Rosa's inquisitive face fitted neatly between the grown woman's legs. Auntie Flowers raised herself from the bed and walked towards the mirror. The springs above Rosa's head gave a bowful bounce, a salute which seemed appropriate since Uncle Tuckie's military boots seemed to ask for one. The urine pot got the stares from Rosa. Rosa's attention was soon fixed on Auntie Flowers who slowly removed the pins from her circular bound hair. Rosa had never seen Auntie Flowers with her hair down. Although Auntie Flowers was quite fond of her, now was not a good time to talk about Auntie Flowers' many hair pins. The child was silent. She was mesmerized by the sequence of events, most of which she would never have observed had she not sought the privacy of a small space under Mrs. Hood's bed. Rosa's mouth fell open as she counted, "Aaah ... 15 ... 16 ... 17 ... 18 ..." Tasting the urine stench against her palate, she shut her mouth instantly, placing both her hands over her tight-lipped mouth. She continued counting by nodding and memorizing, so that she could remember to tell Nita and maybe write it on one of her favourite walls. Auntie Flowers started singing, "Wait by the river, wait by my side," as she brushed in long, silent strokes. She sang in a funeral voice, Rosa thought, the kind of voice that vibrates, makes waves, and causes for everyone to cry. Auntie Flowers' voice was deep and passionate. "Wait till the moon is right, wait up all night, wait till it's morning, come hold me tight, wait till we kiss good-night, come let's not fight." Opening and closing her mouth was more agonizing than Rosa had anticipated. She wished she had told Mamma Zila that she was ill and could stay home to watch Auntie Flowers under better conditions. The urine lay still in its place. Glancing at it reminded Rosa of how her excitement was hampered by its presence.

She watched carefully as Mrs. Hood brought the metal bath into the bedroom. Mrs. Hood moved towards Auntie Flowers and stroked the woman's hair. It was not unusual for Rosa to see Mrs. Hood plant a kiss on Auntie Flowers' cheeks. This kiss was long and wanting. Auntie Flowers was still singing, "Wait till the birds are singing, wait till my heart is ringing." "Flowers, gimme a hand wit der water please." "Wait for the morning sun, wait till the birds are done." Auntie Flowers wrapped a towel around her hands and assisted Mrs. Hood with the pot of hot water. Rosa heard the noises of the women's feet dragging the huge pot of hot water from the coal stove. As she waited for them to enter the room something started moving on her head. Rosa, for fear of missing out on the bathing events, shook her head sideways until the eight-legged creature fell to the ground. It was a small spider. Its presence distracted Rosa immensely. Auntie Flowers hated spiders and seeing one now would cause for her to run out of the house and for Mrs. Hood to go running after this harmless creature, finding yet another under her bed – an eight-year-old, more dangerous one between her overdue urinal and her husband's military boots. Rosa grabbed the spider and placed it smilingly into the urinal. It died instantly. The two women had brought the big cast-iron bath into the room. Mrs. Hood kept pouring cold water into the bath. Rosa, in the meanwhile, found a pair of Uncle Tuckie's shoes and placed them over the

urinal, preventing the smell from leaving its temporarily destined place. Auntie Flowers went into the backyard and came
back with some lavender violets and yellow daisies. She gently
removed the petals and threw them into the water. Although
its floating glory was not visible to Rosa, the child smiled a
pleasant smile, thinking that Auntie Flowers was finally going
to announce the name of her love and ask, like female-children do, "He loves me yes, he loves me no, he loves me yes?"
and at the pluck of the last petal, a positive answer is blessed
with a scream of joy. Instead, Auntie Flowers placed the last
petal on Mrs. Hood's head. The woman exhaled from deep
within her bosom and blew the petal until it floated, then
rested on her dress.

Rosa watched attentively as Mrs. Hood undressed. Her
dress was the first garment she lifted over her head. It fell softly
to her feet. As Mrs. Hood bent to pick it up, Rosa saw Mrs.
Hood's kadoematjie.[1] Unlike Rosa's that was tied to her vest,
Mrs Hood's was tied to her bosom. Her breasts were large and
full and held her petticoat firmly. The woman removed her
petticoat by removing her arms from the garment. This she
did not pull over her head. She slipped it off her shoulders and
wiggled around with both her hands between her legs. Without much ado, the full contents of Mrs. Hood's underwear
were removed and Rosa's mouth gaped open to meet its
nakedness. It was Mrs. Hood's belly that fascinated Rosa most.
It was similar to Uncle Tommy's. His had scars of war, physical
fights, operations, and many other journeys he had been on.
Rosa thought about her geography lesson and how Mrs.
Hood's stomach resembled a map, with mountains and all.
Mamma Zila's flesh was firm for her sixty years and she had no
scars of any sort. And like Mamma Zila, Mrs. Hood had not

cupped her breasts either. It was their resistance to white settler-colonial culture and the need to remain untainted by it which was not observable or understood by the eight-year-old female-child, since she had rubbed her breasts with onions – a local remedy – with the hope that hers could soon fit a commoditized, prepackaged, cotton cup. Mrs. Hood's skin was lighter than Mamma Zila's and Rosa could see her freckles clustering around the nipples. Rosa felt her own face and thought about how her freckles clustered around her nose, a small protrusion. Mrs. Hood's were darker and clustered around her nipples, a larger, orally-celebrated protrusion. Mrs. Hood's breasts lay straight against her belly and her warm fingertips gently smoothed the clustered skin until the fullness of her nipple was visible to Auntie Flowers. It looked warm and comforting. Rosa was moving her hands around, thinking about how much the long extensions of breast reminded her of winter hand gloves – the ones she wore during July and August when her hands were sore and remained stiff, in snake-like position.

Auntie Flowers unbuttoned her dress and there, nakedly, the two women faced one another, each with her own shape. Each put her left foot into the bath at the far side of it, allowing for some space for the right foot. Auntie Flowers was standing at the back of Mrs. Hood, who had her arms round both of them so as to embrace Mrs. Hood. As both women placed themselves in the bath, splashes of water fell to the floor and small lavender petals stuck to the outside of the bath. The two women remained locked together for quite a while, their silence perturbing Rosa greatly. Mrs. Hood lifted her head backwards and placed it gently on Auntie Flowers shoulders. Her clavicles made their appearance and her long grey hair made big circles on the nape of her neck, sculpturing her clavicles in a somewhat vivacious manner. The room was silent. Both women were breathing deeply. The release of their breaths shook the room. "Wooooooow," they both breathed out repeatedly. It was not like a voice lesson Mrs. Jacobs gave, the female-child thought, this was very different. Auntie Flowers did not sing again and Mrs. Hood held the woman behind her tightly. When Auntie Flowers moved forward keeping Mrs. Hood at some distance from her, it enabled her to unlock herself from the firm grip she needed relaxation from. As she removed Mrs. Hood's arms and hands, she stroked them rhythmically, like the voetvrou[2] does with babies. The strokes were long and, unlike with babies whose strokes are accompanied by words of wisdom and pray, Auntie Flowers hummed a song. It was unfamiliar to Rosa who had her eyes fixed on Auntie Flowers' knees. They were round and big like Mamma Zila's and told Rosa that it was Auntie Flowers who did the scrubbing and polishing of floors in the house. Auntie Flowers stroked Mrs. Hood's hair and made rings with it, placing water on the already curly bits. Some of the droplets nestled themselves onto Mrs Hood's lips. The two women put each's finger in the other's mouth. Rosa thought it was exciting to see grown women exchange spit. She wondered whether they did the same with food. Although this was an exchange of water, the female-child thought of it as equally defiant. Mamma Zila had warned Rosa so many times about exchanging food already chewed and Rosa thought about telling Mamma Zila about this incident.

The thought left her mind immediately as the gushing water jolted her attention to the two women exchanging places in a bathtub too small to contain one grown woman.

They sat facing one another now and Rosa could only see Mrs. Hood's back and some parts of Auntie Flowers. The urinal was beside her and although moving her head from right to left did leave room for greater vision, this did not quite fulfill the little girl's curiosity. It was the way in which Auntie Flowers cupped her hands and poured water over Mrs. Hood's breasts that fascinated Rosa most. It reminded Rosa of Father John and baptism at St. Marks, where the family attended church regularly. Auntie Flowers did utter a few words – silent words, warm words, judging by the serene smile on Mrs. Hood's face – although not exactly in the same tone as Father John. Both women's eyes were cast towards the ceiling. Are they talking to God? Rosa wondered, almost aloud. Both the women embraced one another tighter. The water squirted out between their legs and the overflow ran under the bed to meet the unwelcome gaze of Rosa's shoes, both of which were still stuck in her bosom. Suddenly, like a stroke of lightning, Mrs. Hood raised herself. Rosa closed her eyes for fear of what was going to happen to her. With her eyes closed and waiting for her punishment, Rosa heard Mrs. Hood's hands moving and grabbing something, then moving its contents swiftly with her hands. A ray of sunlight shone on the right side of Rosa's face. The sun, although not casting its fullest power, had enticed the woman towards the greater acceptance of its rays. Boldly she drew the curtains, wrapped them around her wet legs, and danced a childlike dance – a tantalizing, somewhat naughty teasing motion, while Auntie Flowers giggled. The rays of sunlight shone brightly on Auntie Flowers' face and enhanced the sharpness of her clavicles, its wetness bronzed like a medal, waiting patiently to be touched and admired. Mrs. Hood's teeth met the temptation, sucking dearly at its warmth until blood filled the gaps between her teeth. Her kiss planted a red glowing print on Auntie Flowers' face and the woman's sparkling eyes made Dracula seem like a hopeless case for seduction against the wishes of frightened, chaste women. Both women ate graciously from the blood, their tongues curling with lust and their palates seeping with its nutritious contents. There was passion, love, admiration, an exchange of caring moments, stolen from the heavy load which the constraints of marriage bore. No body of blood of Jesus Christ could fulfill the spirituality of body, of being, that these two women felt and allowed themselves to indulge in.

As the blood coloured the water, Auntie Flowers scooped a handful and poured it over her face. Rosa's tilted face and opened mouth allowed for the sun to shine on her palate – it gulping the air from which these two love-drunk women breathed. Rosa's eyes were still; her body lay motionless. And like a mother feeds a child, Mrs. Hood lifted her breasts from the waist up, holding onto their length with her knees while Auntie Flowers' mouth enveloped the quivering protrusions. Heavy breathing like a voice lesson, Rosa thought again, was the medium through which these two women communicated their desire. Mrs. Hood's partner's desires were fulfilled and, slightly salivating, eyes closed, and fingers clenching the rims of the bathtub, Auntie Flowers moved her body forward, lifted her legs and feet out of the bath, and wrapped them around Mrs. Hood. Auntie Flowers' feet, crossed one over the other, made the shape of a bow. Is this what Auntie Spider spoke about when she referred to white women being scared of Black women's powers and how our women can wrap men up like Christmas presents? It was no idle thought. Rosa lay watching every movement of Auntie Flowers' toes, each cracking joint succumbing to the vibrant touch of its beholder. She recognized the visual image implanted in her mind, one created by the words of Auntie Spider, also known as Auntie Legs, who regularly told stories about Black women's sexuality to girls in the neighbourhood, preparing them for their approaching womanhood. Is this like sex? the female-child asked herself, having been told that it being when a woman allows a man into her vagina.

Slowly Mrs. Hood moved her head back as her breasts extended themselves into the mouth of her lover. Auntie Flowers bore no resemblance to a child any longer. Her whole body was wrapped around Mrs. Hood who accepted its passionate, lubricious glory. Both women held each other close and and kissed every freckle, every inch, every part of the other's face. Rosa lay still, motionless, with a smile on her face. There were no hands visible to Rosa; but, to the women who each had their folds unfolded, stroked, and stimulated, the organs attached to their arms fulfilled every libidinal desire. Transmitting their otherwise clandestine sexual appetite, their voracious tongues sweeping every morsel. Several soft cries were muttered, then louder ones filled the room – each with distinctive sound and echo from all of the four flabbergasted lips – then a cry of relief, accompanied by laughter and softer outcries, each intermittent one exhaling more joy than the one before.

There was a knock on the door. Both women looked at one another. The knocker decided to let itself into the house – a common practice – to see what was keeping the inhabitants of the house from answering. Remembering their arrangements for a ride to Hanover Street, both women gasped, looked towards the window to access the brightness of the light – telling the time of day – and answered the caller. "Just wait Peter, we're getting dressed." Rosa could hear the person stopping in their tracks. "Okay, Mrs. Hood, I jus wannit to know if you ladies were ready for Hanover Street." It was Peter Jantjies, a neighbour who worked at the dockyard and sold fish to the vendors in Hanover Street. He was taking several women down to Hanover Street and offered women in the neighbourhood the option of selecting the finest pieces of fish and, on occasion, would give them a ride in his cart. Both women raised themselves simultaneously and silently hugged as the water ran over their firmly held arms. The towels brushed their skin lightly and slowly, reluctantly, both women clothed themselves in silence. Mrs. Hood opened her wardrobe, groped among the many items, removed her money cloth, and clutched it under her arm. It had several knots in it and the woman, feeling a bit of discomfort, removed the cloth and relocated certain portions. In the far right corner the rent money lay knotted until the end of the month; in the far left corner lay the food knot, which did not include money for purchasing fish. Mrs. Hood located the fish knot just below it, its proximity strategically placed so that, whenever possible, small transfers could be made, especially since Peter was the more gullible peddler and known for his kindness, and sometimes, not often, the money scored on bargaining would be used for buying stockings and rose water. Peter left the door open and Rosa could hear him calling women in the neighbourhood. The two women lifted their tub of passion and released it in the backyard, where the water removed splints of wood and took then down the drain. Auntie Flowers and Mrs. Hood departed and met Peter at the door, each lifting herself individually into the cart and assisting Peter with the calling of their equally late peers.

Rosa was relieved that she was finally alone to make decisions about the rest of her day. She removed herself slowly from under the bed, looked around to absorb her surroundings since she had not been able to enjoy them laying under the bed. The female-child giggled softly to herself, then louder and louder until the sound filled the room with panic. She became silent, bit her lip, pouted a bit, and nodded to herself. "It's a secret and noborry knows anyting," she uttered. It had dawned upon her to speak to one of her many walls – her companions – and this event needed to be recorded. Rosa walked into the backyard and placed herself on the concrete step, pulled her dress down so as to protect her body from the coldness of the cement bricks, and sat down. She stared at the wetness of the cement floor, seeing the reflections of the two lovers whom she had thought, and people in the neighbourhood thought, were cousins. She undid her buckled shoes, removed her socks, and stuck her right toe into the wetness. She pulled it back instantly still staring at the reflection of her thoughts. Did she now partake in this event by placing a part of her body into the water? Several thoughts occupied her mind, most of which seemed to suggest that the events she had just witnessed were for secrecy. She raised herself almost graciously, in adult fashion, and found a piece of wood at the back of the yard and took a splint from the dry log. Having pricked her finger, as she usually did when writing on walls and implanting her print, she swore to secrecy and vowed never to talk about the events she had witnessed. She remembered Mamma Zila's words: "Child, when you grow older, you'll find out that there are some things you just doan talk about." Rosa had always thought this a strange saying since everybody exchanged stories and, as far as the female-child knew, there were no secrets – only ones not told to white people, if you worked for them.

Touching her nipples and remembering the fullness of Mrs.

Hood's breasts, she climbed over the wall and rested herself among the wooden logs in Mrs. Benjamin's backyard. There was nobody home and she could climb all the walls to the end of the street, and when the sun shone way over Ospavat indicating that it was twelve noon, Rosa would go to the Hopelots forest and play in the trees, where she could again see where the sun was, wait for the sirens to sound after lunch, and return home promptly, as expected.

1. Kadoematjie: A piece of cotton cloth filled with earthly soils, herbs, plants, and indigenous mixtures. The cloth is sewn together and worn around children's (and sometimes adults') necks and most times pinned to their vests or any piece of underwear. It is meant to protect children from harm and colonial evil.
2. Voetvrou: A woman who delivers babies and who is known for walking the streets fulfilling her role in the community.

"No Rosa, No District Six" is an excerpt from a novel in progress.

GUY MALET DE CARTERET

Rainy Day

I approached the farm across the fields. It was dark. At each new field I had to walk in a little way and feel with my hands for any crop before walking across. The ground was slightly frozen and I could feel my breath on my hand when I bent down. The earth was crisp and the only noise was the crunch under my feet. It was easier to walk around on the path next to the hedge, but I preferred to head out into the open field and try and guess the corner where I knew the gate would be.

It was the middle of the school holidays and I had spent the days walking in the fields, out of the house, away from the depression at home. Dad had walked out. I knew he would. And now there was a strange quiet in the house. There were no longer any shouts of rage, just the sound of the TV to fill the empty space and break the stale alcoholic air. That was two months ago. Mum spent most of the time in the kitchen, sitting. At first she hid her drinking from me. She would pretend and start chattering to me in a fake jolly way which made me feel uneasy. I didn't know how to reply to her. Once I asked her why we always had to have sausages for dinner, and she started crying, slowly at first. Then she turned around and started to sob, her shoulders hunched up in a funny way. I stood looking at her shoulders moving up and down. I wanted to say I was sorry. I wanted to go up and hug her and tell her that she didn't have to pretend anymore, that we would get by, the two of us. But I just put my empty plate in the sink and closed the kitchen door behind me, thinking how much older she looked. Later, when I had turned out my light, she came and sat at the end of my bed. She sat here for a long time without saying anything, her hands on her lap. Again I felt I should say something but I didn't feel old enough. Then she leant forward, trying to find my face. She kissed me on my cheek, and I could smell wine on her breath. She left, leaving the door ajar, and I listened to her getting undressed before I fell asleep. Things seemed to get worse after. I spent more time in front of the TV and she spent more time in the kitchen drinking.

I opened the gate and stepped into the lane, then turned right. It was noisier now. My boots echoed on the tarmac. The sound seemed to bounce back from the darkness. Occasionally there was a rustle from the hedge. A bird or a rabbit, I couldn't tell. The road led to a small wood where the summer before I had found a frame for a swing. I had cut branches and tied them to the frame, making a camouflaged shooting-post from where I tried to pick off pigeons with my air-rifle.

I turned left onto the track which led to the farm. It was beginning to get lighter. The darkness seemed to turn in on itself. I could make out the dark glint of the reservoir below.

There was a light on in the building spreading a sickly glow into the farmyard. I stepped onto the orange square of light and looked into the kitchen. Martha was at the stove making tea. I could hear the radio tuned to the weather forecast.

"Up early with the birds this morning," she said as I entered.

"I woke early," I said, not knowing what else to say.

I sat down at the table and watched her hands as she took down some mugs and turned off the stove. She moved uneasily. It was as if she had to think first before shifting her weight. On her feet she wore slippers, the kind that have no back, which scraped along the floor as she moved. Her feet seemed to spill out of the fur, and rose, missing out the ankles, into fleshy columns as thick as table legs. An apron which reminded me of nursery curtains was tied at her waist by a scarf. She handed me a cup of tea, saying that Jim and the others would be here soon. Then she let out a sigh and sat down next to me.

"How are you getting on, then?" she said after a while.

"Fine," I said. I moved my feet closer to the bar-heater. "Though my back hurts a little," I added.

"Bound to for a bit," she said. "But you'll get used to it. Anyway it will be over soon and you'll be back at school."

I watched her hands take the mug up to her mouth. Then I looked back at the lino floor. It had begun to peel in places. Dirty brown bits between red and white squares. The thought of school seemed far away, as far away as the strange places being read out on the weather forecast. It was only three days ago that I applied for the job and only two days that I had been working. Everything seemed longer. My back hurt and I wondered whether I would last the week. I began to feel tired. I regretted that I had woken up early and hadn't stayed in bed longer.

I heard the windows of the back door rattle and then the scraping of boots before Jim came in. He smiled through his pipe and patted me on the back as he sat down. Martha got up to get him his tea.

"Bit of frost out there this morning," he said to her back. I remembered the crunch of the fields earlier. Even that seemed far away.

"Forecast for rain this afternoon. That's all we need. Got to get them in by the end of the week or there'll be trouble," he added.

Martha didn't look at him. Instead she began to put a scarf round her head. A scarf of faded blue. She asked him if the cows were ready. Then she knotted the scarf twice under her chin. I silently prayed for rain, for a rest, while I watched Jim prepare his pipe with tobacco. There was a little bit of spittle on the chewed mouthpiece. At the tip it had faded to a colour that reminded me of bone. He wiped his mouth and I could hear the hairs on his chin. He was in no hurry when it came to his pipe. He lit his pipe and we waited for the others to arrive.

Looking at Jim, I remembered the first time I had seen him. It was when I had gone to the farm to ask for work. He had approached me from one of the outhouses and I immediately sensed that something was odd about him, something not quite right.

The day before I had been out in the fields after rabbits. I had positioned myself next to a large warren and waited. Ever since the day I had shot a diseased one I had been after one properly. It had cowered against the hedge, its ears pulled down along its back. It didn't move when I brought the gun close to its head. I told my father and he told me the name of the disease. He said that it was merciful to shoot it, that shooting it put it out of its misery, and stopped the disease spreading. Even so I felt somehow wrong when I rolled it into the hedge with the barrel of my gun and covered it with leaves.

Two fields across and sloping away from where I sat, they were planting cauliflowers. I watched the men, three of them, sitting behind the tractor bobbing up and down putting cauliflower plants into the ground. When the tractor reached the end of the field the planter was raised and the men got up. Then the tractor turned round so it pointed in the other direction. The planter was lowered. The men got on and the same thing started all over again. It suddenly seemed funny. I laughed. They weren't planting cauliflower but hair. The tractor was really combing the bald scalp of the land and the men were planting hair roots between unploughed fields that wore wigs of green. At their backs a white scarf of seagulls flapped in the wind, then dropped to the ground, littering the earth like golf balls. It was then I decided to go and ask for work the next day. There wasn't much else to do, and the only reason why I was after rabbits was to get out of the house. Besides, I wanted to buy a bike, a racer like Jimmy Beard had, so I could ride to school without waiting for the bus.

I arrived at the farm around lunch-time. Nobody was about, so I decided to take a look in one of the sheds that made up a side of the farmyard. It was built of corrugated iron and was painted a dull red. There was no door, just a large opening at one end, with a central support made of stone. Weeds sprouted at the edges. It was dark inside and had a strange shut-up smell like a cupboard. It seemed hollow somehow, echoey. Machinery – some muddy, some clean – stood idle on the earth floor. I recognized a few items – the large potato-harvester at the back, a plough a little rusty – and made guesses as to what the others were used for. Above the machinery, approached by a ladder, was another floor where boxes were stacked on top of each other. I stepped forward and pulled at a lever on one of the machines. Nothing happened. I turned and saw a pile of bluish pellets. Rat poison, I thought. When I went out into the yard again I saw him as he stepped out of one of the buildings. He spotted me immediately and walked towards me, carrying a bucket.

"Snooping, are we?" he said as he approached. He was a tall man but there was something odd about him. I noticed a pipe which stuck out at an angle from his mouth.

"No, I'm just looking," I said. "I'm interested."

"Are you? What can I do for you?" He had a flat, low voice. He stopped and looked down at me from a great height.

"I'm looking for work," I mumbled. I felt uncomfortable at feeling so small. I looked into the bucket and saw a mixture of vegetables. Bits of cabbage and carrots gave colour to the brown swill of potato peelings and other things. It smelt off, like blocked drains.

"Are you?" he said again. Then he continued to walk past me. I followed him. It was then that I noticed that he only had one arm. The spare arm of his coat was tucked into his pocket. I walked close behind him. He seemed all wellington boots which wobbled below the knee.

"I thought I could help out. With the cauliflowers, I mean. Planting," I said. I watched the wellington boots.

"School holidays?" he said over his shoulder.

"Yes," I said. I quickened my walk so I came alongside the bucket.

We had come out of the farmyard and had turned right along the red corrugated shed. The stone of the yard gave way to concrete. It had a small gully running down the side, forming a drain at the end. To our left was the road running to the village. I heard a car pass. We approached a small building, not very tall, with a low wall in front that then ran back and joined the building on either side. Behind the slanted roof I could see an orchard with long uncut grass between the apple trees. The orchard was bordered by trees covered in ivy. And behind, fields.

All of a sudden I heard pigs grunting. Jim emptied the bucket over the wall, and started to uncoil a hose from a tap on the side of the building. I stepped onto a stone so that I could lean on the top of the wall and look over. I had never seen a pig in real life before. In a strange way, they looked almost human. I watched them feeding while Jim began to hose down the pen.

I thought that he had forgotten me until he handed me the hose and told me where to direct the spray. He took a stiff broom and climbed in, knocking the pigs out of his way with his knee. He put the handle to his shoulder and started to walk forward, leaning into it. Raising the broom every so often, he swept the muck towards a small hole in the wall. Then he walked back and started moving towards the hole again. When his back was turned I tried to get a reaction from the pigs by increasing the force of the water and spraying them where I thought their arsehole was, somewhere under their tails. But they were too busy sniffing for more food to move out of the way.

When he finished I asked him again about the job. He put the broom back and turned off the tap and then started to coil the hose. When he was done he turned round and looked at me and said nothing. It was as if I hadn't asked him before, and he was thinking about it for the first time. I looked up at him, trying to read his face. Then I felt my eyes searching for his other arm, seeking an answer. It could have been strapped to his chest or his back, if he had one, but I knew that was silly.

Then I looked at his boots, for I felt he knew what I was thinking.

"It's hard work, you know," he said.

I looked up and saw that he was looking at the pigs. Some had gone back into the building, while others were still sniffing around.

"Think you can manage?" He turned and looked at me – not really at me, but over me. I nodded. With that he picked up the bucket, saying that he couldn't stand around talking all day.

"Be here at 5:30. If you do okay then it will be for a week, maybe eight days. It depends on the weather," he said, and headed back up to the farmyard.

I don't know why, but I looked up at the sky. Then I watched him, the bucket, the boots, and the arm pass the red corrugated shed and turn the corner.

Henri was the first to arrive. As he shut the kitchen door a small gust of wind disturbed the pipe-smoke that hung in the air. He said hello in French to Martha and Jim, then nodded to me. He stood leaning against the doorpost, his arms folded. Martha had told me that he was a labourer from Gaspé when I asked about the tattoos that covered his arms and rose above his collar on his neck. He had frightened me the first day I arrived for work.

Jim finished his tea and we went outside. It was lighter now, but the buildings were still dark. Paul and David arrived. I heard their voices and saw the glow of their cigarettes as they walked into the farmyard. I could tell by the way they walked that they were still half-asleep. We began to load the trailer with boxes of cauliflower plants while Jim drove the planter to the fields. When he returned we attached the trailer to the tractor. Jim told Henri to dig some more plants and for Paul, David, and me to get on the back of the trailer. Martha had already gone to look after the cows.

I hadn't worked with David or Paul before. It was their first day. They told me that they were going back to the city in a week or so's time. They asked me if I went to school and what my favourite subject was. Everybody asked me that. They said that they went to college, that they were going to be doctors. Then they started using long words. First one saying a word, then the other. I asked them what they were talking about. "Diseases," Paul said, and showed his teeth. I told them the one disease I knew. I told them about the rabbits.

"Well, what's it like then?" Paul said.

"It makes them go limp. It's like they are too scared to move," I said.

"No, not the rabbit," Paul said. "Planting cauliflowers."

We were still riding on the back of the trailer, driving past the football pitch. It had been closed down and the nets had been taken from the goal posts. I had gone a couple of times with my father, and stood watching the game on the sideline. The men used to smoke and pass whisky round. I remembered my father's whisky flask. My mother had given it to him for his birthday. It had his initials and the date on which she gave it to him.

"It's hard work," I said. "I haven't done much, I've only been working two days. First time," I added.

"Ours too," Paul said. He looked at David. David nodded towards Jim. He said they had told Jim that they had planted cauliflowers before. They needed to earn some money to pay for their trip home. They wouldn't be doing it otherwise.

"You better show us how it's done," Paul said.

I thought of Martha and her hands, and how she had shown me the first day. It wasn't difficult. It was just bending. A lot of bending every time the machine clicked. Henri was there too, at the other end of the seat. Martha was between us. I watched her hands putting plants into the ground. The three of us hadn't talked. We just bent down and put cauliflower plants into the earth every time there was a click. The only other sound was the seagulls. Martha only talked to me once after she told me how to plant. It was at the end of the day. I couldn't get off the planter so it could be raised and the tractor could turn round. I didn't have the strength. I just leant over till I fell off, and lay there on the ground, waiting for the tractor to get into the position. "Don't worry," she said. "Everybody does that the first day." I felt relieved. I thought that in the silence they had been thinking that I couldn't do it, that I wouldn't last the week.

We pulled off the road and into the field. We took the trailer off and put the planter on. Then we loaded the planter with three boxes of cauliflower plants, one for each of us. I showed them where to put their feet. I showed them the wheel that moved round and clicked. I told them every time it clicked you had to put a plant into the hole. I told them it was better to put it in at an angle because when the planter moved forward it brought it upright. Martha hadn't told me that, but I told them anyway. I knew other things. I knew that it was better to vary the way you picked the plants out of the boxes. Either to grab a handful or just one, and to use different hands for taking the plants and for putting them in the hole. That way you didn't use your back the same way all the time.

"How do you think he did it?" David said to me. We had just finished one row of the field and had turned back. I was sitting in the middle. I let them sit on the ends so they could lean over and fall off if they wanted.

"Do what?" I said.

"His arm," David said.

"I don't know," I said. "It must have been an accident."

"He drives a tractor well for someone who only has one arm," Paul said.

"Of course it must have been an accident," David said. "But what accident? What type of accident?"

"Could hardly have been anything else," Paul said. "I mean, he couldn't have chopped it off out of a sense of duty." He turned to me. "In Japan they cut off their little fingers out of a sense of duty." I missed a click.

"Of course, he could have misjudged. Slipped," David laughed.

"Or was disloyal a lot," Paul said.

"Or it could have been out of love, an arm instead of an car. Could you imagine carrying his other arm to his loved one and laying it at her door?" David said.

They both laughed. I did a bit too, even though I didn't understand. That morning I laughed some more. I didn't really want to. I knew you were supposed to laugh at jokes even if you didn't understand. All morning Paul and David talked about Jim's arm. I was glad someone was talking as it made you forget about the clicks and about your back. But I wished it was about something else. I didn't want Jim to hear. I liked Jim. I liked helping with the pigs at lunch-time. And then after the pigs we'd go up to see his pigeons.

He kept them in one of the outbuildings. There were no

stairs and to get to them we had to climb a ladder which went through a trap door up to the next floor. Each floor was a long empty room stretching the length of the building. On the top floor, in a cage in one of the corners, were his pigeons. It seemed a private place when our feet sounded on the wooden floorboards. The would flap around the cages as we got closer and the room would come alive with shadows. The cage as well as the floor was covered in shit. The first time I saw them I had thought of the swing frame, of whether I might have shot at any of them. Jim told me that he had raced them. He never had a winner but one had come in third, he said. He showed me how to attach the ring to their legs. I'd watch him through the wire, talking to the birds. That was the only time Jim really talked. He didn't need another arm when he was with his birds. They liked him and let him pick them up and hold them. He'd hold them close to his face and call them by their names. Blue, Mister, Will, Jinx, Flyer. I couldn't tell the difference but Jim knew.

We stopped for lunch and picked up the trailer. We needed more plants which Henri would have dug. There was more traffic on the roads as we drove back to the farm. We had been working towards the farm as we planted, so we hadn't so far to go. Cars tried to pass us. David stood up and waved them on when the road was clear. He said Jim would have his hand full.

When he got to the farm, David and Paul asked if I wanted to go to the pub with them, that they would buy me a drink. The only way they would be able to get through the afternoon, they said. But I stayed. I had a routine with Jim.

In the afternoon we planted more cauliflowers. David and Paul talked about their college and their girlfriends. But mostly it was about Jim's arm. They said he could get an artificial one if he wanted. That it would be better. You could do things with a glove hand like hold a glass, they said. Then Paul said you didn't need two hands to drink. They laughed. A hook would be more useful, or one that had a prong so you could lift things. He could even fill his pipe with that, if he wanted.

It didn't rain that afternoon. But it rained the next day. David and Paul had come back from the pub a bit drunk. We had been planting for about an hour after lunch, and then it began. We carried on at first as it was only a drizzle. But it got heavier and the sky blacker. The wheels spun up spray as we drove back to the farm.

The farmyard was covered in rain water. One of the gutters was blocked, and the rain water fell down in a heavy stream, smacking the stone. We drove into the building opposite the red corrugated shed and waited for it to stop. Jim stood in the doorway looking up at the sky. He was silhouetted, and all around him I could see the slanting rain dropping hard onto the stone, breaking up and splashing. Occasionally rain would come in and hit his boots and hit the earth floor, making a different sound. My hands were red from the cold and the rain. I could hardly feel them. I cupped them to my mouth and blew. I looked around and saw David wipe some wet hair away from his face. He swept it back over his head with his hand. Paul was sitting on some boxes, scraping them with a nail. We didn't talk. We just waited, glad for the rest. David looked up at Jim. And then he said it.

"What happened to your arm, Jim?" he said. Paul stopped scraping. David and Paul looked at each other. "How did you lose it?" David asked.

Jim turned around and looked at him, then Paul, and lastly me. He took a few paces forward. I could see him better now. But I couldn't see his face properly. I thought then that he was going to hit David. I thought he was going to step forward and whack him one right in the face. But he just stood there. There was a pause. Nobody spoke. It seemed to last a long time. Jim took his pipe out of his mouth and looked at it.

"An accident. Some time ago," he said finally.

"What type of accident? A farming accident?" Paul asked.

"Yes, from a combine." He stopped, then went on. "Pulled me in. Just about took it off. Went right through muscle and bone. Everything."

"Must have hurt," Paul said.

"I haven't seen one of those combines, but I imagine one of those machines could easily do something like that," David said.

"Accidents were common in those days," Jim added. He lit his pipe. He pulled at the pipe a couple of times and let out a stream of smoke. The smoke reached the end, then broke, swirling upwards in strands, and drifted towards the doorway.

"Can we see your arm?" David said. "Paul and I are medical students. We'd be interested on medical grounds. If you don't mind, that is."

Something hit me in the stomach when he said it. I felt my throat swallowing. He had gone too far this time, I thought. Jim would surely hit him. Paul got up from the boxes. Both of them looked at Jim.

Jim began taking off his coat. He walked over to the wall and hung it on a nail. There was a wet patch between his shoulder blades that pointed down his back, making his shirt stick to his skin. He turned around, and I watched his hand unbutton his shirt. I felt my heart beat faster. I suddenly realized that I wanted to see it too.

He finished undoing his buttons. Using his one arm, he twisted out of his shirt. I saw it then. It was small, not very long. It hung down about five inches. It had been cut above the elbow. He walked forward towards David and it wobbled. Each step Jim took seemed to go up his legs, through his body, and out into that shaking piece of flesh. He stopped in front of David. Then David reached out a hand and touched it. It seemed to fold, to turn in on itself. He said nothing. We all said nothing. Jim walked over to Paul. His shirt was still tucked in and hung down the back of his legs. Paul also touched it, and said something to Jim. I didn't hear what he said.

Jim turned towards me. My heart jumped and I felt the thump in my stomach again.

"And how about you? I suppose you want to look too," he said.

He stopped in front of me. I was sitting on the trailer and his arm, his bit of an arm, was right in front of me, still wobbling. I didn't know what to say. I just looked at it. A piece of flesh but more than a piece of flesh. It was sort of knotted at the end and looked raw and reddish, wrinkled like a newborn baby's skin. It looked unformed, something not complete, something that might grow. But I knew it couldn't. What was missing had been ripped away.

"Touch it," he said. I didn't move. I just looked, and felt the saliva in my mouth.

"Go on, touch it. It won't bite." He turned his head to look at David and Paul, and laughed. David and Paul laughed too. Touch it, they said.

I lifted my arm and stretched out my hand. I knew it was

wrong but I was curious too. It felt soft, slightly warm, moving back at my touch, offering no resistance.

We finished planting cauliflowers within the week. It didn't rain again. We didn't talk, Paul, David, and I. We just planted in silence. It was like the silence in the red corrugated shed. It was like the silence when you put your head underwater in the bath. I didn't hear the seagulls. I didn't hear the clicks.

MARIA A. BILLION

No Miracles Sweet Jesus

The sea is rolling rough today. When Nena and her brother jump off their rock platform, arms and legs feel like seaweed, no good to steer them anywhere. Seaweed pods battered against barnacles, mussels, rocks.

Nena can feel a sweetness in her mouth from a cut lip.

Nena and Paul, the only two in the sea, in the whole world. Wait till they got home, they'd get it for sure, even if they dusted their knees to fool Papa into thinking they had been to school.

"Did you go to school today?"

"Yes," Paul would say, shaking his head, "yes," no matter how many times Nena drilled him to nod "yes" and shake "no." Only a year younger but you'd think he was just a baby the way she had to drag him around ever since that first time they went down to the sea.

What about bathing suits?

Who needs them?

What if we get caught?

Don't worry.

Smell that sea, the wind is up, the crabs are running.

For many days now, she's lost count. Nena has forged notes in her father's name, looked for crabs in the seaweed patches, built stone turrets against Turk and Nazi, swum and sunned all day. And not once listened to Sister Donatus tell how Jesus came to call her to be a nun. You got to go if he calls you, Sister Donatus said.

A white sun today, wind up, whitecaps foaming round her. Only a few arm lengths away, her brother. She calls out to him but he doesn't hear, his head now and then hidden by the waves, the hot sirocco blowing from him to her, he can't hear. He's not used to deep water, not like this, rough. If he drowns it will be all her fault, you have been trouble to me from the start, her mother said, wait till your time comes, her mother said, and she wasn't talking about becoming a nun.

"Trouble to me even before you were born a month late I almost died and even as a toddler you almost killed your brother."

A hissing in her ears. The waves suck at seaweeds and mussels clinging to the rocky shore.

"Yes you, you pulled him off the table when my head was turned a minute as if I hadn't lost one baby already before you were born, a baby boy. Mark my words your time will come."

Nena must keep her brother in sight but not get too close, not until she has figured what to do. Paul nearly pulled her under once when Nena was teaching him to swim and he started to sink.

Holy Virgin Mother of God help them get to shore. She'll say a novena, she'll go to school every day, she'll obey her mother. Not like yesterday at house blessing, before the priest came. She'd made herself scarce, played up on the roof and down in the back garden. Not scrubbing the stone stairs, not rinsing the tile floors, not polishing the glass balconies.

Nena slits her eyes against the white glare. She must come up on her brother unawares, grab him, before anything happens to him. He's drifted farther away from her now. His head bobs like a glass ball loosened from its fishing net. Wavetops glint silver, a million pieces of a broken mirror. The sound of her voice calling her brother is swallowed by the wind. She scans the beach. Deserted. Except for a solitary figure sitting on their rock platform.

Eyes burn against the sun, she senses more than sees the man, his image afloat in the red haze behind her eyelids. The apparition strikes her dumb for a minute, the better to hear the voices siphoning into her ears along with the sea. The voices of her grandmothers and mother mix with her own.

Beware of the Turks.

The pirates'll get you.

The Nazis.

They'll skin you alive.

Not helping your mother.

Your time will come.

Immaculate conception.

Pray for me.

Nena feels the whole world shrink to the size of her small island in the Mediterranean, that middle island in the middle sea her grandmothers were always telling her stories about, stories going far back, even from before the time they were born. And right in the middle of the island in the middle sea sits this man.

"You just wait, wait till some man comes along and ruins

your life, just like that, no rhyme no reason. Mark my words your time will come."

Nena fixes her eyes on her brother's head, takes a deep breath, and plunges underwater.

"Not me. That's not gonna happen to me. I'll become a nun."

She surfaces, shakes her head, hair spraying prisms before her. She still cannot see Paul's arms moving above the water. Maybe he's too tired to swim, maybe he's floating on his back.

But. To become a nun, she would have to go to school. "Go to school, get an education," Papa said, "then you can become anything you want, anything at all."

But look at him, he'd lost his chance. Her mother had a baby every time he looked at her, her mother said, he had to quit politics, work overtime at the dockyard. Even that didn't stop him from stirring up the dockyard workers. "Are you going to let the British walk all over you? Are you men?"

Nena had heard that story many times.

"Do like I say, not like I do, go to school." He made her a special schoolcase, mahogany with brass hinges, made it shine like a mirror with their faces in it. The same schoolcase waits for them now, hiding under a rock ledge with lunch inside it. Tomatoes, olives, hard crusted bread. She feels a scratching inside, hungry.

Do like I say. Easier done. No time to do anything at all Nena wanted to, go down to the sea at high noon for one thing, have the beach and the foreshore to herself and her brother. Except today that man sitting on their rock platform.

As she is lifted and lowered by the turbulent sea, Nena ventures a sideways glance at the man sitting there. Can't he see they're in trouble, why doesn't he jump in to save them?

A breaking wave forces water down Nena's throat, makes

her face feel hot. Or is he waiting until they're knocked sense-less against the rocks before he makes his move, is this going to be the day her time would come? The eight arms of an octopus tear at her insides. Will she go under, will the sea be too much for her this one time?

No. No. The sea cannot wash away the holy water sprinkled on her just yesterday afternoon. The priest blessed crucifixes, holy pictures, and votive offerings, blessed the silver-framed photographs of Nena and Paul in First Communion white, cheeks retouched a queer pink, blessed the large sepia angels in the background. "The angels will safeguard you against all harm from now on." And just last Sunday at Communion the body and blood of Jesus came alive inside her. And the Bishop himself gave Nena and Paul a smart tap on the right cheek with his two fingers when they were confirmed. "You are now soldiers of Christ, ready to do battle bravely with all evil from now on."

Can't her brother see her? Where is he now she needs him? She'll hit him or hold him, whichever comes first. Why did she have to fight more evil than he had to? His day would not come. Why did he have to obey all the time, help all the time? Make her mother curse Nena all the more.

A frenzy of coughing wracks her chest as she heaves to spit out the alien sea.

When the priest left yesterday her mother just about fainted with fatigue.

"This is it. I'm at the end of my rope. You'd better. Mark my words."

Her mother, red in the face, in one of her fits.

"Your brother, he helps even if he's younger, only seven, a boy too. I never had a chance."

Like saying the Litany.

"When I was your age I never had a chance to go to school. I was always doing for others, not just my mother, my sisters too, me, the youngest of thirteen, shunted from household to household, never knowing where I was going to sleep next, never knowing which brother-in-law I would be fighting off next."

A rage of recitation upon her mother.

"Making myself useful when my sisters had their children, and now with the lot of you, one died already, one on the way, my own mother old enough to be my grandmother, my own daughter an ungrateful wretch, you mark my words, your time will come." The litany rushes headlong, the rage pushes out. Her brother petrified, Nena frozen. By now Mother has one leg over the banister on the third storey landing. Her voice bounces off the white walls.

The wind hurts Nena's ear. She plunges underwater for relief. The salt water makes Nena's cut lip sting. She sucks her lips back over her teeth. The cold vertical sun turns everything white, sky and sea, the cold white sun beats down on her, sends shafts of cold trembling through her arms, legs, her whole self. She holds her hands out of the water, palms facing her. Ashen and wrinkled like an old woman's. She cannot see the rest of her body in the roiling sea. She's only a head, adrift like her brother's.

"This is it. I'll jump. I'm going to jump." A scream pushes past her mother's constricted throat, a sound coming from an underground cavern, until her rocking back and forth against the banister sets up a vibration under Nena's fingers where she stands, and releases her mother's voice to its full, frenzied pitch. "I'll jump." The noonday sun streams stark through the large central skylight above, the white stone stairs, the white iron railings standing shadowless, hard bright, mother, daughter, son in slow-motion pictures.

Nena cannot see Paul. One moment he's floating. It's only been a few minutes, hasn't it, she's lost track. He's got to be all right. Maybe he's floated ashore. She wills her eyes shorewards. The man sits like a statue, except for a scarf lifted and set down by the wind. Though his features appear blurred to her, she can see that he sits with back straight, feet apart, palms on his knees, his whole figure angling forward.

Like another man she once saw. She in the room on the roof of her house, watching through a dusty windowpane. He on a white wooden chair inside a large wire cage. Scores of pigeons fluttering round him. More pigeons perched on his hands, thighs, shoulders, head. Cooing an infernal hubbub. Unseen neighbours on the floors below shouting curses.

Stop your daydreaming, watch where you're going. Watch your brother.

Maybe Paul has made it to shore and is hiding on her. Playing tricks on her. One time he held his breath, turned purple, pretended he was choking to death. "I just wanted to see what you would do." Nena nearly choked him for real before her mother pried her fingers loose. "Trouble to me from the start."

"I'll jump."

Nena three floors below, frozen. "No, Mummy, no." Nena never says those words, though they sound loud enough in her head. She never utters them, though they ring so clear she is sure she actually hears them said. Must be her brother.

"Jump," Nena spits out. "You must jump."

Don't look back. Move, foot, move, one in front of the other, turn your back on the scene.

At any moment her mother's body will hit her retreating form, both of them landing on the hard tiled floor, silent. A melon splatting from a height. They'll still be in one piece, a miracle, you won't be able to tell there'd been such a mess, even if their arms and legs and necks lie at weird angles and there's blood trickling from ears, nostrils, mouths, may they both rest in peace amen. Amen.

He sat on the edge of the chair, the man in the wire cage, legs apart, his sex a serpent rising from a dark bush, livid against the white of belly. Her eyelids fixed, her heart still, Nena drew back from the windowpane and scrambled down the spiral staircase to the back garden, leaping over the stone wall to be with her best friend next door. Not to say anything, she never told anyone, not even her Father Confessor, just to be somewhere else, safe.

Nena lengthens her strokes, away from the man on the rock platform, but she can't resist a backwards look. No pigeons. Now he looks like a statue she'd once seen of Jesus embracing a lamb. Or was it a small child? Words seen on holy pictures tumble in her ears. "I am the word, the word made flesh, the lamb of God. Suffer little children to come unto me." Safe.

She faces the horizon again, feels her innards sink as she spots her brother's bobbing head. So all the while he was still out there, for real, he was not playing tricks on her. Whatever Paul did, she would always be her brother's keeper.

Nena skims the sea towards her brother, hands glinting like the wings of seabirds. She cups one hand under Paul's chin, slides underneath him so his back lies on her front, his head resting on her chest. He does not resist.

"That's it, lie back, let the sea support you, don't fight it."

Wasn't that the way Papa had taught her to swim in the first place, leaping into the water on faith.

'Jump. Come on. Jump in. I'll catch you." And she had, a new creature in her new element.

"That's it. Lie back. Don't fight it, but don't forget to kick your legs."

Nena sees the both of them float on the sea swell alongside the shore, past Stella Maris Church, past the iron railings above the limestone cliffs, past the fishing boats moored at the marina, sees them float on into the sheltered curve of Balluta Bay where her father once sat her down on a bench to tell her where her mother was going to get her next baby. "See that tanker over there with the yellow stripe? That's where."

Nena can see them pull themselves along the shallows and lie panting, heads on the sand like fish out of water. Paul's face looks cracked from sobbing between breaths.

"See what you did. Now we're gonna get it. It's all your fault."

"It's okay." She smooths the water off his body, then hers. "We're okay." They lie back, offerings to the sun till the last drops burn away.

As Nena's head dips in and out of the sea, she is lulled by the gurgling in her ears. A shivering again takes hold of her body, her brother's too. They are now an eight-legged creature riding the glassy sea.

Behind her eyelids Nena can see just how it'll be.

At supper that evening Paul won't even try to lie.

"The sea was awful wild today. There was a man out there today."

"A man? What man? Did he touch you?"

"No, we're okay, nothing happened, nothing."

"Nothing! You could have been killed, you could have been – . That's the last time you're going to drag your brother with you. The last time. She goes. To boarding school. Or I go."

Papa sits silent, looking at a spot on his wine glass just beyond his fingertips resting on the white tablecloth.

A soft whistle of wind blows in and out of the vents of the central skylight. The light coming through the thick glass turns their faces aquamarine. Nena sits silent too, waiting for her father to speak. She cannot read his face today, what he would do.

The waves broaden, the wind dies down, Nena and Paul a sea creature winding shorewards.

She will give thanks first thing in church in front of a small niche alight with votive candles. She'll draw a large penny out of her uniform pocket and hear it clink as it joins the others, the clinking reminding her of all those other souls who made offerings to the Sacred Heart. She kneels before the statue, her eyes fixed on the Heart itself, a brilliant vermilion, trickling brilliant vermilion drops of blood on the white robes of Jesus.

Cradled by the soft sea swells she can picture herself there, mesmerized by the dismebodied Heart. "The inside made manifest," Sister Donatus said of the Sacred Heart, "Love Incarnate." Words that always baffled Nena. Now they fall into place, coins in an offering box. The inside out, love you can see. From inside one into another. That man. The Sacred Heart. Her own heart ready to come out right in the middle of herself.

Paul has separated himself from her and is dogpaddling his way towards the shore.

Her eyes fix on the halo of flame around her votive candle.

It flashes a white brightness. A sign. "Jesus. Mary. Joseph." She crosses herself. "No miracles, sweet Jesus," she prays, "not now. Sweet Jesus, don't call me."

She looks at their rock platform. As deserted as they'd found it that morning. Release and loss, one fish devouring another. Alive behind her eyelids, no one sees her, not at all.

She follows her brother with slow, silent strokes and comes to rest on the shore, half in half out of the water.

EDEN ROBINSON

Traplines

Dad kills a marten.

"Will you look at that," he says.

It is limp in his hands. A goner.

We tramp through the snow to the end of our trapline. Dad whistles. The goner marten is over his shoulder. From here, it looks like Dad is wearing it. There is nothing else in the other traps. We head back to the truck. The snow crunches. This is the best time for trapping, Dad told me a while ago. This is when the animals are hungry.

Our truck rests by the roadside at an angle. Dad rolls the white marten in a grey canvas cover separate from the others. The marten is flawless, which is rare around here. I put my animals beside his and cover them. We get in the truck. Dad turns the radio on. Country twang fills the cab. We smell like sweat and oil and pine. Dad hums. I stare out the window. Mrs. Smythe would say the trees here are like the trees on Christmas postcards. They are tall and heavy with snow. They crowd close to the road. When the wind blows strong enough, the older trees snap and fall on the power lines.

"Well, there's our Christmas money," Dad says, snatching a peek at the rearview mirror.

I look back. The wind ruffles the canvas that covers the martens. Dad is smiling. He sits back, steering with one hand. He does not even mind when we are passed by three cars. The lines in his face are loose now. He sings along with a woman who left her husband. Even that doesn't make him mad. We have our Christmas money. There will be no shouting in the house for a while. It will take Mom and Dad a while to find something else to fight about.

The drive home is a long one. Dad changes the radio station twice. I search my brain for something to say to him. He watches the road, and looks at the back of the truck. I watch the trees, the road, the cars passing us.

One of the cars has two women in it. The woman that isn't driving waves her hands around as she talks. She reminds me of Mrs. Smythe. They are behind us, then beside us, then ahead of us and gone.

Tulka is still as we drive into it. The snow drugs it, makes it lazy. Houses puff cedar smoke and the smell of it gets in everyone's clothes. Sweet and sharp. When I am in school in town, I can close my eyes and tell who is from the village and who isn't just by smelling them.

When we get home, we go straight to the basement. Dad gives me the ratty martens and keeps the good ones. He made me start on squirrels when I was in grade seven. He put the knife in my hand saying, "For Christ's sake, it's just a squirrel. It's dead, you stupid knucklehead. It can't feel anything."

He made the first cut for me. I swallowed and closed my eyes and cut.

"Jesus," Dad muttered. "Are you a sissy? I got a sissy for a son? Look. It's just like cutting up a chicken. See? Pretend you're skinning a chicken." Dad showed me, then put another squirrel in front of me and we didn't leave the basement until I got it right.

Now Dad is skinning the flawless white marten. He is using his best knife. His tongue is sticking out the corner of his mouth. He sits up, and shakes his skinning hand. I quickly start on the next marten. It is perfect except it has been in a fight that left a scar across its back. It isn't a good skin. We won't get much for it. Dad goes back to work. I stop, clench, unclench my hands. They are stiff.

"Goddamn," Dad says quietly. I look up, tensing. Dad starts to smile. He has finished the marten. It is ready to be dried and sold. I have also finished mine. I look at my hands. They know what to do now without me having to tell them. Dad laughs as we go up the creaking stairs. When we get into the hallway, I breathe in, smelling bread. Fresh baked homemade bread.

Mom is sprawled in front of the TV. Her apron is floured and she is licking her fingers. When she sees us, she stops and puts her hands in her apron pockets.

"Well?" she says.

Dad lifts her up and dances her across the living room.

"Greg! Stop it!" she says, laughing.

Flour gets on Dad and cedar chips get on Mom. They talk and I leave, sneaking into the kitchen. I snatch two buns and take three aspirin and go to my room. I stop in the doorway. Eric is there. He is plugged into his electric guitar. He sees me and looks at the buns. He pulls out an earphone.

"Give me one," he says.

I throw him the smaller one, and he finishes it in three bites.

"The other one," he says.

I give him the finger and sit on my bed. I see him thinking

about tackling me, but he shrugs and plugs himself back in. I chew on the bun, roll bits of it around in my mouth. Fresh bread has a taste I have never been able to name. Something that makes it different from day old, or store bought. It is still warm, and I wish I had some honey for it, or some blueberry jam.

Eric gets up and leaves. He comes back with six buns and wolfs them down, cramming them into this mouth. I watch him, then watch the walls. He can't hear himself eat. I plug my ears and glare at him. He looks up. Grins. Opens his mouth so I can see.

Dad comes in. Eric's jaw clenches. Dad pulls himself straight. I leave, go into the kitchen, grabbing a hunk of bread. Mom smacks my hand. We hear Eric and Dad starting to yell. Mom rolls her eyes and puts three more loaves in the oven.

"Back later," I say.

She nods, frowning at her hands, not looking up.

I walk. Think about going to Billy's house. He is seeing Elaine, though, and is getting weird. He wrote her a poem yesterday. We all laughed at him and he didn't even mind. He didn't find anything nice to rhyme with "Elaine" so he didn't finish the poem.

"Pain," Craig said. "Elaine, you pain."

"Pain Elaine," Jer said.

Billy smacked Jer and they went at it in the snow. Billy gave Jer a face wash and that ended it. We let him sit on the steps and write in peace.

"Elaine in the rain," I say. "Elaine, a flame. Cranes. Danes. Trains." I smile, "My main Elaine." I shake my head. Billy is on his own.

I let my feet take me down the street. It starts to snow, tiny ladybug flakes. It is only 4:00 but it is getting dark. Street lights flicker on. No one but me is out walking. Snot in my nose freezes. The air is starting to burn my throat. I turn and head home. Eric and Dad should be tired by now.

Another postcard picture. The houses lining the street look snug. I hunch into my jacket. In a few weeks, Christmas lights will go up. We have the same set every year. Dad will put them up two weeks before Christmas. We will get a tree a week before Christmas. Mom will decorate it. She will put our presents under it on Christmas Eve. In the morning, some of the presents will be wrapped in aluminium because she never buys enough wrapping paper. We will eat. Mom and Dad will go out and we will not see them for a few days. Eric will go to a lot of parties and get really stoned. Mom and Dad will go to a lot of parties and get really drunk. Maybe this year I will too. Anything would be better than sitting around with Tony and Craig, listening to them gripe.

I stamp the snow off my sneakers and jeans. I open the door quietly. The TV is on loud. I can tell by the announcer's voice that it is a hockey game. I take my shoes off. The house is really hot after being outside. I pull off my jacket. My face starts to tingle as the skin thaws. I go into the kitchen. I take a few aspirins and stand near the stove. The kitchen could use some plants. It gets some good light in the winter. Mrs. Smythe has her kitchen crowded with plants. The cats usually munch on the ferns, so she has them hanging by the window. They have a lot of pictures of places they have been all over their walls. Europe. Africa. Arctic. They have been everywhere. They can afford it, she says, because they don't have kids. They had one, a while ago. On the TV, there is a wallet-sized picture of a dark haired boy with three missing teeth. He was their kid, but he disappeared. Mrs. Smythe stares at the picture a lot.

Eric tries to sneak up behind me. His socks make a

slithering sound on the floor. I duck just in time and hit him in the stomach.

"Oof," he doubles over, hands over his belly. He has a towel stretched between his hands. His "Choking" game. He punches at me, but I hop out of the way. He hits the stove. Yelling, he jerks his hand back. I race out of the kitchen and go down to the basement. Eric is screaming my name. "Come out, you chicken," he says. "Come out and fight."

I stay still behind some plywood. Eric still has the towel ready for me. After a while, he goes back upstairs and locks the door behind him.

I stand. Eric turns the TV off. Mom and Dad must have gone out to celebrate. They will find a bootlegger and go on a bender until Monday, when Dad has to go back to work. So. I am alone with Eric. He'll leave the house around 10:00. I can stay out of his way until then.

The basement door slams open. I scramble under Dad's tool table. Eric must be stoned. He probably has been toking up since Mom and Dad left. Pot always makes him mean.

He laughs. "You baby. You are a fucking baby." He doesn't look for me that hard. He thumps loudly up the stairs, slams the door shut, then tiptoes back down and waits. He must think I am really stupid.

We stay like this for a long time. Eric lights up. In a few minutes, the whole basement smells like pot. Dad will be pissed off if it ruins the perfect white marten. I smile, hoping it does. Eric will really get it then.

"Fuck," he says and disappears upstairs, not locking the door. I crawl out. My legs are stiff. The pot is making me dizzy.

The wood stove is cooling. I don't open it. Its door squeals. It will be freezing down here soon. Breathing fast, I go upstairs. I crack the door open. There are no lights on except in our bedroom. Eric must be playing. I pull on my jacket and sneakers. I grab some bread before I hear the bedroom door being opened. I stuff it in my jacket and run for the door. Eric is blocking it, grinning.

"Thought you were sneaky, hey," he says.

I back into the kitchen. He follows. I wait until he is near before I bend over and ram him. He is slow because of the pot and slips to the floor. He grabs my ankle, but I kick him in the head and am out the door before he can catch me. I take the steps two at a time. Eric stands on the porch and laughs. I can't wait until I'm bigger. I'd like to smear him against a wall. Let him see what it feels like. I'd like to smear him so bad.

I munch on some bread as I head for the village exit to the highway. The snow comes down in thick, large flakes that melt when they touch my skin. I stand at the exit and wait.

I hear One Eye's beat-up Ford a long time before I see it. It clunks down the road and stalls when he stops it beside me.

"You again. What are you doing here?" One Eye yells at me.

"Waiting for Princess fucking Di," I say.

"Smart mouth. You keep it up and you can stay out here."

The back door opens anyway. Snooker and Jim are there. One Eye and Pete Wilson are in the front. They all have the same silver lunch buckets at their feet.

When we come into town I say, "Could you drop me off here?"

One Eye looks up, surprised. He has forgotten I am here. He frowns. "Where are you going?"

"Disneyland," I say.

"Smart mouth," he says. "Don't be like your brother. You stay out of trouble."

I laugh. One Eye slows the car and pulls over. It chokes and sputters. I get out and thank him for the ride. One Eye grunts. They pull away and I walk to Mrs. Smythe's.

The first time I saw her house was last spring when she invited all her English classes there for a barbecue. Their lawn was neat and green and I only saw one dandelion. They had rose bushes in the front and raspberry bushes in the back. I went with Tony and Craig, who got high before we got there. Mrs. Smythe noticed right away. She took them aside and talked to them. They stayed in the pool room downstairs until the high wore off.

I wandered around. There weren't any other kids from the village there. Only townies. Kids that Dad says will never get their pink hands dirty. They were split into little groups. They talked and ate and laughed and I was walking around, feeling like a dork. I was going to go downstairs to Tony and Craig when Mrs. Smythe came up to me. It's funny, I never noticed how nice her smile was until then. Her blue sundress swayed as she came up to me, carrying a hotdog.

"You weren't in class yesterday," she said, smiling.

"Uh, stomach ache."

"I was going to tell you how much I liked your essay. You must have done a lot of work on it."

I tried to remember what I had written. "Yeah."

"Which part was the hardest?" she said.

I cleared my throat. "Starting it."

She gave me a funny look. "I walked right into that one," she said, laughing. I kept smiling.

A tall man came up and hugged her. She kissed him. "Sam," she said. "This is the student I was telling you about."

"Well, hello," Mr. Smythe said. "Great paper."

"Thanks," I said, trying hard to remember what I had written about.

"Is it William or Will?" Mr. Smythe said.

"Will," I said. He held out his hand. We shook.

"Did you ever find out what happened to him?" Mrs. Smythe said.

Oh no, I thought, remembering what I'd written. I had a dog in grade three that I named Stinky who got lost. We had to write about a real life experience and it was the night before the deadline and that was all I could think of. I blushed and shook my head. I was glad Tony and Craig weren't here.

"Karen tells me you've written a lot about fishing, too," Mr. Smythe said, sounding really cheerful.

"Excuse me," Mrs. Smythe said. "That's my cue to leave. If you're smart, you'll do the same. Once you get Sam going about his stupid fish stories you can't get a wor –"

Mr. Smythe goosed her. She hit him with her hotdog and left quickly. Mr. Smythe put his arm around my shoulder, shaking his head. He asked if I'd ever done any real fishing. We sat down on the patio. He told me about the time he caught a marlin, and about scuba diving in the Great Barrier Reef. He went down in a shark cage once, to try to film a Great White eating. I told him about the halibut I caught on Uncle Bernie's gilnetter. He wanted to know if Uncle Bernie would take him out. I gave him Old Marty Gladstone's number, because he takes charters. He asked me what gear he was going to need. We ended up in the kitchen, me using a flounder to show him how to clean a halibut.

I finally looked at the clock around 10:00. Dad had said he would pick me and Tony and Craig up around 8:00. I didn't even know where Tony and Craig were anymore. I couldn't believe it had gotten this late without me noticing it. Mr. Smythe said he would drive me home. I said no, that's okay, I'll hitch.

He snorted. "Karen would kill me. No, I'll drive you. Let's phone your parents and tell them you're coming home."

No one answered the phone. I said they were probably asleep. He dialled again. Still no answer.

"Looks like you've got the spare bedroom tonight," he said.

"Let me try," I said, picking up the phone. There was no answer but after six rings, I pretended Dad was on the other end. I didn't want to spend the night at my English teacher's house. Tony and Craig would never shut up about it.

"Hi, Dad," I said. "How come … oh. I see. Car trouble. No problem. Mr. Smythe is going to drive me home. What? Sure, I —"

"Let me talk to him," Mr. Smythe said, snatching the phone. "Hello! Mr. Bolton! How are you! My, my, my. Your son is a lousy liar, isn't he?" He hung up. "It's amazing how much your father sounds like a dial tone."

I grabbed the phone. "They're sleeping, that's all," I said. I dialled again. Mr. Smythe watched me. There wasn't any answer.

"Why'd you lie?" he said quietly.

We were alone in the kitchen. I swallowed. He was a lot bigger than me. When he reached for me, I put my hands up and covered my face. He stopped then took the phone out of my hands.

"It's okay," he said. "I won't hurt you. It's okay."

I put my hands down. He looked sad. That annoyed me. I shrugged, backing away. "I'll hitch," I said.

Mr. Smythe shook his head. "Karen would kill me, then

she'd go after you. Come on. We'll be safer if you sleep in the spare room."

In the morning, Mr. Smythe was up before I could sneak out. He was making bacon and pancakes. He asked if I'd ever done any freshwater fishing. I said no. He started talking about fishing in the Black Sea and I sat and listened to him, eating slowly. He is a good cook.

Mrs. Smythe came into the kitchen dressed in some sweats and a T-shirt. She ate without saying anything and didn't look awake until she finished her coffee. Mr. Smythe phoned home, but no one answered. He asked if I wanted to go up to Old Timer's Lake and try my hand at his new Sona Reel. I didn't have anything better to do.

Mr. Smythe has a great speedboat. He let me drive it around the lake a few times. We even went water-skiing. Mrs. Smythe looked great in her bathing suit. We lazed around the beach in the afternoon, watching the people go by. Sipping their beers, they argued about who was going to drive back. We rode around the lake some more and roasted hotdogs for dinner.

Their porch light is on. I go up the walk and ring the bell. Mrs. Smythe has said to just come in, don't bother knocking, but I can't do that. It doesn't feel right. She opens the door, smiling when she sees me. She is wearing her favourite jeans and a fluffy pink sweater. "Hi, Will. He says he's going to beat you this time."

"Dream on," I say.

She laughs. "Go right in. He's waiting." She goes down the hall to the washroom.

I go into the living room. Mr. Smythe is not there. The TV is on loud, some documentary about whales.

I find him in the kitchen, scrunched over a game of solitaire. His new glasses are sliding off. With his glasses like that, he looks more like a teacher than Mrs. Smythe. He scratches the beard that he is trying to grow and looks up.

"Come on doooown," he says, patting the chair beside him.

I take a seat and watch him finish the game. He wrinkles his nose and pushes his glasses up. "What's your pleasure?" he says.

"Pool," I say.

"Feeling lucky, huh?" We go down to the pool room. "How about a little extra this week?" he says, not looking at me.

I shrug. "Dishes?"

He shakes his head. "Bigger."

"I'm not shovelling the walk," I say.

He shakes his head again. "Bigger."

I frown. "Money?"

"Bigger."

"What?"

He racks up the balls. Sets the cue ball. Wipes his hands on his jeans.

"What?" I say again.

Mr. Smythe takes out a quarter. "Heads or tails?" he says, tossing it.

"Heads," I say.

He slaps the quarter on the back of his hand. "I break."

"Where, let me see that," I say, laughing. He holds it up. The quarter is tails.

He breaks. "How'd you like to stay with us?" he says, very quietly.

"Sure," I say. "But I got to go back on Tuesday. We got to check the traplines again."

He is quiet. The balls make clunking sounds as they bounce around the table. "Do you like it here?"

"Sure," I say.

"Enough to live here?"

I am not sure I heard him right. Maybe he is asking a different question from the one I think he is asking. I blink, opening my mouth. I don't know what to say. I say nothing.

"Those are the stakes, then," he says. "I win, you stay. You win, you stay."

He is joking. I laugh. "You serious?"

He stands up straight. "I don't think I've ever been more serious."

The room is suddenly very small.

"Your turn," he says. "Stripes."

I scratch and miss the ball by a mile.

"We don't want to push you," he says. He leans over the table, squints at the ball. "We just think that you'd be safer here. Hell, you practically live here already." I watch my sneakers. He keeps playing. "We aren't rich. We aren't perfect. We —" He looks at me, looks down. "We thought maybe you'd like to try it for a few weeks, first."

"I can't," I say.

"You don't have to decide right now," he says. "Think about it. Take a few days."

It's my turn again, but I don't feel like playing anymore. Mr. Smythe is waiting though. I stare at the table, and pick a ball. Aim. Shoot. Miss.

The game goes on in silence. Mr. Smythe wins easy. He smiles. "Well. I win. You stay."

If I wanted to get out of this room, there is only one door and Mr. Smythe is blocking it. He is watching me. He takes a deep breath. "Let's go upstairs."

Mrs. Smythe has shut off the TV. She stands up when we come into the living room. "Will —"

"I asked him already," Mr. Smythe says.

Her head snaps around and she glares at him. "You what?"

"I asked him."

Her hands fist at her sides. "We were supposed to do it together, Sam." Her voice is flat. She looks at me. "You said no."

I can't look at her. I look at the walls, at the floor, at her slippers. She stands in front of me. Her hands are warm on my face. "Look at me," she says. "Will? Look at me."

She is trying to smile. I shouldn't have come tonight. I should have waited for Eric to leave. "Hungry?" she says.

I nod. She makes a motion with her head for Mr. Smythe to follow her into the kitchen. When they are gone I sit down. It should be easy. It should be easy. I watch TV without watching it. Faces, words, names, places, cars all flash by. I wonder what they are saying about me in the kitchen.

It is almost 7:00 and my ribs hurt. Mostly, I can ignore it, but Eric hit me pretty hard and they are bruised. Eric got hit pretty hard by Dad, so we're even, I guess. I can't wait until Eric moves out. The rate he is going, he will be busted soon anyway. Tony says the police are starting to ask questions.

It is a strange night. We all pretend nothing happened and Mrs. Smythe fixes some natchos. Mr. Smythe beats me at Monopoly, then at poker, then at speed. Mrs. Smythe gets out a pack of Uno cards and we play a few rounds and watch *Sixty Minutes*. Mrs. Smythe wins. We go to bed.

I lie awake. My room. This could be my room. I already have most of my books here. It's hard to study with Eric around. I have a headache now, too. I couldn't get away from them long enough to sneak into the kitchen to get an aspirin. I wait for a few minutes then sit up. I pull my T-shirt up and take a look. There is a long bruise under my ribs and five smaller ones over it. I think he was trying to hit my stomach but he was so wasted he kept missing. It isn't bad. Tony's Dad broke three of his ribs once. Craig got a concussion a couple of weeks ago. My Dad is pretty easy. It's only Eric that is bothering me. Mr. and Mrs. Smythe get mad and fussy when they see bruises though. You have to keep quiet about it or they will start talking your head off and won't shut up until you're bored half to death.

They keep the aspirin by the spices. I grab six, three for now and three for the morning. I am swallowing the last one when Mr. Smythe grabs my hand. I didn't even hear him come in. I must be sleepy.

"Where'd they hit you this time," he says.

"I got a headache," I say. "A bad one."

He opens the hand that has the aspirins in it. "How many do you plan on taking?"

"These are for later," I say.

He sighs. I get ready for the lecture. "Go back to bed," he says. He sounds very tired. I wish I could say something. I don't think they will want me around after this. I don't know why they let me come in the first place. I guess it's okay. Tony and Craig and the rest were starting to bug me about it anyway.

"Will," he says. I look up. He smiles. "It'll be okay."

"Sure," I say. "It'll be okay."

I leave around 5:00. I leave a note saying I have a really bad headache. I catch a ride back home with some guys coming off the graveyard shift.

No one is home. Eric had a party here last night. I am glad I wasn't here. They have wrecked the coffee table and the rug smells like stale beer and cigarettes. Our bedroom is worse. Someone puked all over Eric's bed and there are two used condoms on mine. At least none of the windows are broken this time. I start to clean my side of the room then stop. I sit on my bed. Mr. Smythe will be getting up soon. It is Sunday, so he will make waffles or French toast. He will make a plate of crispy bacon and eat it before Mrs. Smythe wakes up. He thinks that she doesn't know that he does this. She will wake up around 10:00 or 11:00 and will not talk to anyone until noon or until she's had about three coffees. She starts to wake up around 1:00 or 2:00. They will argue about something. Who took out the garbage or who did the dishes or the laundry last. Mrs. Smythe will read the paper.

I crawl into bed. The aspirin are not working. I try to go to sleep but it really reeks in here. I have a biology test tomorrow. I forgot to get the book from their place. I yawn. Our truck pulls into the driveway. Mom and Dad are arguing. I close my eyes. They sound plastered. Mom is bitching about something. Dad is not saying anything. Doors slam.

Mom comes in first. She doesn't notice the house is a mess. She goes straight to bed. Dad comes up the stairs a lot slower.

"What the – Eric!" he yells. "Eric!"

I pretend to sleep. The door bangs open.

"Eric, you little bastard," Dad says, looking around. He pulls me up. "Where's Eric?"

His breath is lethal. You can tell he likes his rye and vodka straight.

"How should I know?"

"Where the fuck is he?" Dad says. "I want to talk to him."

I say I don't know. Dad gets up and rips Eric's amplifiers out of the walls. He throws them down and gives them a good kick. He tips Eric's bed over. Eric is smart. He won't come home for a while. Then Dad will have cooled off, and Eric can give him some money without Dad getting pissed off at him. I don't move. I wait until Dad is out of the room before I put on a sweater. I can hear him down in the basement, chopping wood. It should be around 8:00 by now. The RinkyDink will be open in an hour. Billy will be there because Elaine is there.

Mom is up. She is looking behind the stove. She sees me and makes a shushing motion with her hand. She pulls a bottle from behind the stove and sits down at the kitchen table.

"You're a good boy," she says, giggling. "You're a good boy. Help your old old old mother into bed, hey."

"Sure," I say, putting an arm around her. She stands, holding the bottle with one hand and me with the other. "This way, my lady."

"You making fun of me?" she says, her eyes going small. "You laughing at me?" Then she laughs and we go to their room. She flops onto the bed. She takes a long drink. "You're fucking laughing at me, aren't you?"

"Mom," I say, annoyed. "You're paranoid. I was making a joke."

"Yeah, you are reeeally funny. Really funny. You are a laugh a minute," she says, giggling again. "Real comedian."

"Yeah, that's me," I say.

She throws the bottle at me. I duck. She rolls over and starts to cry. I throw the blanket over her and leave. The floor is sticky now and stinks. Dad is still chopping wood. They wouldn't notice if I wasn't here. Maybe people would talk for a week or two, but after a while, they wouldn't notice. Only people that would notice is Tony and Craig and Billy and maybe Eric, who would miss me when he got toked up and didn't have anything for target practice.

Billy is playing Pac-man at the RinkyDink. He is chain-smoking. When I walk up to him, he turns around quickly.

"Oh. It's you," he says turning back to the game.

"Hi to you too," I say.

"You seen Elaine?" he says.

"Nope," I say.

He crushes out another cigarette in the ashtray beside him. He plays for a while, loses a pac-man, then shakes a cigarette out one-handed. He sticks it in his mouth, loses another man, then lights up. He sucks deep. He looks at me. "Relax," I say. "She'll be here. Her majesty's limo is probably stuck in traffic."

He glares at me. "Shut up."

I laugh and go play pool with Craig. Craig has decided that he is James Dean. He is wearing a white T-shirt, jeans, and a black leather jacket that I think is his brother's. He has his hair slicked back. A cigarette is dangling from the corner of his mouth.

"What a loser," he says.

"Who you calling a loser?" I say.

"Billy. What a loser." He struts down to the other side of the pool table.

"He's okay."

"That chick," he says. "What's her face. Ellen? Erma?"

"Elaine."

"Yeah, that's the one. She going out with him cause she's got a bet."

I look at him. "What?"

"She's got to go out with him a month, and her friend will give her some coke."

"Billy's already giving her coke."

"Yeah. He's a loser."

I look at Billy. He is lighting up another cigarette.

"Can you imagine a townie wanting anything to do with him?" Craig says. "She's just doing it as a joke. She's going to dump him in a week. She's going to put all his stupid poems in the newspaper."

I see it now. There is a space around Billy. No one is going near him. He doesn't notice. I look around me. I catch some guys I used to hang out with grinning at me. When they see me looking at them, they look away.

Craig wins the game. I am losing a lot this week.

Elaine gets to the RinkyDink after lunch. She's got some townie friends with her that are staring around the RinkyDink like they are going to get jumped. Elaine leads them right up to Billy. Everyone is watching them without seeming like they are watching them. Billy gives her his latest poem. I wonder what he got to rhyme with Elaine.

They leave. Billy holds the door open for her. She gives her friends a look. They giggle. The same guys that were watching me start to howl. They are laughing so hard they are crying. I feel sick. I think about telling Billy but I know he won't listen.

I leave the RinkyDink and go for a walk. I walk and walk and walk and end up back in front of the RinkyDink. There isn't anywhere else to go. I hang out with Craig, who hasn't left the pool table.

I spend the night on Craig's floor. Craig's parents are Jehovah's Witnesses and preach at me before I go to bed. I sit and listen because I need a place to sleep. I am not going home until tomorrow when Mom and Dad are sober. His Mom gets us up two hours before the buses come to take the village kids to school. They pray before we eat. Craig looks at me and rolls his eyes. People are always making fun of Craig because his parents stand on the corner downtown every Friday and hold up the *Watchtower* mags. When his parents start to bug him, he says he will take up Devil worship or astrology if they don't lay off. I think I'll ask him if he wants to hang out with me on Christmas. His parents don't believe in it.

I see Mrs. Smythe in the hall between classes. Craig nudges me. "Go on," he says, making sucking noises. "Go get your 'A.'"

"Fuck off," I say, pushing him back.

She is talking to a girl and doesn't see me. I think about skipping English today but know that she will phone home and ask where I am. It isn't fair. She doesn't do that for anyone else. Craig can skip as many times as he wants and all she does is make a note of it, and sends it to the principal's office.

At lunch, no one talks to me. I can't find Craig or Tony or Billy. The village guys at the science wing doors snicker as I go by. I don't stop. I keep going until I get to the headbanger's doors in the shop wing. I don't have any money and I don't have a lunch so I bum a cigarette off this girl with really tight jeans and to get my mind off my stomach I try and get her to go out with me. She smiles, but doesn't say anything. When she walks away, the fringe on her leather jacket swings.

I flunk my biology test. It would have been easy if I studied. It is multiple choice. I stare at the paper and kick myself. I know I could have passed if I had read the chapter. Mr. Kellerman reads out the marks from lowest to highest. My name is called out third.

"Mr. Bolton," he says, raising an eyebrow. "Three out of thirty."

"All-riiight," Craig says, slapping my back.

"Mr. Duncan," he says to Craig, his voice becoming resigned. "Three and a half out of thirty."

Craig stands up and bows. The guys in the back clap. The kids in the front laugh. Mr. Kellerman reads out the rest of the marks. Craig turns to me. "Looks like I beat the Brain," he says.

"Yeah," I say. "Pretty soon you're going to be getting the Nobel Prize."

The bell rings. Last class. English. I go to my locker and take out my jacket. If she phones, no one is going to answer.

I go downtown. I don't have any money so I walk. The snow is starting to slack off and it is even sunning a bit. My stomach growls. I haven't eaten since breakfast. I wish I had gone to English. Mrs. Smythe would have given me something to eat. She always has something left over from her lunch. I hunch down in my jacket. I guess it isn't right to mooch off her now that she doesn't want to see me anymore. I am glad I didn't mooch off her, but I am still hungry.

Downtown, I go to the Paradise Arcade. All the heads hang out there. Maybe I will find Eric. Maybe he'll give me some money. More like a belt. It's worth a try. I look around for him, but he isn't there. No one much is here. Just some burn-outs by the pinball machines. I see Mitch. I go over to him, but he is soaring. He is laughing at the ball going around and around the machine. I turn and walk away. There is no one here I can mooch off. I head for the highway and hitch home. Mom should be passed out by now and Dad is at work.

Sure enough, Mom is passed out. She is on the living-room floor. I get a blanket for her. The stove has gone out and it is freezing in here. I go into the kitchen and look through the fridge. There is a bottle of pickles and some really pathetic looking celery. There is also some milk, but it is so old it smells like cheese. There is no bread left from what Mom made this

Saturday. I find some Rice-a-roni and make it. Mom wakes up and asks for some water. I bring her some and give her some Rice-a-roni. She makes a face but eats it slowly.

At 6:00, Dad comes home. Eric comes home with him. They have made up. Eric has bought Dad a six-pack and they watch a hockey game together. I stay in my room. Eric has cleaned his bed by dumping his mattress outside and stealing mine. We have a grammar test this Friday. I know Mrs. Smythe will be unhappy if she has to fail me. I read the chapters on "nouns," "verbs," and get through "the parts of speech" before Eric comes into the room and kicks me off the bed.

He tries to take the mattress but I kick him in the side. Eric turns. He grabs me by the hair. "This," he says. "Is my bed. Understand?"

"Fuck you," I say. "You had the party. Your fucked up friends trashed your bed. You sleep on the floor."

Dad comes in. He sees Eric push me against a wall and hit me. He yells at Eric, who turns around, his fist frozen in front of my face. Eric lets me go. Dad rolls his sleeves up.

"You always take his side!" Eric yells. "You never take my side!"

"You pick on someone your own size," Dad says. "Unless you want me to pick on you."

Eric gives me a look that says he will make this up to me later when Dad isn't here. I pick up my book and get out. I go for a walk. I keep walking around the village, staying away from the RinkyDink. That is the first place that Eric will look.

I am at the village exit. The sky is clear and the stars are popping out. Mr. Smythe will take out his telescope and he will try to take a picture of the Pleiades. Mrs. Smythe will be marking papers while she watches TV.

"Do you need a ride?" this guy says. There is a blue pick-up in front of me. The driver is wearing a hunting cap.

I take my hand out of my mouth. I have been chewing my knuckle like some baby. I shake my head. "I'm waiting for someone," I say.

He shrugs and takes off. I stand there and watch his head-lights disappear.

They didn't really mean it. They would get bored of me quick when they found out what I am. It should be easy. I should have said yes and then stayed until they got bored and then come home when Eric cooled off.

Two cars pass me as I walk back to the village. I can hide out in Tony's until Eric goes out with his friends and forgets this afternoon. My feet are frozen when I get to the RinkyDink. Tony is there.

He says, "So. I heard Craig beat you in biology."

I roll my eyes. "Didn't it just impress you?"

"A whole half a point. Way to go," he says, grinning. "For a while there we thought you were getting townie."

"Yeah, right," I say. "Listen, I pissed Eric off –"

"Surprise, surprise," he says.

"– and I need a place to crash. Can I sleep over?"

"Sure," he says.

Mitch wanders in the RinkyDink and a crowd of kids slowly drift over to him. He looks around, eyeing everybody. Then he pulls out something and starts giving it away. Tony gets curious and we go over.

"Wow," Tony says, after Mitch gives him something.

"What?"

We go outside and behind the RinkyDink where a crowd of kids is gathered. "Fucking all-riiight," I hear Craig say, even though I can't see him.

"What?" I say. Tony lifts up his hand. He is holding a little vial with small white crystals in it.

"Crack," Tony says. "Man, is he stupid. He could have made a fortune and he's just giving it away."

We don't have a pipe, and Tony wants to do this right the first time. No one will share with us though, so Tony decides to do it tomorrow, after he buys the right equipment. I am hungry again. I am about to tell him that I am going to Billy's when I see Eric.

"Shit," I say and hide behind him.

Tony looks over and sees Eric. "Someone's in trou-ble," he sings.

Eric is looking for me. I hunch down. Tony tries to look innocent. Eric spots him and starts to come over. "Better run for it," Tony whispers.

I sneak behind some other people but Eric sees me and I have to run for it anyway. Tony starts to cheer and the kids behind the RinkyDink join in. Some of the guys follow us so that they will see what happens when Eric catches up with me. I don't want to find out so I ignore everyone behind me and start pumping hard so I can get home before Eric catches me.

Eric used to be fast. I am glad he is a head now because he can't run that far anymore. He used to always beat me in the races we had. I am panting now, and my legs are cramping. I run up the stairs to our house.

The door is locked.

I stand there, hand on the knob. Eric rounds the corner to our block and starts to smile. There is no one behind him anymore. I knock on the door but now I see that our truck is gone. I run around the house but the basement door is locked too. Even the windows are locked.

Eric pops his head around the corner of the house. He grins

when he sees me. He disappears. I grit my teeth. Start running across our backyard. Head for Billy's. Eric lets out a hoot. He has someone with him. I think it is Brent. I duck behind our neighbour's house. There is snow in my sneakers and all the way up my leg. I am sweating. I rest for a while. I can't hear Eric. I hope I have lost him, but Eric is pissed off and when he's pissed off he doesn't let go. I look down. My footprints are clear in the snow. I start to run again, but I hit a thick spot and have to wade through some thigh-deep snow. I look behind me. Eric is nowhere. I keep slogging. I make it to the road and run down to the exit.

I have lost him. I am shaking now because it is cold. I can feel the sweat cooling on my skin. My breath goes back to normal. I wait for a car to come by. I have missed the night shift and the graveyard shift won't be by until near midnight. It is too cold to wait that long.

A car, a red car. A little Toyota. I start to run again. Brent's car. I run off the road and head into a clump of trees. The Toyota pulls over and Eric gets out of the car and starts yelling. I reach the trees and rest. They are waiting by the side of the road. Eric is peering at the trees, trying to see me. Brent is smoking in the car. Eric crosses his arms over his chest and blows into his hands. My legs are frozen.

After a long time, a cop car cruises to a stop beside Eric and Brent. I wade out and wave at the policeman. He looks startled. Then he looks at Eric and Brent and asks them something. Eric shrugs. It takes me a while to get to them because my legs are slow.

The cop is watching me. I swear I will never call them pigs again. I swear. He turns to Brent, who digs around the glove compartment. Eric glares at me. The cop says something to his partner. I scramble up the embankment.

Eric has no marks on his face. Dad probably hit him on the back and stomach. Ever since the social worker came, Dad has been careful. Eric suddenly smiles at me. He holds an arm out and moves to me. I move behind the police car. Eric is still smiling. The policeman comes over to us.

"Is there a problem here?" he says.

"No," Eric says. "No probulum. Li'le misunnerstan'nin'."
He grins.

Oh shit. He is as high as a kite. The policeman looks hard at Eric. I look at the car. Brent is glaring at me. He is high, too.

Eric tries again to get to me. I put the police car between us. The policeman grabs Eric by the arm and his partner goes and gets Brent. The policeman says something about driving under the influence but none of us are listening. Eric is watching me. His eyes are very clear. I am not going to get away with this. I am going to pay for it. Brent is swearing. He wants a lawyer. He stumbles out of his car and slips on the road.

Brent and Eric are put in the back seat. The policeman comes up to me and says, "Can you make it home?"

I nod. He says, "Good. Go."

His partner says something to him, but I don't understand what it is because it is numbers. The policeman looks at me.

"My partner wants to know if you're going to press charges."

I look at Eric. He is flushed. I shake my head. It would only make him madder and he would only be in jail a few weeks. It would only make things worse. The policeman shakes his head and says, "I told you so."

They drive away and I go home. I walk around the house, trying to figure a way to break in. I find a small screwdriver and jimmy the basement door open. Just in case Eric gets out tonight, I make a bed under the tool table and go to sleep.

No one is home when I wake up. I scramble an egg and get ready for school. I sit beside Tony on the bus.

"I was expecting to see you with black eyes," he says.

I shake my head. My legs are still raw from last night. Freezer burn? I rub my head and sigh. I have something due today but I can't remember what. If Eric is in the drunk tank, they will let him out today.

The village guys are talking to me again. I skip gym. I skip history. I hang out with Craig and Tony in the Paradise Arcade. I am not sure if I want to be friends with them after they cheered last night, but it is better to have them on my side than not, so I am friends with them again. A couple of guys get a two-for-one pizza special for lunch and I am glad I am friends with them because I am starved. They have some five finger specials from Safeway. Tony is proud because he got a couple of bags of chips and Pepsi and no one even noticed.

Mitch comes up to me when I go to the bathroom.

"That was a really cheap thing to do," he says.

"What?" I say, frowning. I haven't done anything to him.

"What? What? Getting your brother thrown in jail. Pretty crumby."

I laugh. "He got himself thrown in jail. He got caught when he was high. Him and Bre –"

"That's not what he says." Mitch frowns. "He says you set him up."

"Fuck." I run a hand through my hair. "When'd he tell you this?"

"This morning," he says. "He's waiting for you at school."

"I didn't set him up. How could I?"

Mitch nods. He hands me some crack and says, hey, I'm sorry, and leaves. I look at it, but know it will make me sick. I can't smoke anything. I'll give it to Tony.

Billy comes into the Paradise with Elaine and her friends. He is getting some smug looks but he doesn't notice. He holds the chair out for Elaine, who sits down without looking at him. I don't want to be around when he finds out he is a joke. I go over to Tony.

"I'm leaving," I say.

Tony shushes me. "Watch," he says.

Elaine orders a beer. Frankie shakes his head and points to the sign that says We Do NOT Serve Minors. Elaine frowns. She says something to Billy. He shrugs. She orders a Coke. Billy pays. When their Cokes come, Elaine dumps it over Billy's head. Billy stares at her like she has gone stark crazy. Her friends start to laugh, and I get up and walk out.

I lean against the wall of the Paradise. Billy comes out a few minutes later. His face is still and pale. Elaine and her friends follow him, reciting lines from the poems he wrote her. Tony and the rest just laugh. I go back inside, and trade the crack for some quarters for the video games. I keep remembering how Billy's face looked, and I keep losing the games I play. Tony says let's go, and we hitch back to the village. We raid his fridge and have chocolate ice cream coconut sundaes. Angela comes in with Di and says that Eric is looking for me. I look at Tony and he looks at me.

"Boy, are you in for it," Tony says. "You'd better stay here tonight."

When everyone is asleep, Tony pulls out a weird-looking pipe and does the crack. His face goes very dreamy and far away. A few minutes later he says, "Christ, that was great. I wonder how much Mitch has?"

I turn over and go to sleep.

❑

The next morning Billy is alone on the bus. No one wants to sit with him so there are empty seats all around him. He does not look like he has slept. Tony goes up to him and punches his arm. Billy looks at him, then looks out the window. Tony says, "So how's Shakespeare this morning?"

The guys in the back of the bus laugh, but a lot of the girls don't. I don't want to watch it, so I look out my window too. I hope Eric isn't at the school. I don't know where else I can hide.

Mrs. Smythe is waiting at the school bus stop. I sneak out the back door of the bus, with Tony and the guys making enough noise and pretending to fight to cover me.

We head down to the Paradise again in Binky's car. I am starting to smell bad. I haven't had a shower for days. I wish I had some clean clothes. I wish I had some money so I could buy a toothbrush. I hate the scummy feeling on my teeth. I wish I had enough for a taco, or a hamburger. I wish I had a Pepsi.

Eric is at the Paradise, so I hide in the mall. I find Dad in Safeway, looking for Eric.

"Let's go to the Dairy Queen," he says.

Dad orders a coffee, a chocolate milkshake, and a cheese-burger. We take the coffee and milkshake to a back table, and I take the order slip. We sit there. Dad stares at his hands.

"One of your teachers called," he says.

I sigh. "Mrs. Smythe?"

"Yeah," he looks up. "Says she'd like you to stay there."

I try to read his face. It is very still. His eyes are bloodshot and red rimmed. He must have a big hangover.

I shrug.

The cashier calls out our number. I go up and get the

cheeseburger and we split it. Dad always eats slow to make it last longer.

"Did you tell her you wanted to?"

"No," I say. "They asked me, but I said I couldn't."

Dad nods. "Did you tell them anything?"

"Like what?"

"Don't get smart," he says, sounding beat.

"I didn't say anything."

He stops chewing. "Then why'd they ask you?"

"Don't know."

"You must have told them something."

"Nope. Just asked."

"Did Eric tell them?"

I snort. "Eric? No way. They wou – He wouldn't go any-where near them. They're okay, Dad. They won't tell any-body."

"So you did tell them."

"I didn't. I swear I didn't. Look, Eric got me on the face a couple of times and they figured it out. They aren't go –"

"You're lying."

I finished my half of the cheeseburger. "I am not lying. I didn't say anything. And they won't say anything."

"I never touched you."

"Yeah, Eric took care of that," I say, smiling. Dad doesn't smile back. "You seen him?"

Dad nods. "I kicked him out."

"You what?"

"Party. Ruined the basement," Dad says grimly. "He's old enough. Had to leave sooner or later."

He finishes his cheeseburger. Eric will be really pissed now. I'll have to lie really low for a while. We go check the trapline, and get some more martens, and even get a little lynx. Dad is happy. We go home. The basement is ripped apart. I wonder if he was looking for me.

Next day at school, I spend most of the day ducking from Eric and Mrs. Smythe before I finally get sick of it and go down to the Paradise Arcade. Tony is there with Billy, who asks me if I want to go to Vancouver with him until Eric cools off.

"Now?"

"No better time," he says.

I think about it. "When you leaving?"

"Tonight."

"I don't know. I don't have any money."

"Me neither," he says.

"Shit," I say. "How we going to get there? It's a thousand miles at least."

"Hitch to town, hitch down to Smithers, then hitch to Prince George, hitch to –"

"Yeah, yeah, but how are we going to eat?"

He wiggles his finger. Five finger special. I laugh.

"You change your mind," he says. "I'll be behind RinkyDink around 7:00. Get some thick boots."

We are about to hitch home when I see Mrs. Smythe peer into the Paradise Arcade. It is too late to hide because she turns and sees me. Her face becomes stiff. She walks over to us, and the guys start to laugh. Mrs. Smythe looks at them, then at me.

"Will?" she says. "Can I talk to you outside?"

She stares around like the guys are going to jump her. I look at them and try to see what she is nervous about. Tony is grabbing his crotch. Billy is cleaning his nails. The other guys are snickering. I suddenly see them the way she must see them. They all have long, greasy hair, combed straight back. All of us have jeans on, T-shirts, sneakers. They don't look nice.

I look back at her. She has on her "school uniform" as she calls it. Dark skirt, white shirt, low black heels, glasses. She is watching me like she hasn't seen me before. I hope she never sees my house.

"Later?" I say. "I'm kind of busy."

She blushes, and the guys laugh hard. She takes a step back, and I want to take the words back. "Are you sure?" she says.

Tony nudges my arm. "Why don't you introduce us to your *girl*friend," he says. "Maybe she'd like –"

"Shut up," I say. Mrs. Smythe has no expression now. She pulls herself up.

"I'll talk to you later, then," she says, and turns around and walks out without looking back. If I could, I would follow her out.

Billy claps me on the shoulder. "Stay away from them," he says. "It's not worth it."

It doesn't matter. She practically said she didn't want to see me again. I don't blame her. I wouldn't want to see me either.

She will get into her car now and go home. She will honk when she pulls into the driveway so Mr. Smythe will come out and help her with the groceries. She always gets groceries today. The basics and sardines. Peanut butter. I lick my lips. Diamante frozen pizzas. Insta-oodles-o'-noodles. Eggo waffles. Captain Crunch.

Mr. Smythe will come out of the house, wave, come down the driveway. They will take the groceries into the house after they kiss. They will kick off their shoes. Throw something in the microwave. Watch *Cheers* re-runs on channel eight. Mr. Smythe will tell her what happened in his day. I wonder what she will say happened in her day.

On the way home with Billy, I wonder what Christmas in Vancouver will be like. Billy yabbers about how great it's going to be, the two of us, no one to boss us around, no one to bother us, going anywhere we want to go. I smile. Turn away from him. Watch the trees blur past. I guess anything will be better than sitting around, listening to Tony and Craig gripe.

DAVID BERGEN

The Bottom of the Glass

I do not suffer well, and this, in the final totalling up of my life, may be my greatest failure. To suffer well, I have been taught, is to find joy in pain, to be steadfast and fly beyond the temporal, to bear one's cross. Suffering well, it seems, is the young Anabaptist man, in A.D. 1528 at Bruck, on the Mur, in Steyermark, about to be drowned for his faith by the papistic Roman church and laughing at the water. Of course, some held that the devil had hardened his heart.

Lately I have caught myself gritting my teeth at the strangest of times. For instance, when I am relaxing: I will have been sleeping or reading and suddenly I become conscious of my mouth, that I am clenching my teeth as if I am lifting something heavy or bracing myself for a fall or heavy blow. Aware of this I force myself to relax; I drop my mouth open, yawn, breathe past my teeth, think of soothing images, but all I seem to get are balloons popping, the ocean pounding into me, and water drip, drip, dripping onto my forehead. So I bite my teeth once again.

Vange, my wife, says I should take drugs, Indocid, because this it what she uses for her period cramps and she swears by it. She says this to me across the supper table as I am feeding Leslie, our daughter, who is spitting everything back at me.

"Take two," Vange says, "it'll knock you out."

"I don't want to be knocked out," I say, although I don't sound too convincing. My jaw hurts. Our son Daniel used to grind his teeth at night; in the deepest of sleeps he'd suddenly be pounding away so hard you could hear his teeth popping through the walls. When I was young my uncle told me that a person's teeth never rot after they die, that death in fact preserves teeth, that you could exhume the body one hundred years later and you'd still see the teeth, the mouth full of molars. He grinned at me as he said that, clicking and showing his fat purple tongue. The other day I again thought of my uncle as I put my ear to the freshly dug black earth and listened for my son's teeth pounding up to me. Because he died this summer, my son did, just after his fifth birthday. And that's about that.

Ted Schmidt next door is an alcoholic. As is his wife and as was perhaps the wife before that. Personally, I used to like to drink with Ted because he was so generous and good-natured, so happy to have someone sit beside him and nurse some Johnny Walker. We would sit on the front porch in the late afternoon and look at the setting sun through our drinks as we tipped our glasses and Ted would say something about the beauty of the earth and I would nod in agreement. Ruthie, his wife, sometimes joined us and she would sit down beside me, stretch her long legs down the stairs and bang ice against her teeth. We would sit tripled and maybe we would talk about baseball or Marxism — Ruthie liked to talk about Marxism; she said once she'd like to be a good Marxist Christian. I wasn't sure why she said good. Anyways, I haven't had a drink with Ted and Ruthie since Danny died, which is over two months now. I don't mean to harp on this but it's at the core of what I'm saying. You see, he drowned in Ted and Ruthie's swimming pool. I suppose he thought he could swim. I imagine he thought, Hey neat, water, I'll swim. I'm not sure what I suppose or think or imagine anymore except I do know this is the reason I no longer drink with Ted. Also, two weeks after Daniel's funeral, Ted became a Christian. He came over and showed me the Four Spiritual Laws and I said, I know Ted, I've seen those before. He said he wasn't drinking anymore, that he was going to go to church only he hadn't decided which one. It shouldn't be hard, I thought, our town of ten thousand had twenty-six churches. I said, "Good for you, Ted," as if he was sixteen and had just passed his driver's test. And then I asked, "How about Ruthie?" and he smiled a dry, thirsty smile and said, "No, Ruthie is still Ruthie."

One of these days Vange is going to fly apart. She's been too calm, too reasonable, as if she is trying to tell me that this too is life, that grief can turn you inside out so you don't let it, you turn your back on it, you shoulder it, or you spit it out like bad fruit. I sat on the toilet tonight and watched her bathe Leslie. Leslie lay back on a frame of cloth and metal and she gurgled and pushed plastic ducks into her mouth and she punched at the lights above our mirror. I could smell Zincofax and baby powder and I looked at Vange's back, her spinal cord speed-bumping through her T-shirt, and thought how easy it was to make children. Vange wanted to last night. She said, Now, and though we met and came apart I felt I was somehow deceiving the one who was gone, as if he could be so easily replaced. "It's good this," Vange whispered into my throat, "this is what we need," and I shuddered because she sounded desperate and her face was wet and I was unable to say Yes or No and so I thought of Ruthie, across the street, drinking alone while her husband pored through the Bible. I have nothing against the Bible. I know the stories by heart. I told them to Daniel as he squeezed his hot little body in beside me on our green arm-chair. David fucked Bathsheba, Lot's daughters fucked Lot, Herod butchered babies, Salome asked for John the Baptist's head on a dish. Great. But really, no, for Daniel I kept things simple. Painstakingly I tried to erase any of the messages of sin and salvation from the stories that had once converted me at a young age. And, after all that effort, one night he lifted his face and breathed on me, his head still damp from his bath and he asked why Grandpa said that Jesus died for all the little Daniels of the world?

Grandpas. My father, who lives in this same town, is retired now. A religious and pious man, my father suffers well. My father would gladly have been a sixteenth-century martyr. For him the kingdom of God is in heaven not on earth and to have been drowned in a sack or burned alive would have given him great joy. Sometimes when I visit him at his home he watches my face and he is ashamed of me; he sees his own image and he shudders. So I think maybe I should hit him or walk away but I don't, I stay longer and make him suffer. It was at Daniel's funeral, watching my father grieve, that I realized there was not much difference between my glass and his heaven.

Funny. Vange is going to church with Ted. From the kitchen window I watch them disappear around the corner of Oak and Henry; Ted with his short red hair, his orange neck, and

Vange, her hair long and blonde, her skirt swaying at her calves. Vange is still breast-feeding so she takes Leslie in the big red Gendron. This Sunday, after they are out of sight, I wander around the house a bit and then I lie on Daniel's bed. We've cleaned out his room for possible guests but I can still smell him. Then, as these August nights can bring frost, I go out to check the garden. I'm crouching over the cherry tomatoes when suddenly Ruthie is there. She's wearing shorts so I'm staring at her bare legs and when I look up, follow her smooth thighs up past her crotch to her stomach and neck I see she is dressed warmer on top, a grey kangaroo sweatshirt. She's wearing red lipstick, smiling or perhaps pouting, and she's holding a drink of something that could be vodka or water. I know what it is.

"Ted's gone," she says.

I stand and nod, stretch my back, and Ruthie's hair is wet and smells good and I am aware of liking the look and smell of a woman just out of the bath.

"Wanna drink?" she says, and I'm not sure if she says "wanna" or "want to," or if she's aware of the difference.

I hesitate, look down at my tomatoes, see her toes which are painted purple, and I say, Okay. So we go to her house where I sit on a stool at the kitchen counter and watch her long fingers crack ice out of a tray and drop them into a glass. From where I sit I can see the pool and it's really quite nice, in the shape of a light bulb with the shallow end the screw-in part and I force myself to look at it, study its length and imagine its depth. Ruthie sits across the counter from me, sees where I'm looking, and she says, Sorry. She stands to draw the curtain on the view but I tell her that it's fine, that it's just a goddamn pool so she shrugs and says Ted wants to fill it in, make it into a tennis court. They've put locks on all the gates now, she says and then she says more but I'm concentrating on my drink which feels like it's the first of a few for the day.

Ruthie stops talking. I say: "Ted seems happy these days."

Ruthie says, Yaa, and then says she's hot so she takes off her kangaroo top. She's wearing a pink tank top underneath and when she swivels on her stool and reaches for the bottle I see the white of her breast and her nipple. Her nipple is small and her breast is tight and young looking. She's never had children. Normally, I would glance away but today I don't. Perhaps she feels she owes me something and if this is it I'll take it because obviously she's aware of her own body and what it does. She swings back at me and while she pours another drink I look at her. She has a small stingy mouth; it's as if she needs to keep things in. Her neck is long and her body is still fine but it's her face and eyes, her hands too, that tell me who she is. She lights a cigarette, offers me one and I take it. She smiles at me, touches my hand which is lying on the counter. She says, "Ted's on the edge. To be honest, he was happier before. This Christianity is wearing him out." Ruthie doesn't sound happy or cynical. She is matter-of-fact and I wonder if she wants Ted to start drinking again. I imagine, Yes and No, always yes and no. Personally, I admire Ted. He's not hiding anything, never has, and that goes against the rules in our town. On the surface, our town is a perfect little place – excellent lawns, no slums (perhaps because there is no railroad track), houses freshly painted – it fairly gleams. But beneath the surface it's an ocean teeming with its own life; a life of imperfections and rot and failures that in any other place would be quite accepted (or if not accepted, accommodated) but here people either ignore the life underneath the surface or they coldly chase the culprits out, all the while saving the appearances; except they have never really gotten to Ted Schmidt, and I have to admire him.

Ruthie begins to talk about the second Donut Shop she and Ted are starting, about hiring young, irresponsible girls, and while her little mouth grimaces I wonder why I'm sitting in her house on a Sunday morning drinking and looking down her pink tank top. I mean, if I want to look at breasts I just have to ask Vange, she's good to me. "I have to go," I say. "I promised Vange I'd pick her up from church and then we're going out to eat."

"Oh," she says, sorry it seems to see me leave. "I guess Ted'll walk home on his own."

"I guess," I say, becoming aware at the door of Ruthie's smell of liquor, smoke, and shampoo, and how tall she is and how her eyes slant down to her nose and the sheen of her legs and how all I'd have to do is pull her near whichever way I wanted and push my knee up between her legs, but it's her mouth that decides me. So I touch her cheek, rosy, rosy, and tell her not to worry about Ted, which is silly because she's not.

We go to eat at the hotel. Normally, we'd have stopped at McDonald's but Leslie doesn't care where we eat. Vange is wearing a white skirt and a loose yellow top. She has on white sandals and her tanned feet glow under the dash. I touch her leg as I drive and she takes my hand. The Gendron is stashed in the trunk where it bumps and clangs through the corners. Leslie nods off in the carseat in the back.

"Lots of stares today," Vange says.

"Well, what did you expect?" I say, and then, "How about Ted?"

"Ted has moved beyond all the guilt and the shame and his conversation is, in their eyes, the fruit of all this. And maybe that's the way we should see it too. People get pleasure in seeing Ted and me in church together, even though I can smell their desire to ask where you are."

I say: "Why is it that believers are the last to see the irony in things? Is life that simple for them?"

Vange isn't paying attention. She says: "One woman, Mrs. Wiebe, well-intentioned I'm sure, pulled me aside today and whispered that she was sorry, so sorry, and asked how we were, and before I could say that of course we were fine, why not, she was explaining that there were two ways we could deal with this: I could be angry and bitter or I could see this as an opportunity, like Ted Schmidt, she said. Like Ted. She actually said that."

"Which Wiebe?" I ask, curious about this.

"I don't know, don't care." Vange sighs and trails my knuckles with her nails as we pull into the hotel parking lot.

"What," I say, "that I should stop drinking too?" Then, not waiting for an answer, knowing what it will be, I say I saw Ruthie.

Vange looks surprised. "Oh, where?"

"Outside. In our garden."

"She actually came outside?"

"Yes, and then I went to her house for a drink."

Vange doesn't say anything. She kneels on the front seat and reached back to unstrap Leslie. She cradles her and climbs out. Vange doesn't like Ruthie. For some reason she thinks Ruthie is unsafe, in fact she said once that Ruthie was too sexy (if that's possible, I thought), as if warning me and she said too that Ruthie cared only about Ruthie and that made her dangerous.

Actually, I do see what she means but I find Ruthie more pathetic than dangerous, like Ted, or maybe like me, I think. After we're seated and we've ordered I ask Vange if she thinks she's grieved enough. She drinks some water, looks at me and says, Yes. When she says this she looks just like Daniel used to when he would be trying to convince me of something: not a lie, Dad. Then, she says that grieving is like climbing a mountain, that you reach a certain level and then you descend, how she has peaked, how she will never grieve enough but that she has gone high enough.

I believe her, because for her life has two laws, natural and human, and Danny's death falls under natural. I wonder if she considers habitual and driven drinking a natural law too because for me I still hold Ted and Ruthie responsible. I mean, how does a sodden son-of-a-bitch like Teddy apply mouth-to-mouth? Through a bottle? Right now, sitting across from Vange I am angry at her fatalism. I remember a night several weeks after Danny died. Vange was looking for something to take hold of and she was going on about these natural laws and I harumphed and said, "Solomon Grundy, born on Monday, christened on Tuesday, married on Wednesday, took ill on Thursday, worse on Friday, died on Saturday, buried on Sunday. This is the end of Solomon Grundy." I paused and then said, "I'd say that was a full life, wouldn't you?"

"Don't do this to me," Vange said, "You can't leave me out of this. I'll end up hating you."

I backed off then, scared suddenly, and even now if I am angry at her I will not walk that edge of her. I reach across the table and hold the sleeve of her yellow top between my thumb and forefinger. Vange looks at me, I can feel her soft skin on the back of my finger, and she smiles, a kind of grieving smile.

❑

The bottom of the glass is a bit of a paradox. In the right light, with the right drink and right glass, the bottom can bend and twist just perfect so that you want to put your tongue down there and stroke it, or maybe drink quickly in order to reach the bottom, but then the beauty of it is already gone, disappeared with the liquor. So you get more, there's always more, and you sniff it, inhaling the fumes, but the bottom is still swimming there so pretty and it'd be good to see it again. Only this time you maybe drop a marble in there for further effect, reach in two fingers, remove the fingers, savour them in your mouth, watch the marble spin round and round and you drink quickly, absurdly, trying to reach the bottom of the glass.

I attempt to explain this all to Vange but she has little patience for theories involving alcohol. She wonders how long I will go on using the glass as my way of mourning. And me, I don't know. I want to tell her that she, Vange, has always been my salvation, but that would be admitting that these days she's not enough.

Ed, one of the reporters at the paper where I work, says I should take a holiday. He watches my hands shake at 10 o'clock in the morning and he say I should do something. He says take a holiday but he means something else. I shrug and laugh nervously but still go for lunch and have a few drinks and before getting back to work I reach under my car seat and take a few pulls of Scotch. So, for the afternoon I'm fine and when I get home I fix a drink and moon over it before settling into the kitchen and helping Vange with the supper. I tell her Ed says we should take a holiday. She says, Fine, and suddenly we're planning two weeks at the lake, which frightens me because it's too close to water and too far away from the secrecy of the bottle.

"It'll be good for us. My Mom and Dad said we could use their cabin any time," Vange says, wedging tomatoes, the light glancing off the burnished knife.

I get two weeks. Vange works as an accountant out of the house so there's no problem there and Leslie's all gung-ho for the cabin and mosquitoes and fires in the evening. I can see the excitement in her blue eyes as I bend to rub noses with her. "Heeeeah, Lessey, betchabetchabetcha." She throws her head back, grabs a fistful of my cheek and says, "Bung." I go over to ask Ted and Ruthie to watch the house and water the lawn. Ruthie answers the door. She's eating doughnuts and icing sugar lies like dandruff on the shoulders of her black top. Then Ted is there too, hovering behind Ruthie, one hand on her backside and when I say what we're doing, Ruthie says, Sure no problem, but Ted looks surprised, as if we're deserting him. I'm not sure why he feels that way. "Wanna come in?" Ruthie asks, but I say, No, gotta pack.

In the early morning, around 5:00 a.m. when light begins to filter the tops of the trees and touch the bedroom curtains, Leslie and I leave Vange sleeping in the cabin and we walk down to the boardwalk that leads to the big campground at Falcon Lake. As I bump the stroller slowly over the rotting wood, Leslie giggles, claps her hands, oohs at the rushes and birds, the muskrats, and at her own ability to ooh. We tread the dewy grass at the edge of the beach, listen to the tock of axes beating on wood and smell bacon. Here at the lake I find I can manage without the fumes rising constantly from the glass to my nostrils. The back of my throat doesn't ache as badly either. Sure the edge is always there, especially in the late afternoon, after a swim and while contemplating supper. But I can handle it. Vange says it's Ruthie, we live too close to her and Ted and maybe we should move. Yes, she says again, we should move, and her cheeks round at the thought. When she says things like this I wonder how much longer she will put up with who I am; although, here, away from there, we are warming to each other again.

On the beach in the afternoons Vange and I lie side by side and touch hands as we watch Leslie burrow in the sand. Then Vange swims. She walks selfconsciously to the edge of the lake. I watch her move, study her shoulder blades, the roll of her bum. Sometimes I whistle. Once in the water she smiles back from her bodiless head. She bobs, she dunks, she seals, she disappears. I hold my breath and smell my arms which give off a mixture of lotion and sweat. I stoop and smell Leslie and she is a bun freshly drawn from the oven. Vange surfaces way out past the buoys and I breathe easier now that I can see her head plowing along. She was the one teaching Daniel to swim. He'd just come off the water wings and this summer was going to learn. Vange turns on her back. Leslie piles sand on my thighs. A young girl, maybe eighteen, runs by. She's wearing a black bikini and her stomach is flat and tanned and her teeth are white. She is beautifully awkward; coltish. Two boys, her age, follow and they are young and foolish and hopeful. I pat Leslie's head and ask if she's hot. "Gig," she says, so I help her dig.

Eating supper on our last evening before heading back home, Vange looks up at me and says that today it is exactly three months. "Yes," I say, "I know," and wonder if there comes a time when one stops counting, when the sight of a shoe lying matchless at the door is simply that, a shoe. I would like a drink. Not the cold beer sitting before me, but something whitish or yellowish in a heavy glass with ice floating at the surface, something that brings with it a shuddered warmth, a deep familiar sadness. But there is nothing in the cabin. I consider the possibilities of driving into Falcon to purchase some peace but it is raining hard tonight and Vange hates to be left alone with Leslie. Vange is watching me; she senses my thoughts but says nothing.

While she puts Leslie down I build a fire and open a book. I close the book. I check the shutters for leakage. I sit down and poke at the fire. I put on my jacket and go outside and start the car. Lightning screams in off the lake and rolls up on our dock. The lights go out in the cabin and come back on again. I turn the car off and go back inside. I shake my jacket off at the door and drops of water float back into my face. Vange is at the fire stirring it like a cauldron and from where I am I can see her shoulders shake. I push my wet hair behind my ears with icy fingers. I think about icy fingers for a while as I watch my wife cry. She is wearing an old grey sweater of her father's and it has a big collar that comes up to Vange's crown and from where I sit it makes her head look small, her back crooked. Finally, she turns and her face is ugly and raw and she calls my name, Saul, and this makes me move. It takes me a long time but I reach her and hold her and I say, "Good girl, that's a good girl."

"Good girl," I say.

My father, trying to keep busy, reads the Bible and *Martyr's Mirror.* I walk into his musty house, sit beside him, and stare at his white hair and his trembling fingers holding his books, one of which is opened to stories of martyrs: Richst Heynes,

A.D. 1547, "thrust into a bag like an irrational brute, and cast into the water and drowned"; Claes Lecks, A.D. 1548, burned alive; Elizabeth, A.D. 1549, "to be drowned in a bag – and thus offered up her body to God"; six brethren, at Amsterdam, on the 20th of March, 1549, "ended their lives in great joy, and were burned alive." I have read these stories and I think I understand why my father is so disappointed in me; he sees Daniel's death as useless (as do I) but he also blames me for his death (as do I sometimes) because I have failed to carry the seed, to pass on the necessary, the good, the essence of life. Fate, fortuity, and chance are words my father does not use. For my father a martyr's death is the ideal death because it disguises the finality of things – of course he would not admit to this. It produces a credible story, a name and a date to be remembered. A sort of posterity. A martyr's death, as I see it, is an unreal death filled with impossible expectation, idealism, and stupidity. Of course we all want to be remembered. But, we won't be.

We leave late in the afternoon the following day and our normally three-hour drive is extended because of blueberry picking, a flat tire, and a hot front-seat bit of love beneath some shrubs off the side of the highway as Leslie sleeps heavy and oblivious in the back seat. We stop for a late supper and creep into our driveway as the sky is turning dark. I turn off the ignition and feel the heaviness of everything come sliding back into me. Vange feels the same, I can see it. There's loud music thumping over from Ted and Ruthie's and lots of cars parked in their driveway.

"Party," Vange says. She sounds disappointed, aware by now that this is Ted's party too and immediately I want to

apologize, to start the car, to leave this again and for good. But
instead I say, "I'll take Leslie." We do some unloading and
open the house. I carry Leslie up to bed and Vange tucks her in
while I clean out the rest of the car. Then I go inside and lean
on the kitchen sink and look out over the yard to Ted and
Ruthie's where fully-clothed grown ups are jumping into the
pool. I am sure I see Ted, gangly and hoarse-voiced, patrolling
the pool, his arm around whoever comes near, and it must be
this image of his brazen manner, his disregard for holding to
the faith, any faith, that makes me angry and suddenly I am
crossing the lawn and knocking on his front door. I ring and
knock and ring, for some reason refusing to open it myself,
and finally Ted answers, big smile on his red face, hands full of
glasses, and he pulls up, squints and, "Aww, fuck," he says.
"You know, aww shit, Saul." And then, with cunning, he
pushes a glass at me, "Wanna?", and for some reason, I take
one and cradle it like a puppy. It's bourbon, I'm sure, and
though I want to weep with gratitude, I don't touch it. I just
look at it. Ted checks behind me: "Vange?" I shake my head.
He seems relieved. In the living room I see Ruthie slow danc-
ing with Al Krahn; they're both holding each other up, Al with
his hand running her back. The door behind me is still open
and if I turn and walk straight I will reach my own house. Ted
isn't asking me in, nor is he chasing me out. He shifts from
foot to foot and mutters Fuck once in a while, for my benefit, I
guess, but he's not as drunk as he's pretending. His eyes, when
they hold mine, are dark clear holes in which I see all that is
important to him and I understand that right now he hates
me, hates Ruthie and Al Krahn behind him, hates the glasses
he holds, the glass I hold, and most importantly he wants me
to drink from mine.

Without warning I say, "Tell me how you found him."

"How?"

I nod.

"The gate was unlocked," he says, and I say that I knew that. He continues: "I came out for an early morning swim and he was there at the bottom of the pool. The shallow end."

This shocks me and it must be evident because Ted asks me if I want to sit. I say, No. For some reason I had always imagined him floating face down in the water, his blond hair floating like a halo around his head, his shoulders to the open air; that was important, that he have some contact with the air. Ted's revelation makes everything seem further away; now I will have to restructure things in my head, start this futile process again. Ted is babbling, saying something about how heavy he was, mouth-to-mouth, so much water, Ruthie biting her own knuckles until they bled, how this had driven a wedge into his marriage, but I hear only the words, the meaning is unimportant now. Over Ted's shoulder I watch Ruthie kiss Al and I can smell corn chips, can smell my bourbon. I am looking through a viscous liquid or perhaps an imperfect glass while Vange is whispering salvation in my ear from across the lawn, from Leslie's room. Ted suddenly screams at no one to shut the fucking music down, that there's someone suffering here. This brings me around slightly and I look up expectantly, searching for this laughable someone. I realize I'm still holding my glass and that the liquor is untouched. Maybe it should stay that way, but then the glass will stay full and I can see the bottom way down there, there's an angel at the bottom, its image warping up at me and I need so badly to rescue that angel, even though it's a hundred miles away.

STEVEN HEIGHTON

How Beautiful Upon the Mountains

TŌKYŌ: From now on, Japanese who are too busy or live too far from family grave sites can pay to have professionals visit and clean the graves and burn incense in their place. The new service, provided by Clean Cemetery Co., has been in high demand since it became available last month.

[From *The Japan Times,* February 10, 1989]

After the funeral my father said to me, "As long as she was alive I felt my home was here."

My grandmother is buried on a bleak escarpment near the airport on the edge of the city. The day after the funeral I drove out again with my brother and sister, and afterwards, drinking coffee in her favourite restaurant, we found we'd all felt the same thing while standing above her grave: hunched together in the icy air we'd wanted to gather her in, to retrieve her from the frozen turf and hold her, take her somewhere warm. But none of us had spoken. In the restaurant my sister wondered aloud if we'd feel different about things in summer, when the wind would be mild, the graves green, and the headstones festooned with wreaths and fresh flowers – but we all live a long way from North Bay now, and none of us went up the next summer, or the summer after that.

My sister's fingers fluttered over the arborite as if hunting for the cigarettes she'd given up years ago. She asked us if we thought we'd be able to go up in the summer.

"I should be able to find time," I told her. "Dean?"

"It's a long drive from Detroit," he said. "It's a long way from anywhere."

My sister cupped her palms around her coffee mug and shivered. "I don't like to think of her never having visitors. You saw those graves behind her? Nobody's been out to them in years."

"You'll miss the lake, Dean," I said.

"In Detroit we got the river." He tried to grin. His eyes had a raw, invaded look – it wasn't long since he'd set his childhood behind him, the fledgling of the clan; he thought he'd escaped us, and that part of himself we would always keep alive. Now these reminders, this baring of a nostalgia he should have been too tough for.

He blinked down at his coffee. His eyes, as relatives had been telling him for years, were his grandmother's.

"Anyway," I said, "I should be able to find time. Maybe I'll fly up with Dad – he still comes up now and then."

"Maybe I'll come with you," my sister said.

We must have imagined our grandmother eavesdropping, or that Carla, the waitress who'd always served her, would tell her everything we'd said next time she came in. Because we all live a long way from North Bay now and it's not easy to go up for a weekend. Not the next summer, or the summer after that.

On a sunny morning in October 1947 the principal of my father's school swaggered into a classroom accompanied by an officer from the mountain airbase. The principal instructed all boys to rise and stand at attention. The officer, his broad chest gleaming with badges and winged decorations, saluted the principal then turned to the boys and told them to follow on the double; he cracked his black boot heels on the tiles and strode emphatically from the room. Frowning, the principal levelled a long arm toward the door and urged the boys to hurry. At first they had to run to catch up with the long-striding airman.

The boys filed down the main hall of the school through a gauntlet of ravenous eyes – their younger schoolmates, gathered at the classroom doors, envious, applauding, or else leering and full of taunts, depending on the rumours that had hatched among them. My father heard them speculating as he passed by.

They got the day off to go visit the airbase.

Lucky buggers. Must of done something to help during the war.

Yeah, like what? Collecting garbage? Cleaning toilets?

I say Herman Weiner's a Nazi spy after all. And the others must of helped him.

They're all gonna be taken out and shot.

The boys were trooped single-file into a camouflaged bus past a hawk-nosed driver who started the engine and steered them from the parking lot before they were properly seated. The officer from the airbase rose and stood at the head of the aisle. Smoothing his moustache and sweeping the cap from his bald head, he called for silence and began to brief the agitated boys. At 0400 hours this morning, while the city slept, an RCAF Hurricane fighter on a training mission had for no apparent reason crashed into the hills behind the airbase, killing the pilot on impact. The boys had been granted a brief reprieve from their scholastic duties (here the officer paused momentarily, as if for a smile he could not quite execute) – a brief reprieve so they might help the Air Force gather evidence pertaining to this strange accident. The boys would be required to search a densely wooded mountainous sector for pieces of the aircraft. No souvenirs, it went without saying, were to be looted from the site.

The speeding bus hummed and crackled like a wireless with the boys' excitement, but James Merritt, the biggest boy of all, urged them to be wary.

The sector's densely wooded, he winked. *We'll have to look out for Kraut snipers.*

The other boys smirked and giggled or shaped their hands into Lugers and fired them out the window at make-believe foes. But Herman Weiner's smile was forced.

It's the Japs I'd watch out for, he said. *The Japs and the land-mines. Blow your balls off.*

James Merritt leered at the other boys, then glared at Herman. *We all know there's no Japs around here,* he said. *But even one Kraut's too many as far as I'm concerned.*

Before the boys could join James in laughing, my father interrupted and told them he'd seen some Japs the year before while driving in the hearse with his cousin Hal, the under-taker. My father liked to remind the boys about his cousin as often as possible, and for their part they seemed to respect and even fear this connection, as if Death were the boy's personal acquaintance or not-so-distant relative who might be ex-pected to guarantee the safe conduct of his kin. And since North Bay was smaller then, and the hearse had to moonlight as the local ambulance, my father held another enviable and exotic post: second cousin to the city's ambulance driver.

The day he saw the Japanese, my father was driving up the

mountain with his cousin to pick up an air cadet hurt in a brawl with a veteran pilot. *An odd one, that pilot,* his cousin said. *Hear he's always getting into trouble. The War, I guess....*

What do you mean? My father wanted to hear more of what had happened to the pilot, but his cousin couldn't tell him very much. There were rumours about bad experiences in combat, how his fighter squadron had flown on costly raids with the bombers over Dresden and Cologne before being transferred to the Pacific in the last months of the war. But no one knew the details. *Maybe he flew with the Enola Gay,* my father said – but cousin Hal told him the Enola Gay had carried out its mission alone.

At a level crossing he and Hal passed a party of Japanese workers standing by the road, resting chins and folded hands on the grips on their spades, smoking cigarettes with languid, half-closed eyes. *Japs,* his cousin told him. My father still recalls how they looked at him through the hearse window with dull apathetic faces, like men watching the funeral procession of a stranger. Their amber skin was stamped with fatigue. Suddenly one of them, much younger – a boy no bigger than my father – grinned at the hearse, a cigarette drooping from his lower lip as he smiled; and before he could stop himself my father smiled back, the reaction as automatic as returning an enemy's fire.

Those were the first foreigners he had ever seen.

But they're not even foreigners, he told the boys in the bus. *Not really. My cousin said. They're fishermen from B.C. and they were born here and brought East for logging and to work on the railroad.*

Once a Jap, always a Jap, Herman Weiner said – and in spite of himself James Merritt had to agree.

The bus laboured up an incline, then began to pick up speed as it pitched breakneck into a valley. The driver geared down and the engine roared but the bus continued to accelerate, the chassis rattling and wind hissing through hidden flaws in the metal and it was just like flying, all the boys agreed. None of them had ever flown. The bus shuddered to a stop at the base of another hill and the officer from the airbase leapt up and ordered the boys to follow him out.

The year I turned eleven my father took a course and learned to fly – small planes, Mooneys, Cessnas and Pipers, Beechcraft Musketeers. He bought into a secondhand Musketeer with seven others so that every two months, technically, the plane was his for a week. But he only had time for it on weekends. And one weekend it came my turn to go up with him.

We were planning to fly to North Bay – my grandmother's heart problems had started earlier that year, and besides seeing her my father wanted to drop in on his cousin Hal and a few old friends. He'd charted a course that would take us north-northwest over Nottawasaga Bay and Christian Island then due north over the Magnetawan to the French River and northeast over Lake Nipissing to the city.

I grinned and wriggled in my seat as the engine caught and the propellor melted into air. I was to see this stunt performed again and again in the future, but the sorcery of that vortex where steel became sky, where things invisible could kill you and cut you to pieces or haul you birdlike through the heavens – for me that magic never disappeared. I pored over our map. I'd been appointed navigator, and now tracing the flight path my father had drawn and savouring the exotic syllables of Iroquois names, I felt important, much older, involved at last in the distant, billowing adventure of adult lives.

And it was just us – for the whole weekend I would have him to myself, my father, the guardian who now depended on my navigation, my co-pilot.

I had never flown before and at first it was even better than I'd imagined. The Musketeer seemed to bolt over the runway like a racing car along a dragstrip, there was a bellying sense of loft then a sudden weightlessness as we took flight; I held my breath and waited for schoolbook laws to strike us down. The windshield was a planetarium of open space and in the mid-day light the full moon hovered like a destination. Gravity tackled me to my seat as our engine fought the thinning air. And all the time my father seemed calm, unaroused, his features as still and impartial as the dashboard's face of glowing dials and gauges; it took me years to see that he would always compose himself, as he did until the end of the funeral, whenever he knew I was watching.

The city, our home, had fallen away beneath us so that all I could see was a flashing cinematic backdrop of densely ranked towers so unlike the common, squalid concrete boroughs we passed through on our drive to the island airport. This was another city altogether, a fabulous and magical sprawl, like New York, where my father had gone to work for a year, like Cologne or Bombay or Ōsaka. Beyond the receding skyscrapers Lake Ontario sparkled like a tropical gulf and already Lake Simcoe was visible ahead, sleek with sunshine, shot through with highlights of coral, indigo, and amber.

I had never flown before, and now I saw that the earth showed a different face to all creatures of the air – to birds, to angels, to gods and pilots. It was the face of a foreigner, and I could not take my eyes off it.

"You like the view, son?" my father glanced down at me. "You're looking a little green."

And as I returned his gaze I felt the pain lift off – a headlong, swooping nausea that would hold an air-show in my belly for the next half-hour till we turned back and made an emergency landing in Buttonville. In the future it would make all flight an agony, and at one point impossible, so I would learn that even the most innocent of escapes had their price – and that ecstasy is soon followed by nausea.

"Not in the cockpit!" my father cried, as the stunt-plane inside me executed another impossible loop.

How beautiful upon the mountains, Uncle Hal declaimed in his resonant responsible mortician's voice, *How beautiful upon the mountains are the feet of him who bringeth glad tidings, who publisheth peace....*

My mother leaned against me in the pews and whispered, "This sounds a little cheerful for a time like this. Didn't we hear it last month? The Christmas service ... you and your sister home...."

I shrugged, trying to hear the rest of the words. *Who bringeth glad tidings, who publisheth peace.* "It's fine," I whispered. "Really. Maybe she requested it."

For eye to eye they see the return home of the Lord God to Zion.

"I think this is a Christmas reading," someone behind us said.

And so it turned out. Uncle Hal had confidently recited the wrong passage from the Book of Isaiah. After the funeral my grandmother's only surviving friend was furious, but I heard my father say to my mother *I'll have to add something to my will about that. Have them read the same thing for me, will you?* And my mother, who had been so stolid until then, embraced him and hid her face against his shoulder.

After the funeral my father said to me, "As long as she was alive I felt my home was here. Where my mother was."

Whenever a blast of wind hit the building we felt its frame shiver, as if an earthquake or a bomb were levelling some distant place; with each gust a slight draft drifted in from the walls. The reception was almost over. It was getting dark beyond the windows, but there was still enough light to see my sister's children making angels in the snow.

Wing Commander Morris Kimmett stood stiff as a flagpole beside the camouflaged bus and drafted the boys into six companies of five men each. Each "man" was then issued a camouflaged burlap tote-bag. One member of each company was appointed leader and assigned a small whistle of military issue and a topographical map. The latter was merely a precaution, Kimmett advised them, as the area to be searched was fairly small and had been cordoned off at 0800 hours by Air Force personnel using fine-drawn phosphorescent night-wire.

Wing Commander Kimmett led the boys through a gap in the wire and instructed them to spread out and begin their search. They were to meet at the crash-site – a scorched hollow at the heart of the sector – at 1200 hours – or exactly one-and-one-half hours from the present.

James Merritt had been appointed squad leader and it took no more than five minutes for power to corrupt him absolutely. When Herman Weiner refused to hand over a charred scrap of metal he'd just found, James used his wobbling bulk to bodycheck the younger boy into a birch tree. Herman sat crumpled against the trunk, trying not to cry.

Goddamn Kraut, James said, subduing a smile. *I order you to stand. On the double. Stand and salute me! I'm your commanding officer!*

As Herman faltered to his feet, the boys were distracted by a sharp cry; apparently someone in another squad had made an exciting find. Scowling, James huffed a shrill blast from his whistle and ordered everyone to fan out.

And don't come back, he chided them, *till you got something to show.*

My father soon lost contact with the others. He wandered uphill through a pine grove, scanning the forest floor for things unusual. Suddenly there was a beating of wings above his head and as he glanced up, afraid, he glimpsed through the boughs a low-flying arrowhead of geese, like the great B-29 formations he had seen in the newsreels. He was relieved. This flock would be the last of the season, he thought, to go south.

Looking down again, his heart leapt when a beam of light set off a small metallic object on the ground – a bottle cap. And for a moment he thought a piece of the bottle, lying nearby, was a chip from the plane's windshield. Then he saw something protruding at eye-level from the trunk of a pine: a small sharp sliver of iron, like the bit of shrapnel that had wounded his father in the Great War and was now mounted at home in a trophy case under a parade of chevrons, pins, and decorations.

My father tried to pry the scrap from the tree but it was too deeply embedded. He decided to walk in the direction it was flying when it hit the trunk. This was shrewd, he thought, and his cunning and stealth as he crept forward without a sound made him feel like a crack commando. Squeezing between two large pines he entered a thick bramble of raspberry bushes speckled with fruit the birds had missed – berries gone black, withered and hard, like tiny globs of congealed blood. He could not advance so he knelt and peered under the bushes. And from the far side of the bramble two eyes peered back.

Later he wondered if the scream he heard then actually was his own, though the other boys swore it came from elsewhere in the forest and for better reason. Yet no one ever owned up. My father recalls opening his startled mouth on a dry, mechanical throttling, and then a terrible shriek coming from somewhere to fill it.

Hurtling through the forest a few seconds later, he almost crashed into Herman Weiner. Herman's eyes widened when he saw my father's face. *Hey,* he said, *that wasn't you screaming a minute ago, was it? You don't look too good.*

Let's get out of here, my father said.

No, come to think of it, the scream came from over there. *But* something *must have happened to you.*

Herman —

So what did you see? Geez, you look awful. Did you find the pilot's head or something?

Something, my father said. And he thought again of the eyes he'd seen, almost human eyes, narrowed to anonymity, aglow with an alien, hypnotic light. They'd seemed hungry yet patient at the same time, like the eyes of a predator crouched in ambush — as if they'd been waiting since the day he was born for him to enter the forest and kneel down and peer under the brambles. And he'd thought he knew every animal that lived in the region.

They heard James Merritt's irascible whistling and found him and the others in an open space, squatting in warm sunshine on an outcrop of rock. James was surveying his map with a concise, critical expression. *I know exactly where we are,* he announced, looking up from the map and strafing the surrounding brush with his eyes. Then he saw the approaching stragglers, shuffling quickly like troops in retreat, burlap sacks slung over their shoulders like homeless men.

Weiner and John report! What have you got to show?

My father, still shaken, had nothing to show, but Herman had found a small singed piece of fuselage with writing on it. The boys knelt around the scrap but could make out only a few words, apparently painted on in a shaky, unofficial hand: MERCURY III - FROM HERE TO — the rest had been melted and blurred by the furious heat of the explosion. It looked like scribbles in an alien alphabet, the scrabbling of small birds in the dirt.

So he called his plane "Mercury," one of the boys whispered.

That scream, Herman Weiner said, emboldened by the success of his find, *what was it all about?*

One of the boys raised a finger to explain but James cut him short. *Just rumours,* he sniffed. *We can't pay attention to rumours.*

A hand! cried another boy before James could stop him. *Someone in another group found a hand in a glove!*

And that's not all, another boy said.

From somewhere farther up the slope, Wing Commander Kimmett's whistle, with its characteristically lower pitch, began to shrill. So they were to reassemble already. James ordered the boys to fall in and look smart and keep an eye out for more scraps, and as they trudged through the forest toward the whistle's repeating shriek they found more and more pieces scattered among the pine cones and stuck in the trees and they dropped them like Halloween candies into their clinking sacks. They could see they were drawing closer to the source of the fragments. Now the birch trees they passed were streaked with brown swathes, and in the crotch of an aspen whose bark had bubbled on one side from the heat they found a tiny nest, empty save for feathers and a few particles of shell.

The nest was utterly charred and fell to pieces at my father's touch.

It's like a puzzle, Herman Weiner said, bending over to pick up another metal scrap. *When they have all the pieces they can put the plane back together and they'll know why it crashed.*

I think my father must have wondered then whether the assembled scraps could tell them everything, as Herman Weiner and Wing Commander Kimmett seemed to think. At any rate, I wonder. These days the mountains are catacombed with the relics of fallen shuttles and jetliners and because the pilot is always the first to go we never hear the full story. The jungle digests faulty wiring, rotten struts. Flight-recorders plunge into the depths off Okinawa or settle, like small steel coffins, into unmarked desert graves.

Wing Commander Kimmett stood at attention in the heart of a sizable crater and beckoned the boys in from the forest. My father had thought there would be plenty of wreckage in the crater but there was almost none, and it was rumoured variously that helicopters had lifted out the bigger chunks that morning, that foreign agents had spirited them away before dawn, or that the heat of the blast, like an atomic explosion, had instantly vaporized everything.

But most of the rumours at large that moment and in the following weeks concerned *the hand in the glove.* Drawing shallow breaths, his thin cheeks plausibly pale, little Dawson Parker swore he'd found it by a rock – a black scorched crumpled thing, like a fallen crow. No one else had seen it, but his squad-mates backed him up, and though at first no one believed them when they explained how Kimmett had promptly confiscated the hand, the boys found it useful in time to abandon their incredulity and recount the tale to all who would listen, so that now if you go to North Bay anyone over a certain age will tell you with conviction about The Hand In The Glove.

(At the time it was also rumoured that something had been found in the hand – a photograph, some said of a child, others thought of a parent or else a woman, a *foreign woman* – but back then North Bay was a sober, sensible community, and while The Hand survived by virtue of its solid fleshly weight, the other rumours soon went the way of all romance.)

As he collected the tote-bags Wing Commander Kimmett asked the squad leaders if they had seen during their searches anything worthy of report. James Merritt shook his head No, but Herman Weiner cried out *John did! John saw something scared the living daylights out of him!*

Dawson Parker blushed. His squad leader, Arnie Lukits, sneered from across the crater. What could beat a real live hand? *Shut up, Weimar,* he called. *Go back to Deutschland.* So that Herman Weiner, giggling nervously, had to turn it all into a joke.

You should have seen his face, he snickered, contorting his own features grotesquely. *Said it was a Jap hiding in the jungle who hadn't surrendered yet.* And almost everyone was ambushed by laughter then – even my father. Even James Merritt, demoted to childhood by a boyish grin, gave his Air Force whistle a festive toot.

Wing Commander Kimmett surrendered them a smile.

After the funeral my father said to me, "As long as she was alive I felt my home was here. Where my mother was. As long as your mother is alive, you know, you never really feel the place you're living is home. There's always somewhere else you can go to."

How beautiful upon the mountains are the feet of him....

I left my father with Uncle Hal and strolled through the reception hall to say goodbye to the last guests. Hal was trying to cheer my father up; he'd just poured him another Scotch, and over my shoulder as I walked away I could hear him reviving memories of their rides in the ambulance/hearse when my father was a boy. Did he remember that time an Air Force Colonel from the States fainted on the runway and they'd raced up in the hearse to take him back to the city and he'd come to just as those big black shiny doors swung open and they tried to stuff him inside? Hal's hoarse voice rises at the familiar climax, as if trying to include me too though I am walking away. "And then – you remember? – he starts shouting 'For Christsake not yet, you bastards! For Godsake not yet!' "

I'm wondering if this old standby is really appropriate when along with Hal's studied chuckling there comes a strange unexpected burst of familiar laughter. My father. I can hear how he tries to suppress it, and I'm relieved when he fails. "For Christsake you – you *bastards!*" I hear him reciting the words as both men laugh harder and harder, hysterical now and uncontrolled, a series of gentle explosions, the whisky and a shared past ablaze inside them. "For Godsake," I hear, "not yet!"

I embrace my sister, my brother – both drunk. "Sad place to end up," my brother mumbles, looking away, betrayed again by his grandmother's eyes.

"You used to love it here, Dean."

The walls and floors shake slightly as jets from the base pass overhead. My brother-in-law and my mother are silhouetted against the window, watching the children play by the road. The snow outside now seems the only source of light: the sky is almost dark, and it's getting difficult to see inside the hall.

Someone should turn a lamp on but nobody will – the dimness in here, the last light of this funereal day, is all that still connects us with the absent woman. If the lights come on we'll be able to see each other clearly, and her face will not be among us.

Now and then, even these days, my father plunges and awakes, shot from the clouds of a peaceful sleep by those marksmanlike eyes, tumbling to earth like an exploded shuttle. The dream never varies but he will not describe it, so we are forced to imagine how the eyes look; and even if he told them in detail, or if I did, you would see a different pair, another creature behind them.

More than ever you are haunted. You live in a centrifugal atmosphere, an age of airline passengers, scattered families, flight paths, and far-off destinations....

My grandmother's eyes were inlaid by the time of her death with the tired facets of an adamant, familiar landscape. Over time the slate-blue of her eyes was seamed and subtly altered by the Shield's grey projections, the quicksilver tint of the sky, the quivering light-waves of the deep lake she swam in as a girl and sat watching as an old woman.

"A sad place to end up," my brother mumbles, thinking of the long dismal winters and the bleak graveyard with its frozen ground – but the ground, however cold, was known to her, and would have recognized her in return. I think a parcel of clay behind a subdivision of Ft. Lauderdale condos would have been colder.

Where will my father end up? My mother? Or for that matter, me.

Ft. Lauderdale?

Mt. Pleasant?

Ōsaka?

The loons and geese of Trout Lake fly south in the autumn but don't try to tell me they die there. They have to come home for that. Birds aren't stupid. They have principles. They understand the mechanics of flight.

But then who can really blame us for scattering? If Dean hadn't lit out for the States and disappointed my father, I might have. The skies swarm with ultrasonic waves and satellites and international aircraft bringing rumours of the beautiful invasion, the exotic and now-accessible enemy who becomes a neighbour. How does anyone stay another night in a small town, a small city, a farmhouse on the prairies?

My grandmother never left North Bay, and took to the air only in death. My grandfather left only for the war, which must have been a kind of reprieve for him and his friends, an opportunity, as war has always been, for men to run away from women. And after that too-long, muddy, blood-spattered flight, he never felt an urge to leave home again.

What eyes he must have seen! The story goes that he entered an enemy trench and killed an officer with his bayonet, but it is not recorded whether he looked the dying man in the eyes, whatever colour they were, or what he saw in them if he did.

Home is wherever you're used to the eyes around you so that habit disarms their menacing heat. Home is somewhere below you on the dark plains – a dry nest, blazing.

The breast of a lover is home. A scar, a photograph.

Home is if your mother still lives, and where.

My father and I have discovered that two Gravol and a banana milkshake will settle my stomach enough that we can fly for several hours at a stretch. This is two years after the first flight and many more before the funeral; I've entered that brief and falsely promising phase before the onset of adolescence. Suddenly I'm old enough to wonder why people feel as they do about things but not yet too self-absorbed to care.

Over the gargling of the tiny engine I ask my father what first made him want to fly, and for a moment he seems unsure how to answer. When he finally does, he focuses straight ahead through the windshield as if we're on a crowded highway and he must watch for oncoming cars.

"I suppose it started with the search," he begins, "for pieces of that crashed fighter. I told you all about that…." He pauses for a moment and scans the instrument panel. "But it wasn't the search itself – that just showed me how dangerous it is to fly – it was what we found out after."

"What do you mean?" He hasn't spoken about this before. I turn to face him but he continues to stare straight ahead, his pale eyes in profile translucent, illegible.

"I told you about the pilot, didn't I?"

"Sure. He was going out with the sister of someone you knew. And he was weird, right?"

"Not weird. A little … erratic. Very quiet, and sad. And aggressive when he drank, I heard. No one seemed to know where he was from. People said he'd had some bad experiences during the war, something about the bombing raids, but no one knew the exact details. I remember wondering at the time, you know, what was he doing up there, flying a fighter plane in the middle of the night? But then I guess I must have thought that was a regular part of his training."

"He didn't crash the plane on an official flight?"

"Well, *he* seemed to think it was official. He left behind a complete flight plan. And he mapped out his route in detail."

My father nods, widens his eyes, changes expression while he speaks as if addressing someone face to face, instead of the windshield and the sky beyond.

"So where was he going?" I say.

"No one really knows. No one had heard of any of the places on his itinerary, and he'd drawn his route on a map he'd made himself. But it wasn't of any real place – he'd made it all up. And the names were nonsense too – invented." My father grins lazily and shakes his head as if wanting me to see it's not worth dwelling on, but I know by his evasive manner that the story intrigues him too, puzzles him, won't leave him alone. "And so he went up at 4:00 in the morning and crashed a few minutes later into hills behind the airbase.... Look at that, son."

Glancing down I'm caught off guard by our altitude, the sheer, sunlit fabric of space parachuting away from us, the dizzying tug of the ground; sometimes you wake for the briefest spell and remember that flight is miraculous, impossible.

"Do you see?" my father nods towards Niagara Falls, the American side just now coming into view. Directly below us the escarpment runs – sinuous and ragged, the shattered spine of a crashed jet.

"Beautiful, isn't it?"

"Didn't anyone ever say," I ask, "what the name of the destination was?"

My father casts me a quizzical look, then turns back to the windshield and the invisible steel of the propellor. "Well, I don't suppose anyone really thought much about the actual names. They were words he made up – maybe he'd been drinking, maybe he had a dream. Most people thought he was already half-crazy. I guess the names didn't mean much to anyone else."

"And they never found anything when they put the plane back together? Couldn't something have gone wrong to make him crash?"

"I suppose it could have, yes. But the things we found didn't help them much. They decided he crashed because his instruments malfunctioned in the dark – but I don't know if they had any evidence or not. I don't suppose they would have had to tell us either way."

My father banks the plane sharply so I can look straight down into the falls; a riveting spiral of fierce white, like a hurricane's eye on a weather map. I want to ask him again what it might have been that he saw that day in the forest, but I know by the way he's controlling the plane – with brusque, manly, martial gestures, as if piloting a fighter jet instead of a Musketeer – that he's tired of talking and wants only to fly.

We descend steeply for a few moments and when we level off, Lake Ontario fills the windshield like a gulf or an ocean, seismic, unpredictable, and vast. Sometimes he flies lower than he really should over our neighbourhood, almost buzzing the apartment blocks, a barnstormer, and for a moment I pick out our house and point down at it like a bombardier and tell him I can see my mother, and perhaps I really can – she's hanging laundry in the backyard or standing on the porch with her hands on her hips staring up at us, her face shorn of features by distance and the summer light, like an old photograph, fading. My brother and sister (is it really them?) are falling over themselves as they race our passing shadow up the sidewalk, waving yet running frantically as if we were something to escape. We call this "strafing home."

As we bank sharply to the east, I begin to imagine that other flight, how it might have been. I've never stopped imagining.

How would it feel to light out before dawn for a destination no one else would know – and everyone, perhaps, has imagined? In the chill dark of 4 a.m. you climb into your cockpit on the mountain. Your engine snarls and bites into the cold. To gust over the runway and feel the air sudden beneath you, a weightless irresistible wedge rearing up like a summit as you climb, the early wind and the sun and all that's familiar falling away as the prop cleaves crystals of ice and dim continents unroll beneath … to fly eye to eye with darkness, and see.

About the Authors

MARIA A. BILLION was born and raised in Sliema, Malta. She has lived in the east and west of Canada and also in California, southern Europe, and central Mexico. An M.A. in literature has proved invaluable in work that has included psychiatric research, landscape horticulture, and organizing community projects. One of her stories was a finalist in the 1990 CBC Literary Competition. "No Miracles Sweet Jesus" is part of a cycle set in the old country. Another cycle set in the new is also in the works.

DAVID BERGEN lives in Winnipeg where he is working on a collection of stories. He has had two previous stories published in the first and third volumes of *The Journey Prize Anthology*.

JUDITH COWAN was born on Cape Breton Island, brought up in Toronto, and now lives in Trois-Rivières, Quebec. Her short stories have appeared in English in *Quarry, Queen's Quarterly, Matrix,* and *The Canadian Author & Bookman* (the last won the Okanagan fiction award), and in French in *Liberté, Le Beffroi,* and *XYZ.* Currently she is working toward compiling them in a book. She has translated three collections of poetry, and her translation of Gérald Godin's first novel, *L'ange exterminé,* was published as *Exterminated Angel* in the spring of 1991.

STEVEN HEIGHTON lived and worked in Japan in 1987 and now lives in Kingston where he edits *Quarry* magazine. He has published two books of poetry, *Stalin's Carnival* and *Foreign Ghosts*. In 1990 his story "Five Paintings of the New Japan" won the *Prism international* contest, and it will appear along with the two stories in this anthology and eleven others in *Flight Paths of the Emperor* (Porcupine's Quill, 1992). "How Beautiful Upon the Mountains" will also be included in *Best Canadian Stories,* forthcoming in the fall of 1992.

L. REX KAY was born in Winnipeg and received a B.A. and M.D. from the University of Manitoba. He is currently completing a psychiatry residency in Toronto. He has travelled extensively in Europe and Asia and will be spending the next year in Africa. "Travelling" is his first published story.

ROZENA MAART was born in District Six, Cape Town, South Africa and has lived in England, Colombia, and Canada since 1989. She is a writer, poet, public speaker, and sessional lecturer both in Canada and the United States. She publishes regularly in journals and magazines, and has also published a poetry and essay collection entitled *Talk About it!* (Williams Wallace, 1991). Her areas of work are Black consciousness, psychoanalysis, feminist theory, and violence against women. She teaches Social and Political Thought in the Study of Racism and Feminism, and Sociocultural and Political Issues in International Literature at the University of Ottawa.

CARMELITA McGRATH was born in Branch, Newfoundland in 1960, and has spent most of her adult life in St. John's, where she has worked as a writer, researcher, editor, and teacher. Since 1983 she has been writing and publishing poetry, fiction, and articles. Her work has appeared in *TickleAce, Waves,*

Waterlily, and *The New Quarterly,* as well as the anthology *Digging into the Hill.* Her first book of poetry *Poems On Land and On Water* (Killick Press, 1992) is forthcoming. Winner of several Newfoundland and Labrador Arts and Letters awards, she is currently at work on new fiction, old fiction, and poetry.

GUY MALET DE CARTERET lives and works in Toronto. "Rainy Day" is his first published story.

MICHAEL MIROLLA was born in Italy but has spent most of his life in and around Montreal. He was an Honours Chemistry student at university but wisely came to his senses and switched to English Literature before it was too late. His short stories have appeared in numerous magazines in Canada and the United States, as well as the anthology *Tesseracts* and the *Telling Differences* anthology of Quebec writers. He has published a collection of short stories, *The Formal Logic of Emotion,* and is presently at work on a science fiction novel and a collection of short-short stories that try to balance themselves on the edge of magical realism, surrealism, and speculative fiction.

DIANE JUTTNER PERREAULT was born in Toronto and raised in Winnipeg. She has a B.F.A. (Honours) from the University of Manitoba. Currently living in Winnipeg with her husband and two young children, she teaches Music for Young Children and writes in her spare time. "Bella's Story" is her first published piece.

EDEN ROBINSON grew up on Kitamaat Reservation in British Columbia. She has a B.F.A. from the University of Victoria, and is starting her M.F.A. at the University of British Columbia in 1992. The first draft of her first novel, *Dog in Winter,* was recently completed – a condensed version of its first three chapters won the *Prism international* short story contest in 1991. She is currently researching her thesis project, a non-fiction book on Kitamaat.

About the Contributing Journals

Descant is a quarterly literary magazine which publishes poetry, prose, fiction, interviews, travel pieces, letters, photographs, engravings, art, and literary criticism. Editor: Karen Mulhallen. Managing Editor: Elizabeth Mitchell. Submissions and correspondence: P.O. Box 314, Station P, Toronto, Ontario, M5S 2S8.

Event is published three times a year by Douglas College, in New Westminster, B.C. It focuses on fiction, poetry, and reviews by new and established writers, and every spring it runs a Creative Non-Fiction Contest. Now in its twenty-first year of publication, *Event* has won national awards for its writers. Editor: Dale Zieroth. Fiction Editor: Maurice Hodgson. Submissions and correspondence: P.O. Box 2503, New Westminster, B.C., V3L 5B2.

Exile is a quarterly that features Canadian fiction and poetry as well as the work of writers in translation from all over the world; some the best-known, others unknown. Publisher and Editor: Barry Callaghan. Submissions and correspondence: Box 67, Station B, Toronto, Ontario, M5T 2CO.

Fireweed is a feminist quarterly committed to an editorial policy of cultural diversity. Existing for twelve years as a collective organization of women, *Fireweed* is determined to publish literary and cultural works from a feminist grass roots perspective. *Fireweed* accepts unsolicited submissions from all women and does not publish material considered racist, sexist, or homophobic. Guest collectives have produced some of *Fireweed*'s best issues, such as "Class is the Issue," "Lesbiantics," and "Asian Women." *Fireweed* welcomes ideas for future theme issues. For subscription information, or to send in submissions, write to *Fireweed*, P.O. Box 279, Station B, Toronto, Ontario, M5T 2W2, or call (416) 323-9512.

Grain offers its readers original, exciting stories and poems by emerging authors, nestled beside some of the best, most imaginative works by established fiction writers and poets. Published by the Saskatchewan Writers' Guide, *Grain* has earned national and international recognition for its distinctive literary content and visual style. Editor: Geoffrey Ursell. Fiction Editor: Edna Alford. Submissions and correspondence: Box 1154, Regina, Saskatchewan, S4P 3B4.

The New Quarterly promotes new writers and new kinds of writing with a special interest in work which stretches the bounds of realism. We publish poetry, short fiction, and interviews, with occasional special issues on themes and genres in Canadian writing. These have included magic realism, family fictions, and Canadian writing in the Mennonite context. Submissions and correspondence: c/o ELPP, PAS 2082, The University of Waterloo, Waterloo, Ontario, N2L 3G1.

Prairie Fire is a quarterly magazine of contemporary Canadian writing that regularly publishes stories, poems, book reviews, and visual art by emerging as well as established writers and artists. *Prairie Fire*'s editorial mix is eclectic and frequently features both critical and personal essays, inter-views with authors, and a lively letters section. *Prairie Fire* commissions illustrations for each story and every summer publishes a popular fiction issue. Some of *Prairie Fire*'s best issues have been double-sized editions on various topics and genres, for example, Franco-Manitoban writing (a bilingual issue) and Mennonite writing. Forthcoming are special issues on Ukrainian-Canadian writing, Native writing, and specula-tive fiction. Although *Prairie Fire*'s mission is to "map the region known as the prairies," the magazine is not exclusive and publishes writing from, and has readers in, virtually all parts of Canada. Managing Editor: Andris Taskans. Fiction editors: Ellen Smythe, Margaret Sweatman, and Joan Tho-mas. Submissions and correspondence: Rm. 423 – 100 Arthur St., Winnipeg, Manitoba, R3B 1H3.

For thirty years, *Prism international* has published work by writers both new and established, Canadian and interna-tional. Edited by graduate students of creative writing at the University of British Columbia, *Prism* looks for innovative fiction, poetry, drama, as well as creative non-fiction, in English or English translation. *Prism* also holds an annual fic-tion contest. Request guidelines or send submissions to: The Editors, *Prism international*, Department of Creative Writ-ing, BUCH E462 – 1866 Main Mall, University of British Columbia, Vancouver, B.C., V6T 1W6.

Quarry magazine, founded in 1952, continues to publish short fiction, poetry, essays, and reviews of any length or style by writers new or established from anywhere in Canada and abroad. Publisher: Bob Hilderley. Editor: Steven Heighton, with a board of associate editors. Submissions and correspondence: P.O. Box 1061, Kingston, Ont., K7L 4Y5.

TickleAce is Newfoundland and Labrador's literary magazine. Published semi-annually, it focuses on new writing from contributors in its home province but always includes a significant portion of work from outside. Submissions of poetry, essays, and short fiction (5,000 word limit) are welcomed (with SASE) on any topic. Submissions and correspondence: P.O. Box 5353, St. John's, Nfld., A1C 5W2.

Submissions were received from the following journals:

Antigonish Review
(Antigonish, N.S.)

Border Crossings
(Winnipeg, Man.)

Breakthrough
(Calgary, Alta.)

The Capilano Review
(North Vancouver, B.C.)

Dalhousie Review
(Halifax, N.S.)

Descant
(Toronto, Ont.)

Event
(New Westminster, B.C.)

Exile
(Toronto, Ont.)

The Fiddlehead
(Fredericton, N.B.)

Fireweed
(Toronto, Ont.)

Grain
(Regina, Sask.)

Green's Magazine
(Regina, Sask.)

Malahat Review
(Victoria, B.C.)

NeWest Review
(Saskatoon, Sask.)

Other Voices
(Edmonton, Alta.)

Pottersfield Portfolio
(Fredericton, N.B.)

Prairie Fire
(Winnipeg, Man.)

*The Prairie Journal of
Canadian Literature*
(Calgary, Alta.)

Prison Journal
(Burnaby, B.C.)

Prism international
(Vancouver, B.C.)

Quarry Magazine
(Kingston, Ont.)

Rampike
(Toronto, Ont.)

Room of One's Own
(Vancouver, B.C.)

TickleAce
(St. John's, Nfld.)

The New Quarterly
(Waterloo, Ont.)

White Wall Review
(Toronto, Ont.)

Writ Magazine
(Toronto, Ont.)

Zymergy
(Montreal, Que.)